A Christmas Bluff

Scottish Island Escapes
Book 5

MARGARET AMATT

For Ian and Ossian

CONTENTS

CHAPTER 1

Georgia

Georgia Rose folded her slick Catwoman costume into a storage bag. Halloween was over, which meant only one thing: she could officially mention Christmas. Of course, she'd been unofficially mentioning it since January, but it was a rule drilled into her since childhood; Christmas must never be discussed before Halloween. Georgia grinned as she gave the costume bag a massive shove into the glory hole beneath the stairs. Her older sister, Tamsyn, shared her birthday with old Hallow's Eve, making the day sacred and not to be overshadowed by anything tinselly and tacky – unless it was orange and pumpkin-shaped. She could almost hear her mum's chiding voice saying, 'Georgia, I hope that's not "Jingle Bells" you're singing.' *As if!*

Putting her shoulder to the cupboard door, she rammed it shut. Most of the stuff in there needed to go to the attic but she couldn't face it, not with temperatures barely above freezing. Still, she couldn't hold off the trip up the loft ladder for long; the decorations would have to come out. As she rubbed her hands together with excitement and to warm up, a knock sounded on the front door.

'Coming.' She pulled open the door and beamed at her friend, Beth McGregor. Her smile grew wider still when she saw what Beth was holding. 'Oh, you're a lifesaver.'

Beth stepped inside, carting a portable radiator. 'Where do you want this?'

'Upstairs, if you don't mind. The fire's on in the lounge but my bedroom is a fridge.'

With October gone, Georgia missed the steady stream of visitors searching for unique paintings and photographs from the Isle of Mull. Instead, she tweeted about the fading season with #islandlife, and #artistintheoffseason, trying to sound philosophical while really just wishing she could make a few more pounds without having to take on shifts at the local shop like last winter.

'No problem.' Beth lifted the radiator up the stairs.

'I spent all of yesterday morning making phone calls, trying to get someone to fix the boiler. I can't believe it's on the blink again.'

'Did you manage to get anyone?'

'No. I just got a sore foot from kicking the damned thing.' As temperatures had dropped to three degrees, she was getting desperate. 'Apart from the party last night, this has been a pretty rough week. I've been trying to get photos of sea eagles. I had this amazing idea to snap one with an awesome seascape in the background, but I can't get it right. And when the weather is this grim, they don't always come out.'

Beth plugged in the radiator in Georgia's bedroom. 'Why don't you try near our farm? If you cross the road and walk towards the Ardnish Estate, there's a cliffside walk where you might find what you're looking for.'

Lingering at the door of the spare room opposite, Georgia peered into the space currently set up as her studio, workshop and storeroom. It needed gutting, and the chill hit her like a wall of ice. 'I might try that. I think I walked there with Kirsten last year.' Beth and her sister,

Kirsten, had been good friends to Georgia since she'd arrived on the island almost two years ago. Georgia moved across the landing and into her bedroom, admiring the newly added radiator. Worst-case scenario, she'd grab a blanket and sit next to it all night. 'Can I leave it on overnight?'

'I think so,' replied Beth. 'Just set it on low. It'll smell awful for a bit; it's full of dust.'

Georgia held her nose. 'I can live with it. I'm frozen.'

'I'll take a look at the boiler if you like.'

Georgia smiled. 'Beth, I actually love you and if you hadn't met Murray, I might have considered changing preferences so I could marry you.'

'Shut up.' Beth smirked. 'Sometimes, you're a total nutjob.'

'Haha, I know. But you are amazing. I mean, check you out. You could be a fashion model, but what are you? A farmer, a lifesaver and a miracle worker!'

'Yeah, thanks, but fashion model? You need your eyes tested. And also, I haven't fixed it yet, so don't count your chickens.'

Georgia led her to the boiler, almost dancing. 'I have faith.' Pressing her hands together, she looked heavenward. *Please let her fix it.*

Beth peered into the cupboard and shook her head. 'I might be able to get it going,' she said. 'Do you have a torch and a screwdriver?'

After braving the glory hole under the stairs, Georgia presented them to her. 'You can do this. You can do this,' she intoned.

'We'll see.' Beth prodded something with the screwdriver. 'It's time someone around here helped you after you've helped us all year.'

'What are you talking about?' Georgia furrowed her brow.

'Murray calls you the matchmaker.'

'What? I'm nothing of the sort. I'm thrilled you two got together, you're an awesome couple, but I don't claim any part in it.'

Beth poked around in the cupboard. 'You should. Without your advice, I'd never have had the nerve to get together with Murray. You've been a good friend to me.'

'Aww, that's good to know.' As a newcomer, Georgia had invaded the islanders already set friendships, hoping to fit in and not rock the boat. She wasn't sure she always succeeded.

'And I'm not the only one,' said Beth through her teeth, struggling with something behind the boiler. 'You helped Carl and Robyn, Kirsten and Fraser, and Autumn and Richard. Without you, we'd all still be single.'

Georgia smiled, not giving anything away. She was happy for them, but the irony wasn't lost on her. *I'm the only single one left.* None of them had a clue her heart was already wrapped up. Playing along as the happy-go-lucky single girl was fun, and Georgia liked fun more than anything. But there was also Tony, the man she'd pledged to wait for until the time was right, and she was doing just that: biding her time on the island, making happy connections, pleasant memories, and creating joy whenever she could. It was never meant to be forever.

'There you go,' said Beth. The boiler shuddered; it was a hopeful sound.

'Wow.' Georgia grinned. 'Is it fixed?'

'I think so, temporarily at least. You should still get it seen to properly. It could go again at any time. I'm not an expert.'

'Oh, Beth, I could kiss you.'

'You mad woman.'

Georgia hugged her. As Beth was almost a foot taller than her, Georgia was on her tiptoes. 'Thanks so much.'

As Georgia released Beth, her eyes fell on her calendar and the little blocked out dates. She screwed up her nose.

'Are you ok?' asked Beth.

'Yes, I just remembered, my parents are visiting me in the middle of November. They haven't visited me at all since I moved here. And at this time of year, it'll be icy and cold, they'll hate it. I keep expecting them to cancel.'

'Sounds like Murray's parents. They're coming for Christmas, I can't wait.' Beth gritted her teeth.

'I feel the same way. Much as I love them. Absence makes the heart grow fonder and all that, so I must be extra-super fond of them now, but I'm still not sure I want them to visit.'

'I hear you. Give me a call, if you need anything else,' said Beth. 'I have to get back to the farm.'

'I might come round your way later and try to get some sea eagle photos.' Georgia rubbed her forehead. 'I shouldn't have drunk quite so much last night.'

'Catwoman can't hold her liquor,' said Beth.

'Ha, my sister would agree with you.'

A night from twelve years ago sprang into her mind. 'Mum!' Tamsyn had yelled as Georgia had retched over the toilet. 'Georgia's been drinking and she's thrown up everywhere.' Moments later, their mother had arrived at the bathroom door wearing her cotton pyjamas. Both she and Tamsyn stood with their arms folded, the judges and jury in jammies.

After Beth left, Georgia trailed her finger along the squares on her wall calendar, squinting at the dates. It may be old fashioned to keep a calendar, but she had to have this one as it was filled with her photographs. She couldn't flog them to the tourists without having one for herself.

'So, Mum and Dad are coming in less than a fortnight. Holy crap. And I've still got my exhibition to squeeze in too,' she muttered to herself. She desperately wanted new sea eagle photos. If she could get the angle right, they'd make an impressive showpiece, totally evocative of the island spirit.

The sun made an appearance in the afternoon, but it was bitter. Wrapped up like a polar bear, the lithe Catwoman of the night before was no more. Georgia tucked her blonde bob into a knitted hat with a huge pompom and armed herself with her newest lens, the whopping 500mm. She drove west across the island and left the van at Beth's farm, Creagach. Then, following Beth's directions, she walked at least a mile before she found the path and climbed a ridge leading towards the bluff. She settled towards the edge of it and started to unpack her equipment. Waiting for wildlife was a drawn-out process but she was ready with a flask and a blanket. As she opened her bag to get it out, a voice behind her spoke and Georgia whipped around. She hadn't expected anyone else to be within several miles, let alone on the same hillside.

'Good afternoon,' said a man with a deep mellow voice. What a terribly posh accent. Tamsyn would dote all over him. He was tall and smartly dressed. A proper 'yah' – Tamsyn's affectionate put down of the upper classes.

Georgia smiled at the man as he walked closer, calling two pointers. 'Duchess, Dexter, heel.' They sprang over and sat obediently beside him, making him look like a clipping from *Scottish Field* magazine. Georgia fancied taking his photo; the scene was perfect. His well-cut features, prominent nose and sharp eyes were distinctive and vaguely familiar. Before she could work out if she'd seen him somewhere before, he spoke again. 'You realise this is private property, don't you?'

Georgia looked around at the wide hillside, rolling into the distance in great swathes, covered in scrubby grass and rocks. She raised her eyebrows. 'Really?' It was a struggle to keep her face straight. 'As far as I was aware, there's a right to roam anywhere in Scotland as long as you don't leave a mess or do any damage.'

'That's true, but just be careful there is no damage. The *machair* is very rare.'

Georgia frowned. 'Yes, I know, but this isn't machair.'

'Indeed.' The man gave a little cough and adjusted the collar of his jacket. 'I'd appreciate it if you didn't go shouting about this place. I don't want all and sundry coming up here.'

'Right.' Georgia stared, not sure whether to laugh or cry. Was this guy for real?

'Well, that's all. Have a pleasant afternoon.' He gave a little whistle and carried on along the ridge, the dogs bounding after him.

What? A pleasant afternoon? What a prat. Georgia watched him on his way. His tweed suit had an air of Highland elegance, and the way he carried himself was the essence of a duke on a hunting party. As he disappeared beyond the dip in the hill, Georgia inhaled deeply, holding her breath for a few seconds. Sneaking to the edge of the path, she peered down the hill into the wide glen below. He was striding through the expansive valley, making short work of the narrow track.

Picking up her bags, she swung them over her shoulder and walked the other way. Now she was curious.

Was this private property? Had she strayed onto the Ardnish Estate? She'd heard people talk about it but had never been there or given it much thought. The land was so wild around here, it didn't seem possible anyone owned it. How could you tell? No fences or boundaries marred the wide-open landscape.

After half a mile rambling through the scrubland along the hillside, she came to a white iron gate. How random to find anything so manmade in these surroundings. But a large hedge formed a clear boundary, blending with wild tangling bramble branches. The wilderness continued on the other side. In the distance was a large stone house, bleak and austere in its rugged backdrop and view to the open sea. Georgia shuddered in the wind but also at the house. It had the atmosphere you'd expect in an Agatha Christie novel. Maybe Lord This-Is-Private-Property lived there along with Miss Scarlett and Colonel Mustard. It would suit him if he did: dark, dingy and unfriendly. Checking behind her, Georgia opened the gate and picked her way along the edge of the ridge. Seconds later, she jumped at the harsh shriek of gulls. *Dammit.* She grabbed her camera and wrestled it out of the bag. That sound was often followed by the cries of the sea eagle as it forged a way through its angry rivals. And sure enough, there it was, spreading its gigantic wings and soaring off, completely serene, despite the irate gulls mobbing it on either side. Roughly assembling her lens, Georgia started clicking away.

It was late when she'd finally snapped her fill, and darkness was drawing in. She'd forgotten about Sir Private-Landowner and had a few heart palpitations as she made her way back to the gate and slipped through. Hopefully she wouldn't meet him on her return.

It was a relief to get back in the car. Something about that house gave her the heebie-jeebies. Armed with the photos she needed to make her exhibition shine, she was glad she'd never have to set foot on the estate again.

CHAPTER 2

Archie

Archibald Crichton-Leith had walked the hills around his island estate so many times he could do it in the dark, and had done so on several occasions. The ridge was one of his favourites, but it was becoming more well-known to tourists, especially with the nearby addition of the logging road. He'd campaigned desperately against it in a bid to secure his privacy. But what was that these days?

Even now, tourists still lingered. Perhaps he'd been harsh on the young woman, but so often he'd picked up rubbish and seen the damage people did while trailing over his land, claiming the right to roam but not adhering to the code. That summer he'd had people camping, setting fires and even some despicable visitors who'd emptied their campervan's waste tank into the burn which ran through the estate. If his plans succeeded, he could put a stop to that. Once the Ardnish Estate was back on its feet, he could employ a ranger or a gamekeeper to keep an eye out for potential trouble and possibly prevent it. But that was a long way off. He'd only just mustered the courage to return with a view to staying for the long term, and this was likely to be a marathon, not a sprint.

Archie returned to the house the long way, through the woods and back to the road. It was good to check things for himself. He didn't trust people to report broken fences or the like, not nowadays. The island had changed, and not always for the better.

Messages popped in as he entered the cavernous hallway of Ardnish House, the blessing – or curse – of returning to Wi-Fi. The dogs padded towards the kitchen. Mobile phone signal was a definite no, but there was Wi-Fi. Not the fibre optic superfast version he had in his Edinburgh place, but it was good enough to get by. He'd barely opened his phone when the sound of clipping heels on the stone floor of the passageway echoed in the cold air, adding another layer of chill. A hideous mock roman statue in the corner of the entrance hall hid the view to the corridor, but with only one other person in the house, Archie knew who to expect.

Sweeping a sheet of long black hair across her shoulder, Marcia Turnbull stopped dead. It would have been courteous to smile but Archie's facial muscles failed under Marcia's squinting dark eyes. She resembled a short Italian woman, though her tan was too obviously fake and her black eyeliner just a little too much. She must be around his age; thirties at least and marketed herself as openly single. Archie reeled up the drawbridge between them. Getting involved in an entanglement with her was the last thing he wanted.

'There you are, Archie.'

Why does she persist in calling me that, as though we're bosom friends?

'I've been phoning and messaging you for about half an hour.' Marcia's heavy Glaswegian twang wasn't completely masked by the airs she added to her voice. Archie found his smile at last, mainly because she reminded him of a newsreader as she tried to enunciate every word to perfection.

'I told you I was going out.' He raked his hair. Why did she think he was accountable to her? This was his home and she was a guest, yet here she was bossing him around like his mother. Maybe working for Lavinia Crichton-Leith had rubbed off on the poor woman and he should feel sorry for her, but he didn't.

'That was about three hours ago. I didn't expect you to be so long. Where have you been? I don't want to stay in this house any longer; it's horrible, and it's so cold I'm frozen to the bones. I need to get back to the office.'

'Then go.' God knew he had no desire for her to be hanging around.

'You know I can't. You haven't given me an answer yet.' She walked towards the little office she'd set up in one of the rooms off the lower passageway. Archie followed the clicking heels.

'Actually, I have several times. Just not the answer you and my mother want to hear.'

'I don't understand why you're being so stubborn about this.' Marcia stopped at the door and glared at him.

'Because it's my house, and I'm not selling it.'

'Archie, I've just had your mother on the landline for half an hour. I don't think she's going to accept that. She wants me back in Bearsden, but she wants your assurance you'll sell in the new year. I realise technically the house is yours, but she lived in it for a lot longer and she understands the situation a lot better.'

'Does she?' Archie folded his arms and frowned. At the risk of sounding like a chauvinistic pig, he was sick of women trying to rule his life. And not just his mother or Marcia. Money had made him prey to gold-diggers ever since he'd left his all-boy boarding school. As soon as women had entered his life, his troubles had started. The last one had almost ruined him. It was nothing short of a miracle she'd been caught before clearing out all his accounts, though she'd succeeded in keeping two extremely valuable bottles of vintage whisky. Their sales must have seen her prettily through her despair at landing a short jail sentence for her other offences.

'This place is a drain on the finances. You might have money now, but in a few years, you'll be bankrupt. Just like all the others in your family. Your mother is only trying to protect you.'

Archie rubbed his chin and stared into the middle distance. Protect him? Like women always wanted to *help him, take care of him, be there for him?* Had any of that ever been true? 'For heaven's sake, Marcia, I'm thirty-six, not twelve. I think I know how to conduct my own finances. You can relay that message to my mother and tell her no amount of persuasion will change my mind.'

Marcia didn't reply but clomped into the office and cranked up the dial on one of the three oil-filled radiators she'd set up. Archie didn't like to point out she might save the estate some money herself if she dressed for the weather. Her grey shimmery blouse was verging on see-through and her skirt… sheesh. Archie turned away as she bent to adjust the second radiator.

'I'll tell her, but she won't be pleased. She's already furious you've put a tenant in Gardener's Cottage. It's barely habitable.'

'I'm working on it. The tenant agreed to do some repair work in return for a low rent.'

Marcia let out a long, slow sigh. 'So, you actually think you'll be able to finance the renovation of eight estate cottages, plus Monarch's Lodge, plus this place, by handing out low rents and expecting favours in return?'

'Absolutely not. That isn't my long-term plan. I only enlisted this man's help because his family were tenants on the estate years ago. He approached me when he needed a place to live. He was desperate so I granted it to him.'

Marcia shook her head. 'Your mother will not be amused.'

Archie threw out his hands. 'There's nothing I can do about that. I own the estate now and I'm going to sort it out, one way or another.' How confident he sounded while actually feeling like he was swimming upstream. He didn't have a clue what he was doing. A job in the oil industry had seen him well provided for and he wasn't ready to give it up completely. He needed an escape route if the dormant volcano that was the estate finances decided to erupt and drain away into the sea. But he'd never know unless he tried, and he couldn't sit back and watch his heritage crumble. This estate went back generations; letting it go on his watch wasn't what he wanted. 'So, when are you leaving? Because you have my answer, I'm not selling.'

'On Saturday, once I've sorted out your mother's old rooms,' said Marcia, looking at him like he'd sprouted an extra head. She and his mother obviously thought he was insane wanting to keep the place… They could be right. 'You need to run me to the ferry at eight.'

'Right,' said Archie. Marcia's departure couldn't come soon enough. Then he could get on with his plans, and they didn't involve selling anything except all the old junk his brother had accumulated.

'Maybe you and I should have a nice meal tonight,' Marcia said. 'We can't tomorrow because you have a meeting and Friday's out as we have that silly exhibition thingy.'

'Right.' An exhibition she'd invited herself to, along with a party of people who were sailing over from Oban. Apparently friends of his mother. That translated into the strong possibility of there being a single woman of good fortune amongst the group whom he was supposed to fall head over heels for. Didn't his mother know he'd wised up to her games? How conveniently she forgot that most of the women she'd thrown at him had ended up stealing from him in some way or another or making it blatantly clear they were only in it for the money.

'So, tonight.' Marcia smiled, but it didn't soften her angular face. She looked ready to sharpen her teeth on him before her meal.

Archie stepped back and almost toppled over another radiator. Clutching the neck of his shirt, he composed himself. 'Em, yes. All right. But it's freezing in the dining room.'

Marcia pulled her head to the side. 'I meant we could go out somewhere. There must be some kind of restaurant on this island. Surely?'

'Seriously?' He frowned and loosened his collar. 'And is this going on expenses? That's not exactly helping me save my family's precious funds.'

Marcia leaned on the side of the desk, her low-cut top dropping to display her deeply tanned cleavage. Her pert little bottom stuck out behind, tightly encased in the short black skirt. Archie raised his eyebrow, not daring to move his sightline too far from her face; none of the items on display were appealing to him. What the hell was she playing at? Even in the most unlikely circumstance he fancied her, nothing could come of it. Working for his mother, Marcia would be party to Mrs Crichton-Leith's schemes to marry him off to the latest young heiress. She couldn't think he would yield to her advances, could she? Assuming these were advances. Or was this normal behaviour? Archie was never sure. He was so wary these days. Maybe someone from Marcia's background would like him for something other than his cash savings, or would it be worse?

'I just don't fancy cooking, do you?' she asked.

'Actually, no.' Archie cursed the words as they fell from his lips. This was exactly the reason he'd been so messed about by women; flash him a smile and he couldn't stop himself agreeing to everything. 'Let's go to *Am Bàta.*'

'Wonderful. I need to get dressed. I think I brought my little black number.'

Archie took a deep breath, inhaling the cold musty air in the passageway as he left the office. No doubt Marcia had her black number. Did she ever wear any other colour?

As Archie tended the Aga in the ugly and dated kitchen, he couldn't shake the gnawing niggle Marcia wanted more from him than a three-course dinner. He'd dodged all the women his mother had thrown at him over the years, but after inheriting the estate, the pressure had multiplied. Mrs Crichton-Leith was determined. She wanted her son married to an heiress who might tempt him to remain in the city and sell the cumbersome estate which had bankrupted – and ultimately killed – her husband and elder son.

But Archie was done taking orders. Everything he'd ever wanted out of life had been crushed by his family and their overpowering expectations. For some years, he thought he'd escaped and had kept a low profile, working hard, until Laurence had died, and the spotlight had flicked back to Archie with lightning speed. Now he was master of Ardnish and he was ready to give it his full attention and build it up brick by brick if necessary. And he didn't want anyone getting in the way of his plans.

CHAPTER 3

Georgia

Remember, remember the fifth of November. Georgia hadn't forgotten. The date was wedged in her mind. She had a whistle-stop trip to the mainland planned, then she was helping with the bonfire festivities at the Glen Lodge Hotel. Selling marshmallows on skewers for toasting on the bonfire was the best job, especially if sampling was involved.

She was thrilled when a call came that morning from her new friend, Autumn, offering to accompany her to the mainland for the day.

'Of course! I can't wait to see you again,' Georgia said. Autumn had been at the Halloween party, but with all the dancing to be done, they hadn't had a chance to catch up properly. After Autumn's whirlwind romance with a local man just a few weeks ago, Georgia was more than excited to find out the goss. 'Shall I pick you up at the hotel?'

'Yes, please,' said Autumn. 'Maureen wants me to get some supplies for the bonfire, so I have an ulterior motive.' Since deciding to make her home on the island, Autumn had taken a job at the Glen Lodge Hotel.

'Haha, no problem.'

As soon as Autumn was safely inside Georgia's beloved pink van, their happy chat filled the interior, alongside Georgia's photography equipment and assorted paraphernalia. *I must do a clear out, and soon.* It looked like she was about to head off on a seriously wacky camping trip.

'So, how's it going with Richard?' smiled Georgia. Richard was a tall and broodingly handsome local who didn't give much away but had captured Autumn's heart.

Autumn grinned and tossed her long auburn hair over her shoulder. 'Good. Though it's still a bit tense with my mum, she and I are still working on things.' Autumn's mum had also moved to the island, the reason Autumn had come in the first place, but it hadn't all been smooth sailing.

'Oh, yes. Do tell.'

'She's a bit depressed because my dad's getting married. But I don't think the place she's living with Mike is helping.'

The connection clicked. 'Of course, they rent a cottage on the Ardnish Estate, don't they?' That was how she'd heard of the place.

'Yes. But it's in bad shape. Mike's doing a lot of work, but it's time-consuming and Mum's fed up with leaking roofs and burst pipes. Blair's helping too, so things are moving a bit faster, but it's still not easy.'

'No. I guess not, but what eye-candy.' Georgia grinned. Blair was Mike's particularly attractive young son, who wore his hair in thick blond dreadlocks. With Tony safely tucked in the background, Georgia was free to admire without feeling any need to act. But sometimes it was a lonely place.

'I hope you mean Blair and not Mike. Though I guess Mike's not too bad either.'

'Haha. I meant Blair. He's cute. Did you see him at Halloween dressed as the Viking warrior? Whoa, hottie alert.'

'He's single, why don't you get together?'

'Ha, maybe.' Georgia pulled on the indicator and joined the ferry queue. 'He's a bit too young for me though.' Yes, she always had an excuse. She'd known Tony was the man for her from an early age. Now she just had to play the waiting game and sweep away the flecks of doubt which accumulated more and more as the months went on. She beamed at Autumn. 'I'm glad it's worked out for you.'

'So far, so good. I'd been in a toxic relationship for a long time,' said Autumn. 'Meeting Richard changed the way I looked at things… and myself.'

'Yeah, that's so lovely.' Georgia nibbled a cuticle as the words sunk in. Was she being just as stupid? No! She shoved the thought away. Tony wasn't toxic, this was totally different. They were on a mutually agreed break and everything would work out fine.

Once they were in Oban, Georgia had to abandon Autumn at the shops while she went to the print shop, spending ages choosing the right canvases for her sea eagle photos. She couldn't afford second guessing because she needed them for her exhibition on Friday.

After much hair pulling, she decided on the ones she wanted and waited, hardly daring to look in case they didn't print the right way. She danced for joy when she saw them and almost kissed the print shop owner, before returning to collect Autumn from the supermarket at lunchtime.

'Wow,' said Georgia, surveying several full shopping bags that Autumn had loaded into two trolleys. 'Is this all for the bonfire tonight? Isn't it a bit late?'

'Maureen's a bit stressed.'

'Hmm.' Maureen, the hotel owner, had a history of troubles. 'She can be nice, but sometimes I find her a bit scary,' said Georgia.

'I'm glad it's not just me who thinks so,' Autumn said.

'Well, let's keep her sweet. I have my exhibition there on Friday and I don't want any hitches. Hopefully I'll make some sales and then I might be able to afford Christmas presents.'

'Maybe don't mention the *C* word. Maureen has big plans but they're stressing her out too.'

'Oh, dare I ask what she's planning?' said Georgia.

'She wants to set up all kinds of package deals but she's struggling because Christmas isn't a good time for her.'

'Her husband died last year,' said Georgia. 'This'll bring back bad memories.'

'Oh. I didn't know that,' said Autumn. 'But I know a few people who've lost someone at Christmas.'

'Maybe we just notice it more because people expect you to be happy at Christmas. At least Maureen has Robyn here this year, she'll be able to set up those deals in the blink of an eye.' Maureen's daughter was a marketing whizz. 'And hopefully they'll be there for each other.'

'I hope it turns out well. Maureen always seems close to a meltdown.'

'I wonder what she'll do décor-wise. I wouldn't mind helping. In fact, I'd quite like to have my Christmas lunch there. Last year, I went to my sister Tamsyn's house. She threw one of her Pinterest-perfect parties.'

'Ooh, sounds lovely.'

'Ugh, I wish it was. I mean, I like a party.'

'I noticed.'

'Yeah, but what I don't like is the fact she'd invited about a hundred guests, most of them I didn't know. Some were her husband's relatives, and they are people she views as almost gentry, in fact, they think they are themselves. It's cringeworthy. I get fobbed off as the poor relation. I'm not going through that again. Somewhere on the island I'll find a charitable soul willing to share their day with me.'

'I might have to work Christmas Day, so if you come by the hotel, I'll see you get a proper lunch.'

'Thank you, that sounds much more like me.'

*

Finally back at the hotel, Georgia unloaded her canvases and pictures. Maureen was happy for her to leave them there until Friday.

'I may as well stay and get ready for tonight.' Georgia checked the time as she put the last canvas in the storeroom. For the next two hours, she helped set up some tables outside, thanking the weather gods it was a clear, crisp evening. Her friend, Carl, arrived arm in arm with his fiancée, Robyn. Georgia smiled at them. They had been the first of the lovebirds to get together this year.

'Are you ready for Friday?' asked Carl, rubbing his gloved hands together.

'I think so,' Georgia said. 'I just hope there's a good turnout.'

'There will be, I'm sure. Maureen told Robyn a big group has booked in that night, so they might be here especially for your exhibition, or if not, we'll make sure to drag them along.'

'Sounds like a plan.'

Watching the fireworks, Georgia huddled close to the bonfire, warming her hands, eating as many marshmallows as she flogged, and hoping come Friday, she could make as big an impression as some of these pyrotechnic miracles.

*

After setting up the exhibition on Friday, Georgia rushed home to change. Straightening herself out in the mirror, she cocked her head at her reflection and smiled. Her shoulder-length hair was sitting nicely and, although she'd never be as tall as she wished, her scarlet ankle-length dress showed off the right curves in the right places. She adjusted the front, hoping the strapless style wasn't too brassy. 'It's elegant,' she told herself, but grabbed a black wrap in case she felt too exposed.

Dabbing on some last-minute make-up, she turned her head to see the full effect of the long lashes and sparkly red lips. She flounced up her tousled blonde waves and pouted. 'You'll do,' she said, blowing a kiss to her reflection and heading out, ready for her lift with Beth and Murray. They were also bringing Kirsten, Beth's sister, and Fraser, another loved-up couple. This time last year they'd been a gang of mad singletons. It was times like this when she imagined Tony calling her. When she answered, he'd be standing behind her shouting 'surprise, I'm back'. Because he was coming back, wasn't he? That was the deal they'd made two years ago. Two years? Had it been two years already? With each passing day, they grew further apart. Georgia wasn't one to dwell, so she let it go. Sometimes she wondered if picking up from where they left off would ever be possible. But what was the other option? Make the split permanent? Could she do that? She'd been with Tony since she was seventeen. Ten years they'd stuck it out before his crisis.

'Looking lovely,' Fraser said as Georgia hopped in the back of the Land Rover beside him.

'You always do,' said Kirsten.

'Thanks,' said Georgia. 'I'm a bit nervous. What if no one shows up except you guys?'

'They will,' said Fraser, 'people always want things to do on cold November evenings.'

Georgia raised an eyebrow. 'Are you being serious? Or just cheeky?'

'Both.'

Come seven, however, people started arriving in the hotel's ballroom, cleared to make space for viewing the pictures without crowding. Georgia breathed a sigh of relief and ordered herself a drink. As she waited for it, she glanced around, curious about the punters and listening to the voices rise and fall, mingling with laughter and punctuated by the double doors opening and closing as more people entered. Lots of unfamiliar faces were in attendance so not many of them would know who she was. It might have been sensible to have put up a self-portrait but too late now. She imagined doing herself in Andy Warhol style with big blocks of colour, maybe making her blonde hair a vibrant yellow or turning it pink.

As her drink clinked on the bar, she lifted the elegant glass, thanked the server and wandered over to a group of people. Georgia liked company and didn't mind talking to strangers. Soon she was deep in chat about one of her paintings.

A loud laugh resonated around the room and Georgia looked over, hoping it wasn't the pictures causing the hilarity. A large group of what Tamsyn would term 'yahs' were gathered in the corner, their voices lifting over the gentle clink of glasses. They were dressed in slick suits and satin sheath dresses like they were at a black-tie event – or a funeral. Tamsyn would have been over in a flash, getting right in there, while afterwards claiming, 'Seriously, darling. I can't stand them, so full of themselves. Such terrible yahs! So snooty and above their station.' Oh, the irony! The way she ridiculed them, while aspiring to be one of them with every bone in her body.

Georgia excused herself and sidled towards them. Her bare shoulders tingled, and not from the chill. This group wasn't her usual type. Unlike her sister, Georgia usually steered clear of people like this. What did she have in common with the super-rich and sophisticated? She was a pauper and a proper nutter. Curiosity, however, propelled her high-heeled sandals forward, carrying her closer. What were the yahs saying? If they liked her pictures, she was ready to jump in their midst and start promoting herself; they looked like they had a spare bob or two between them.

As she sipped her violet gin, a man caught her eye. She froze; the cold rim of the glass stuck to her lip. It was Lord Trespass-At-Your-Peril. Georgia lowered her glass slowly and adjusted the wrap which had slipped into the crooks of her elbows. He gave a little cough and turned back to his party.

'Shit, what's he doing here?' muttered Georgia, scanning around the room for someone friendly. She spotted Carl and was about to walk towards him when someone tapped her shoulder. Spinning around, she was eye to eye with a slick black lapel. She raised her gaze until she met the face of Sir I-Love-My-Privacy. His upper lip had a pronounced cupid's bow. He was almost smiling, or was it a sneer?

With a sharp movement, Georgia pushed a strand of hair behind her ear and summoned a worthy hostess smile. *Wow! I have learned something from Tamsyn's parties.* It was her exhibition; it wouldn't do to be standoffish. She needed to make sales, not enemies.

'Hello,' she said.

Having ditched his tweed for the slick black suit, the man looked exceptionally handsome, exquisitely refined, and extremely annoying. Rude men should always be scruffy and uncouth. His gingery brown hair was neatly cropped with a few well-placed and perfectly ruffed up tufts at his forehead. Did he have a stylist perhaps?

'You won't remember me,' he said.

'I certainly do.' Georgia plastered on a grin.

He raised his eyebrows and Georgia squinted upwards. He was quite a bit taller than her, but it was his eyes that caught her attention. The irises were most curious, one was greyish green, the other brown. 'You do.' He nodded, frowning a little as she continued her assessment of his features. From an artistic point of view, he was beautiful. She wanted to grab her paints and a brush. How could she do those eyes justice? The portrait had already started in her head. 'I was a little harsh the other day. I hope you'll understand it wasn't personal.'

'Hmm, what?' She stopped the fantasy painting and took a sip of her gin. 'Oh, that. Sure.'

'Good. So… Did you get some holiday snaps? It's a good time of year to visit. There aren't as many people about.'

Georgia smirked and rolled her tongue around the inside of her mouth. *He doesn't know who I am.* The opportunity for some sport was too delicious. 'Yes, I got lots of great photos, thank you.' She beamed and flashed her eyes at him. 'Would you like to see them?'

'Er, all right.' He scanned around as though waiting for her to pull out a phone or a camera to show him. With a grin, she led him through the crowd, vaguely aware of the drone of background chat and the clink of glasses. On a stand at the window end was the large print she'd had made of her favourite snap. The eagle soared downward with crashing waves beneath it. She pointed, stepping into the lee of the darkened wall to wall window, and watched his expression. 'This is my favourite.'

The man contemplated it for a second, then raised his hand to his face, covering his eyes. As he dragged down his hand, he said, 'Oh god, you're the exhibition photographer, aren't you?'

Georgia raised her glass and winked. 'I am.'

He squinted at the pictures, and Georgia saw his mind working. A frown grew, cutting a rugged line through his otherwise smooth forehead. 'Did you go into the grounds to take these?'

'Pardon? Oh.' Georgia looked away and swallowed a large gulp of gin. 'I eh... don't recall. I just followed the eagle.'

His lips parted as if on the verge of another comment when a short woman with heavy eyeliner and long dark hair touched him gently on the arm. He pulled his mismatched eyes away from Georgia. 'What?' Stepping back from the woman, he adjusted his lapels.

'Come and see this,' the woman said. 'Some of these pictures look like they were taken on the estate.'

'I eh... Excuse me.' He nodded at Georgia, and she watched him and the woman walk towards more of her photographs. All of them products of her illicit hop through the gate onto his private land.

The room seemed too warm. Georgia fanned herself as a slight queasiness bubbled in her tummy. She'd never heard rules about selling photos taken on private estates but then she wasn't exactly a religious reader of regulations and guidebooks.

Before mingling, Georgia spared the man another glance. He was looking back, his jaw tense, his gaze concentrated on her. Georgia flicked her eyes down and headed towards Carl.

'Are you making lots of sales?' He sipped on his drink and eyed the group in the corner. Robyn smiled at

Georgia, her arm draped through Carl's. 'You've certainly attracted the ones with the money. Who's the man? He keeps looking at you.'

'I don't know. I met him on the Ardnish Estate the other day where I took some of the photos. He's annoyed. I wish they'd leave. This is not fun.'

Carl patted her shoulder. 'Don't worry. People like him are like that. More money than sense.'

At the end of the evening, Georgia finally dared to check her sales book. She'd left it open on the table with order forms, hoping a few people might buy a couple of small prints at least. Her jaw dropped as she leafed through them and discovered one order for over £1500.

'Seriously.'

'What?' said Beth. 'Are you ok?'

Georgia handed her the book to make sure she wasn't dreaming.

'Wow, but look who bought them.' Beth ran her finger under a name. 'Archibald Crichton-Leith. He's the prat who owns Ardnish. Murray and I had a run-in with him in the spring. You were with me one time, don't you remember?'

A penny dropped. Georgia held her hand to her mouth. 'Yes. I do. I saw him there, but I didn't click he was the owner. I thought he was a lawyer or something. And he bought the photos? That can't be good.'

'Why? It's £1500 good,' said Beth.

'I know, but I bet it's because he doesn't want anyone else to have them. He thinks they belong to him because I took them on the estate. I bet he sues me or something.'

Beth frowned. 'I hope not, but he doesn't exactly have a reputation for kindness.'

The happiness Georgia should have felt at making so much money was eclipsed by the worry at having to deliver the canvases. Maybe he'd hit her with a lawsuit before she'd even got them out of the van.

CHAPTER 4

Archie

Marcia was gone. Archie punched up the volume on the radio in the Barbarian, wishing he had a ballroom to let out some crazy dance moves that were itching for release now he was free again. 'Christmas music, already,' he muttered as he clicked the remote stick. The usual island fuzz crackled in place of all the would-be channels. With such patchy reception, he had to make do with what was available. Christmas music it was.

Soon he was singing along because, despite his family's insistence, he wasn't a Scrooge. Far from it. He enjoyed Christmas, or at least the vision he had of how it should be. His childhood Christmases had been a bizarre blend of magic and sparkle mixed with a frenzied horror of drunken parties, stress and disappointment; an interesting fusion which left him hovering in limbo every year, uncertain whether to embrace the joy or shove the whole thing in the closet and pray for January. The festivities of two years ago had been typical of his life so far, he'd 'loaned' the woman he'd invited to his company's Christmas soiree almost a thousand pounds to pay for repairs on her car. She'd seemed like a nice person and he wanted to help her out, but he never saw her or the money again.

At least Marcia wouldn't be swooping around when the season kicked off. Having her in the house made him hot under the collar, and not pleasantly. The lingering unease that she might jump him at any second or appear in his room one night claiming to be cold, sent shivers down his spine and had resulted in him buying a strong padlock for his bedroom door. But being alone at Ardnish wasn't great either. The place was a cavernous shell and getting it ready for what he'd planned would require a Christmas miracle. With Marcia's departure, he could get on with it, because he hadn't dared start while she was around. If she and his mother discovered the extent of what he was up to, they'd blow their tops. Doing up the estate was one thing, but his method was another and although he was determined, setting his mother on an episode at this time of year was unwise, not to mention insensitive and unfeeling. She'd been through enough and memories of what happened this time last year would be fresh in her mind.

Back at Ardnish, the ringing buzz of hoovers and the clatter of brushes broke the cold silence as a team of cleaners worked upstairs. A dust storm floated near the window and Archie coughed. This place was worse than the house of horrors.

'Duchess,' he called. The older pointer shot out of the gunroom to greet him, followed by her two-year-old pup, Dexter. Archie clapped them both. 'Let's go for a walk.'

He left via the door in his passageway bedroom. He was basically living in that corridor. Besides the spare room he'd set up as a bedroom, it had the office, the gunroom for the dogs and a bathroom. He only had to confront the main house for the kitchen.

Along a track towards the sea and down a steep incline, the land opened out onto a flat area, surrounded by typical Hebridean bluffs, the kind that were covered in foliage and puffins during the summer, but were bleak and bare at this time of year. Nestled in the flat area was Monarch's Lodge, and – as far as Archie was concerned – the most beautiful house in the universe. When the waves crashed high, they hit the walls at the end of the long rolling lawn. But the house was far enough back to be safe. He stopped for a moment just to look at it and soak in the perfection, remembering doing this as a boy, racing with Laurence, his older brother, unable to wait to open the door and be hit by the delicious scent of gingerbread.

When Archie's father, Alexander Crichton-Leith, had inherited Ardnish, he'd wasted no time in turfing out his old mother, *The Dowager*, as he nicknamed her. She'd been banished to Monarch's Lodge so Alexander and his wife could take over the main house. But Archie's grandmother always seemed happy with her lot, and Archie understood why. He'd much prefer to live in Monarch's Lodge, and he planned to do just that. As the main house was in the midst of its clear out, Archie made daily trips to the lodge. He wasn't a handyman or blessed with skills like that, but he was determined come Christmas, he'd be out of his corridor and in the lodge, while his grand plans unfolded in the main mansion.

He let the dogs loose in the long garden in front of Monarch's Lodge and set to work on his daily tasks. If he dedicated a couple of hours to the place, he felt like he'd accomplished something without infringing too much on his real job. After filling several bin bags and accidently pulling off a windowsill, he decided enough was enough and returned with the dogs to the main house. It was freezing, even without Marcia there to remind him of the fact every ten minutes. In the office, he took off his coat and braved the chill while he waited for the radiators to crank into action. Flipping open his laptop, he lounged back and sighed. Up above, the buzz of a hoover pounded off a wall.

From what seemed miles away, a bell chimed. At first, he thought it was a clock, but realised it couldn't be, not at ten to one. It must be the doorbell. Leaving the office for the arctic zone in the corridor, Archie shaded his eyes; sunbeams dazzled, refracting through the stained glass around the heavy oak front door. They didn't bring warmth and a chill vibrated across his shoulders. His shoes tapped an echoey rhythm on the huge flagstones. He hauled open the door and his gaze fell on a giant white package. Behind it was the young woman he now knew to be Georgia Rose. In the rush of taking Marcia to the ferry then going straight to Monarch's Lodge, he'd forgotten his wallet was £1500 lighter this morning, thanks to this woman.

She wasn't tall and was even more diminished as she waited on a lower step, propping up the giant canvas. Peering over the top of it, she gave a bright and hopeful grin. 'Hi,' she chirruped. 'I have your pictures. Do you want them here or is there a backdoor I should go in?'

'No, this is fine.' This woman had the boldest brass neck he'd ever encountered. She'd wandered into the estate and gone snap happy then sold the results right under his nose. It just happened the photographs were so stunning he couldn't resist. If he'd known someone this talented existed, he'd have paid her to take the pictures for him. They were exactly what he wanted. Still, he wasn't greatly impressed by her methods.

'Great, I'll bring them in then. Stand back.'

Archie looked her over as she clambered up the stairs in her bottle-green coat, passing him into the hallway. She set down the first picture and gazed around. Heat stung Archie's neck. Everything was shabby, cold, gloomy and run-down. A bit of an embarrassment rather than the Highland chic his imagination conjured. If only he could whip the ideas straight from his head and into life.

'So.' Georgia clapped her hands encased in purple gloves. 'I've been thinking, and maybe… I should give you a discount.'

'Why?' Archie furrowed his brow. He half expected his mother's voice to ring out, "Archibald, don't frown, your forehead has a trench deep enough to plant potatoes in, and it isn't a good look."

'Because I went through your gate and I shouldn't have. I just thought it would be the best place to get the photo.'

'Oh, that,' he said, rubbing the back of his neck. 'Well, at least I have custom shots.'

'So, you're not going to sue me?' Georgia smiled wide, her chestnut brown eyes glittering and expectant, filling the hall with instant warmth.

He raised his eyebrow. 'I'm not entirely sure what the grounds would be, so no. Not this time.'

'Great. That makes me feel better.' Georgia clapped and held her purple-gloved hands to her chin. 'So, are you the owner here?'

'I am.'

She shook her head and held her hand to her mouth, covering a grin. 'I didn't realise. I should have, we met once before, in the spring. You were part of a land dispute with the Island Community Woodland Group. I thought you were a lawyer or something.'

'Oh, the logging road. Were you part of that?'

'Not really. I was heading somewhere else and just came by with Beth. You probably won't remember.'

Archie scanned his memories. Nothing from those days was pleasant to recall. He'd been so new to everything and had ploughed in with his monogrammed Crichton-Leith boots, trampling down the islanders just like his ancestors. 'I do vaguely, now you mention it.'

Georgia moved towards the door. 'I'll get the next picture,' she said. 'I had no idea there was a house here especially one this huge. You keep it well hidden.'

Archie ran his finger along his crisp collar and followed her down the steps as she headed for her van. And what a van it was. Bright pink with flower decals all over it. Something about it was just so her. 'Yes. This house was built in the 1880s for my great-great-grandfather. He was very reclusive by all accounts and didn't appreciate locals prying on his business.'

She lifted another canvas from the open boot and smirked. 'Runs in your family.'

'Yes. Very funny.' Though unfortunately true. After being groomed for the role of Crichton-Leith spare, he'd spent years avoiding the place despite harbouring a deep love for it. When he'd been thrust directly into ownership, it was a tough adjustment, no matter how much drilling he'd been subjected to, because he'd never expected it to happen. The history of his predecessors didn't always make comfortable reading, but there were precious moments and stories. His grandfather had bucked the family trend and been quite a philanthropist and a favourite amongst the locals, though sadly his father had lapsed into the old ways. Once the estate had housed a thriving community and something in Archie wanted to recreate that again, but the ins and outs of it were just a vague outline of half-baked ideas. Despite years in business, this was a different ballgame, one closer to his heart and involving a lot more subtle diplomacy. Winning around islanders was a million times trickier than winning over American oil tycoons.

'Do you live in the house?' asked Georgia, passing him a canvas and lifting out another.

'Not all the time.'

As they walked towards the steps, she stared upwards. 'So, are you here for a holiday?'

'No, I'm doing it up for Christmas.'

'Oh, nice. Are you having lots of family over?'

'Not family, no. I'm having other guests.' Archie placed his canvas next to the other one. 'Sadly, the house has fallen into serious disrepair. I only inherited it a year ago, and it wasn't left in the best condition.'

Georgia gazed around with wide, curious eyes. Archie wished she wouldn't. Having an artist nosing over this dead space took his body temperature to below zero. This should be a place full of light and warmth, with music in the hall, singing and dancing in the drawing room and laughter echoing around every corner. But it was the opposite.

Archie used to find poetic inspiration all over the estate. He'd even thought about having some of his work published, but now the best he could write was a few bleak tragedies or sonnets based on how cold a person could get. Since inheriting, he'd hardly been able to set foot in the place. Brief visits had sufficed to keep up to date until he'd finally made the conscious decision to go for it. He couldn't let ghosts haunt him. This was the dream come true. As a boy, he'd fantasised about how he'd run the place if he had the chance, safe in the knowledge he'd never have to.

Before Archie could stop her, Georgia advanced to the corner and ran her finger down a chipped edge of the bust, flicking off some dust.

'You see what I mean.' He winced. 'It's in the process of an overhaul.' He gesticulated around, cringing inside, wishing to throw a giant dust sheet over the room, or Georgia, then he could bundle her out without having to suffer this humiliation. The state of the place wasn't his fault, but he hadn't even dusted the ugly statue and he'd been busted. So much for the team of cleaners.

'It's got potential.' Georgia beamed, ambling around the hall and casting her eye over everything. Whatever she walked past seemed to change from black and white to colour. Archie blinked at the trick of his imagination, but Georgia's vibrancy carried on emitting a cheery glow over the tired space. 'Just think what you could do here.'

'Yes, I am thinking about it. And doing it too.'

'Well, good luck. You have your pictures. Are they part of your master plan?'

'Yes, they're very good… and bespoke.'

'I expect you have plenty of places to hang them.'

'I do. Maybe…' He frowned, feeling the groove deepen across his forehead. 'They might look good in the dining room once it's ready. Would you like to see what you think?' He wasn't sure what had driven him to propose such a thing, but it was out now. Georgia's eyes glinted with surprise.

'Yeah, why not?'

She would, right? Now she'd be examining every layer of dust with her artistic eye. Archie had opened the door to full island scrutiny; he was all too aware of the information network. How long before everyone knew what a terrible state the Crichton-Leiths had allowed the estate to fall into?

'A quick look. And remember,' he said, leading her through the glass-panelled interior doors to the corridor that housed the grand stair. 'It's a work in progress.'

'Of course.' She tugged off her gloves as they made their way along the austere hallway, passing the drawing room, a family room, a guest bedroom, and the study. Archie still steered clear of that room, half-expecting to see his father sitting there surrounded by a cloud of cigar smoke and barking out orders.

Flinging open the door to the dining room, Archie revealed the old banquet table. It wasn't covered in mouldy food and crawling with insects, though it seemed like it should be. Instead, it was piled with boxes of things he needed to sort through.

'What a lot of work.' Georgia peered inside and crinkled her nose.

'Don't I know it. My parents had it done up when they moved in. But that was in the eighties, not exactly a pinnacle period in the history of design. They ripped out the hundred-year-old original pieces they thought were dated to replace it with modern traditional. Now it's stuck in a time warp. Sometimes I expect a nineteen-eighties Miss Havisham, looking like Toyah Wilcox or Cher to step out from behind one of those delightful moth-eaten velvet curtains.'

Georgia laughed. 'Oh dear. That's funny, but not funny, I guess. Not if it's your job to do it up.'

'Exactly.'

Archie hated these old rooms. He wouldn't sit in any of them in the evenings, preferring either the kitchen or his corridor bedsit.

'It's a gorgeous table though.' Georgia stepped forward and ran her finger along it, leaving a streak in the dust. Archie rubbed his hand down his face. What was he paying these damned cleaners for? Georgia flicked the dust off her finger, making no comment, but Archie squirmed as she wandered further into the room. A horrible musty smell lingered in the damp air.

'Yes, thankfully they kept the original table. But the entire house needs work.' And truthfully, he didn't know where to start. He'd made a valiant stab at it, but it was like trying to build a skyscraper with a handful of Lego bricks.

'Are there people working here just now?' Georgia asked as a hoover clattered about.

'Cleaners. It's lain empty for a year so it's not looking too good.'

Georgia bit her lip, possibly considering something. Her eyes flicked back to him, flashing a cheeky glint in his direction. Archie rarely indulged in admiring women these days – fearing the burn – but he couldn't fail to notice Georgia. She was like a light shining in a dark and dingy cave. 'You're very lucky,' she said.

'Am I?'

'Yes. To own a house like this is pretty special. I don't even own a shed. Which reminds me, I have to go or I'll be late for…' She trailed off, pulled her phone from her pocket and checked something.

Archie didn't feel lucky. He was fortunate, but life hadn't exactly been a picnic so far. If his mother's dire warnings were true, this house might become a burden for him too. Looking around with a fresh pair of eyes had opened his. This job was too much for him. How could he ever manage it? He opened the door and let Georgia back into the hall.

After leading her to the main door, he put out his hand. Her skin was even colder than his as she placed her fingers in his palm. She held the handshake longer than he expected until he withdrew and watched her head for her van.

Yes, she was pretty, but was she also sly? She'd snuck onto his land to get the best photos, now she'd wheedled into the house. Perhaps holding his hand a fraction too long was an attempt to intrigue him. She'd made no secret of her situation. She was shedless and poor.

'Get a grip,' he told himself as Georgia threw him a little wave. He'd become paranoid to the point of ridiculous. It didn't follow that every woman he met would fall madly in love with his bank account and do everything in her power to clear it out. But after meeting so many women over the years who'd fallen hopelessly for his cash, fluttering their lashes as little pound signs dinged in their pupils, he was very, very wary. For someone who'd done so well in business, he was ridiculously gullible in relationships. He truly just wanted to find that special someone. The one who liked something about him other than how good his wallet felt in their hands.

Georgia drove off and gave a little toot.

'Goodbye,' he muttered as he hopped up the stairs to the main door. 'Now, what do you think?' He ruffled Duchess's short velvet muzzle and she shook her floppy ears. 'How the hell am I going to sort out this house in just six weeks?'

CHAPTER 5

Georgia

Georgia flew into the Craignure Inn late, but only ten minutes this time, which was good by her standards. Stopping at the bar to order a drink and have a quick chat with the owner, she saw her friends gathered around a table in the corner close to the roaring fire. 'Don't they look happy?' she mused aloud. Three lovely couples. If she could cajole Autumn and Richard into their little group, there would be four, but Richard was working to a deadline and shied away from social gatherings. Georgia smiled as she took her drink – Autumn was working on it.

Throwing back her shoulders, Georgia approached. Being single hadn't bothered her up until now, so why should it change? The reminder that technically she had a boyfriend was usually enough. But more and more it made her uneasy. Two years was a long time, and how much longer might it be? Her thirtieth birthday was next month, and although she'd spent the year telling friends like Beth and Carl age was just a number and didn't mean anything, she couldn't help but start to see some significance herself, like it was lurking in the distance, along with a pair of giant three and zero helium balloons in sparkly fuchsia, waiting to bop her on the head. In many ways she still felt like a teenager and in other ways, she felt like she'd always been old.

'Sorry I'm late.' She slumped into a seat. 'I've had a manic day, and I was just getting ready when my mum phoned.'

'Is she ok?' said Beth. 'You look a bit worried.'

'I'm fine. It was just her cancellation call. I knew it, they always cancel on me, but I couldn't get her off the phone. Honestly, she didn't need to make that many excuses, she could have just said they didn't want to come.' Georgia was so used to this happening it was a foregone conclusion. If she acknowledged the hurt in her chest, she'd probably spend the whole evening crying into her glass, so she decided to let it go or at least mask it with irritation.

'Why don't they?' asked Carl.

'Tamsyn, my sister, again.' Georgia knocked back her drink, annoyingly enough just the soft stuff, but she'd learned to make it work. 'Apparently, she's organised a special Christmas holiday for them and they can't justify coming here as well. So, you know which child will always be dumped if there's a choice.' She raised her eyebrows in mock surprise and pointed both her index fingers at her chest.

'That's like Beth,' said Kirsten. 'She's definitely Mum's favourite.'

'No, I'm not.' Beth flung her a sharp glance.

Kirsten laughed. 'I'm joking.'

Georgia smiled along. 'Yeah, so your kind of sibling rivalry is fine. But this! My parents don't even attempt to hide their favouritism, and worse, they expect me to understand. I mean, who could possibly turn down a surprise Christmas holiday for an already planned trip to see their daughter's new home? Or my once-new home, because I've lived in it for nearly two years and they still haven't been to visit.'

'I guess it's a bad time of year for a visit,' suggested Fraser.

'Oh, it is. Mum reckons there might be hurricanes, tornadoes, freak snowstorms and a plague of locusts. That's apparently normal for the island in November. So, they'll save it until the summer. They must have forgotten they were going to do that this summer but they couldn't because Tamsyn needed them to babysit on her holiday to Rhodes.'

'Ah, we're just not cool enough,' said Carl. 'But hey, we make up for it by being our own kind of crazy.'

'You need a bit of that to live here,' agreed Fraser.

'You certainly do.' Georgia ordered another drink and let the conversation meander onto everything else. It was a welcome diversion from the irritation growing inside her. Part of her coming here was to escape from the constant comparison and the shame of losing the one thing in her life they approved of – Tony.

Raising a glass with her friends, Georgia beamed at them. Even though things had shifted in the dynamic with the new relationships, she was still lucky to have them. And they meant more to her than anything had in her life before Mull… Except Tony, of course.

They passed a pleasant evening; the poached salmon was a delicious diversion from her staple diet of cheese toasties and thanks to Archie Crichton-Leith she was feeling unusually flush. But the following day she still couldn't shift her annoyance. What point was there in bothering about it? It wasn't as if it was the first time it had happened and it was unlikely to be the last, but a seed of wickedness had taken hold and as she sat editing her latest photographs, she grabbed her phone and tapped out a text to her sister.

ME: I hear you're arranging a surprise Christmas holiday for Mum and Dad? Shame it means they won't come and see me now. And where's my invite?

She added the last bit without any desire to go wherever it may be. Even if Tamsyn invited her to the world's most glamorous location, she was not going. No way! This year she was having her own island Christmas, even if it meant lounging around alone in her boring house watching movies all day in her tartan pyjamas. It appealed more than one of Tamsyn's ridiculous extravaganzas.

Barely twenty minutes had passed when Georgia's phone rang. She watched it vibrating on her table. The name TAMSYN flashed in an irate and demanding way. Georgia's hand hovered; she'd love to ignore it. But if she did, Tamsyn probably wouldn't bother calling back and Georgia would miss finding out what was going on.

'Hello.' She tried to sound aloof, but it never worked, she always came across bouncy.

'Hi, darling. Good to hear from you.' Tamsyn had adopted a slow drawl, making her sound like Joanna Lumley and almost unrecognisable from the way she'd sounded when they were younger.

'What's up?' Georgia asked. What amazing excuses would Tamsyn have this time?

'So, this is going to be a bit of a shock for you, I hope you're sitting down.'

What now? Tamsyn pregnant again? Did she need a fourth child to complete the set? 'Yes.'

'All right, so, the holiday. Sorry, it was badly handled and makes me look so insensitive. It was not meant that way at all, darling. In fact, quite the opposite, but I don't think I'm going to be able to pull it off without telling you upfront.'

Georgia tapped her nail on the table, not daring to imagine where Tamsyn was whisking them off to this time. New Zealand? Alaska? It had to be somewhere dramatic; she was making such a scene about it. 'Right.'

'The thing is, I've taken a castle for a couple of weeks. It was a bit of a scoop pricewise. And there's plenty of room for everyone.'

Holding the phone away, Georgia sighed and pulled a silent grimace. A castle! It sounded right up Tamsyn's street and Georgia's worse nightmare. She didn't fancy rattling round an old, cold, gloomy house for Christmas, especially if it was populated with her brother-in-law's pompous family. 'Great, you'll enjoy that,' she said. 'Where is it? Germany? Switzerland?'

'Eh, no. Actually, darling, it's on Mull.'

Georgia took a moment to scrape her jaw off the floor before replying. 'Mull? As in here? Where I live? You're coming here for Christmas?'

'Absolutely, darling. I was going to surprise you, but I see that's not the best idea. I don't want you to feel left out. It'll be so much more fun if you're in on it. That's why Mum and Dad cancelled. They're coming anyway.'

'Eh.' Georgia had a hundred and one objections, excuses – call them what you want – but before she started, she had a question, because it wasn't beyond the realm of possibility that Tamsyn had made a gargantuan mistake. 'So what castle is it? I can only think of three on the island; one's a private house, one's a ruin, and one's a hotel.' Maybe Tamsyn had booked a holiday on the Mull of Kintyre or somewhere else with a happily similar name.

'It's not officially a castle, but it's a huge country pile, and it looks castley enough for me.'

Georgia rubbed her forehead. How could she prevent it? She'd already sworn she wasn't going near them for Christmas, but with them descending on the island, it would be unavoidable. 'And you've booked this already?'

'Yes, last week. It's a new rental, so it doesn't have any reviews yet, but it looks gorgeous and so romantic.'

Cue eye roll. Everywhere on the island looked romantic in the right conditions. Even the village shop had its moments in the right light. Come two weeks of rain and high winds, they'd be singing a different tune. Wait until Tamsyn's kids found out about the poor Wi-Fi, not to mention the lack of soft play centres and McDonald's. How long before the romantic notion went tits up? 'Remember it's cold and wet here in winter, so it might be a bit low on the romance stakes.' She found herself spinning out all the excuses she'd been so annoyed about her mum using the day before. But even the threat of bubonic plague didn't put Tamsyn off.

'We'll get a bit of hygge going, some warm fires and all that. And most of Gordon's rellies are coming too, and they're great at keeping the party moving.'

Georgia didn't restrain her audible groan. *Just bloody great!* That tiresome lot too. 'That sounds... delightful.' It couldn't get any better. The consolation was that Georgia wouldn't have to stay in the 'castle' and as her mother had so kindly reminded her on the phone the day before, her house was far too small to accommodate any of them. She was stacking her escape cards as Tamsyn reeled off the list of who was coming and when. Georgia didn't care. Their arrangements were of no concern and she switched off as Tamsyn prattled on.

'Oh gosh,' said Tamsyn mid-flow. 'There's a delivery man, must be my new iWatch. Listen, talk to Daisy a minute while I go sign for it. Don't hang up, I forgot to tell you something important. Daisy! Come and talk to Aunty Georgia, hurry up.'

Georgia held the phone away from her ear and softly exhaled. How to ruin Christmas in one phone call. This was the worst news she'd had all year.

'Hi, Aunty Georgia,' said the six-year-old.

'Hi, Daisy. How are you?'

'I'm very good. I've been at ballet today. When I come to visit you, I can show you how to do the splits.'

'Ok. You can show me yourself doing the splits, but I don't think I'm going to manage that.'

'It's really easy for me.'

'I bet. So, are you looking forward to coming? You have to go on a ferry.'

'I know. Mummy told me. She says we'll be fine because we were on a big cruise ship this summer and we didn't get sick. But Mummy says we have to watch out for Uncle Tony because he gets really seasick.'

'Tony?' said Georgia, her heart rate increasing. 'But Tony isn't coming.'

'Yes, he is. It's a big surprise and we're not allowed to tell. He's got a big ring and he's getting married to someone. So you better not tell anyone.'

'I won't.' Georgia stared at the pinboard on the opposite wall and the hundreds of island photos covering it. *Tony is coming here?* A surprise. With a ring. *Oh, my god.* She knew what that meant. Her tummy flipped over. Should she expect a 'surprise' proposal under the mistletoe? Another flip. Did she want that? Or could it be a mistake?

'Hello, darling.' Tamsyn was back. 'Sorry to keep you, but I forgot...'

A thousand ideas flashed through Georgia's brain. Tony was coming but had met someone else. Tony wasn't really coming. Tony this, Tony that. Her head was frazzled.

'I forgot to tell you the name of the place.'

'What?' Georgia blinked. That was what she wanted to tell her? Nothing about Tony?

'You might know the place, let me find the name. I doubt you'll know the family. Quite the yahs, as I understand, a long history on the island. Not people you'll have any cause to interact with.' The drawl in Tamsyn's voice got deeper. 'I think some of the family still live on the estate, in one of the cottages, but they won't get in the way. Good to know someone's about, I suppose, in case something goes wrong. Oh, here's the name, it's called Ardnish.'

Georgia dropped her forehead into her hand. 'Ardnish?' *Great.* That was the tatty wreck Tamsyn had booked. Georgia almost laughed through the turmoil tossing about inside her. They were in for a shock; Ardnish was a gloomy old building, cold and soulless. Its owner was a pompous arsehole who rocked his tweeds. Even with his team of professional cleaners, it would never be ready by Christmas. In fact, dynamite and a whole new building would be needed to satisfy Tamsyn's exacting standards.

When Georgia got Tamsyn off the phone, she sat for a moment, listening to the pounding of her heart. Taking slow deliberate breaths, she rebuilt her world in her mind. The world that had been shattered two years ago when Tony announced he wanted to take a break from their relationship. Not forever, just a hiatus. Crushed as she was, she'd agreed. Georgia had found Mull and built a new life. And yet she'd held on, waiting.

As the months had gone on, she'd forgotten for the most part and got on with things, but he was always there, lurking about, unresolved. Truthfully, she hadn't expected 'the break' to last this long, but after a while, she hadn't really missed him, not as much as she should have.

Through the muddle, she wanted to laugh. Tamsyn had paid all that money to stay in an old wreck. *But this is my island.* Georgia felt tears rising and pressed her fingertips to her lips in surprise. Normally only happy things induced tears. How could she bear Tamsyn ripping her home to shreds, criticising it and hating it as she'd done with everything else? The one thing in Georgia's life she'd ever found satisfactory was Tony, and even that came with a string. He'd only been accepted because he happened to be Tamsyn's husband's cousin. Without that illustrious connection, he'd have been shunned and berated like everything else in Georgia's life.

Georgia tapped the desk with her stylus, unable to concentrate. What could she do about any of it? Tamsyn was coming and so was Tony. Georgia could phone him and tell him not to, but what then? Did that mean they'd be finished? Forever? Would that be for the best? Tap, tap, tap went the stylus and Georgia's brain buzzed around trying to find a smart idea or an escape route.

What to do? Sit here and wait until Christmas Eve for the prodigal boyfriend to return with a huge diamond ready to slip onto her finger? For some reason, that idea didn't appeal anything like as much as it should.

CHAPTER 6

Archie

Archie lifted the phone receiver, feeling like he was sitting on the set of a nineties TV series, the office was so dated.

'Oh, hello, Mr Crichton-Leith?'

'Speaking. Can I help you?'

'Yah, defo. I'm Tamsyn Montgomery, I've made a booking with you and I'd just like to check a few of the details.'

'All right, sure.'

'So, can I just make sure you'll have a tree up? I mean it goes without saying, but best to confirm.'

'Er, yes.' Archie rubbed his forehead. *Shit!* There was so much to do and hardly any time before the guests descended. He grabbed a pen and scribbled on his desk pad. *TREE.*

'And the stairs, are they easy? My mother-in-law has the worst knees.'

'There's a downstairs guestroom.'

'No, sorry, that won't do. She can't sleep downstairs, finds it quite improper, you know.'

'I, er, well, there are quite a lot of stairs, but the main stairs have a chaise on the landing so she could have a sit down halfway.'

'Oh, wonderful. That is perfect. As soon as I tell her there's a chaise, she'll be in seventh heaven. Thanks ever so.'

'You're welcome.' As Archie hung up he took a deep breath. *Shit, shit, and more shit.* He needed to do something other than walk around, tearing his hair out. He'd charged them a packet, and they were bound to want a lot more than what he had on offer, such as a tree. Maybe even a lift? Who knew a dusty old chaise would be such a lifesaver? After shifting most of the boxes from the dining room to one of the box rooms, he was warm enough to remove his jumper. He stepped back and frowned; it didn't look like he'd achieved anything. Prising back the flap on one box, he squinted inside. What was all this junk? He didn't have time to go through it. The auction houses could make what they would from them. He closed up the flaps. Laurence had been a hoarder. But instead of displaying his collections, he shipped them to Mull and left them to gather dust in the house he visited twice a year.

Last Christmas had been just that. His last Christmas.

Laurence had married, divorced, repeated the process, and neither time produced issue. Both of his ex-wives were likely stewing at having left before they could cash in on his assets. Archie had inherited it all, along with the responsibility and expectations. But his mother didn't trust him. She'd done her duty and produced the heir and the spare. Maybe because he was her only remaining child, she wanted him away from the place she'd hated.

But he'd followed her rules long enough. If he'd followed his heart, he could have been playing in an orchestra or tangoing on *Strictly Come Dancing*. Ok, so that was a stretch, but there was so much more in him, interests that had been crushed and forced back in their box. He'd done the sensible thing, gone to university, studied hard, and taken a lucrative job in an oil company. It made him bags of money but didn't give him a second's joy.

With the boxes stacked out of sight, Archie did a quick hoover and dust around, but after that, he was stumped. He didn't have a clue how to stage a house or decorate it. Perhaps he should call Marcia. She'd be good at that kind of thing, but his mother wouldn't allow it, not under any circumstances, and Archie wasn't sure he wanted Marcia back in the house.

A moment of colossal fury gripped him and he wanted to grab the nearest heavy object and launch it out the window, but he controlled himself. Wrecking the house wouldn't work. Not this time. He rubbed his forehead as memories nudged him. It hadn't worked the last time either, in fact, it landed him in more trouble than it was worth. He also hoped he'd grown up in the twenty-year interval since his teenage hormones had sent him on a mad rampage; the Christmas he'd returned from boarding school to discover Laurence had burned his folders containing years' worth of poetry notes and writing. Childhood ramblings maybe, but at the time they'd been precious, not to mention private. Archie's fury had stopped just short of throwing his brother out an upstairs window. Laurence had laughed and laughed, claiming he thought it was a pile of old crap and how it had certainly warmed up the room. Such had been their relationship.

This house held nothing but oppressive memories. His father had bullied him for not being tough enough. 'You're not a real man, son, if you don't enjoy boxing. Poetry is for pansies.' So he'd been told on several occasions and if he disagreed he fell foul of his father's left hook. His furious rampage after the poetry-burning had been rewarded with one. His father couldn't understand the fuss. Why would anyone care about something so trivial? It certainly didn't warrant attacking Laurence – though Archie didn't regret it.

After years watching Laurence parading like a peacock and making Archie feel small, he was smugly delighted when he passed him in height. Laurence never forgave his younger brother for being taller, slimmer, and by all accounts better looking. But Laurence got his own back when Louisa arrived on the scene. Archie was easily more her type, but without the estate, he was nothing.

'Your loss,' he muttered to himself. 'Because now I have that too.'

He held his hand to his forehead. Yes, he had the estate, but he didn't have the power to fix it up. He'd rushed in with a half-baked plan and was about to reap the consequences. Years in the oil industry had taught him about the importance of planning ahead, but he'd done this with a degree of spontaneity almost unknown to him. Now he was going to be slapped in the face by his own folly. Maybe selling it was the answer after all and only retain Monarch's Lodge. But the history was too much. He couldn't stand the idea of strangers owning it. His family had built it and he had a duty to maintain it, but where to start? Short of blitzing this monument of ugliness, he couldn't see any way of making it remotely habitable or respectable, especially with less than five weeks to do it.

CHAPTER 7

Georgia

Sitting in Carl's dining room in his new cottage looking out to the sea didn't have the same ambience as the little log cabin in the grounds of the Glen Lodge Hotel, where Georgia had visited him last winter. Something about his rugged outdoorsy look didn't quite gel with this modern open plan surround. But the views were incredible.

Georgia was visiting under the pretence of having a job for Carl, though she really just wanted to offload. On the island, he was affectionately known as The Fixer because of his abilities to piece back together broken treasures of all shapes and sizes. This meant he was also good at making things and Georgia loved creating. He'd already helped her make a driftwood chandelier and clock this year. Now she'd painted an evening snowscape, 'and I want it to light up. I've seen things like it in the shops. There are little holes in the canvas and the lights shine through like stars.'

'Right.' Carl scratched his head. 'I can probably do that.'

'This place is in the cutest location,' said Georgia, trying not to turn green. If a lovely little cottage by the sea came up within her budget, she'd snap it up. But nothing ever did. All she could afford was her boring little two-bed semi in the village of Salen. She couldn't complain about the village, but the house just wasn't her. It was a cop-out to island life, being stuck in that place with the wilderness and the ocean all around but not able to see any of it.

After Carl had got together with Robyn, they were able to afford something much nicer and they'd spent the year doing it up. Since moving in, they'd transformed it from boring 1970s bungalow to modern chic, with the addition of an impressive wooden extension. The external timber recalled the little cabin enough to satisfy Georgia. When she'd met Carl he'd lived there, and she'd always think of him there. Inside, it was hard to believe this cottage had once looked like a granny's house. Now it was like the love child of Grand Designs and Pinterest. They'd taken inspiration from Carl's Norwegian roots, and all the wood and fur blended to make a picture-perfect house. 'I'm so jealous of this place,' said Georgia.

Carl poured hot water in a mug as he stood by the coffee nook, complete with chalkboard, cups on hooks and every variety of luxury beans arranged in mason jars. Wow. Georgia was getting greener by the second. She took a deep breath. No, that wasn't her. Carl was her friend, and he was happy. No use being jealous, it never helped.

'So, what's the other thing you want to talk about?' He placed a mug in front of her and she hugged it, letting the warmth seep into her hands.

'My sister.' Georgia's insides were now in such a state of flux, distinguishing whether it was excitement, anticipation or terror was impossible. Maybe all of them. And even though Tamsyn was part of it, most of it was Tony. No one on the island knew about him. How could she drop that bombshell now? The easiest way was to skirt neatly around it and cover her trepidation by blaming Tamsyn.

'What's she done?'

'She's gone and booked Ardnish for the Christmas fortnight. She and her husband, their three kids, my parents, her husband's parents and several of his relatives are coming here. Just when I thought I was going to be able to avoid them.'

'Maybe she's trying to be nice,' suggested Carl. 'She's finally coming to see you and bringing these people because she's proud of you.'

Georgia raised her eyebrow. 'Hmm. That's the sweet kind of thing people in your family do. Not my sister. And if it is, by some miracle, her being kind, this is her way, something totally over the top.' It was more plausible the whole thing was a ploy to get Georgia and Tony back together. It was what Tamsyn always wanted for Georgia, to have her married into a 'good' family.

'Why don't you just go with it? You normally do. You're the one who can bring laughs to a funeral.'

'Hmm.' Georgia sipped her coffee. 'It's never the same when my family are involved.'

'Yeah. I guess.'

'Hi,' said Robyn, coming in a side door where she had an office. 'I thought I heard your voice, but I was on a conference call. Is everything ok?' She slipped a strand of ashen blonde hair behind her ear as Georgia retold the story, still not mentioning a word about Tony.

'I visited Ardnish as a teenager,' said Robyn. 'The owner used to throw big wild parties every Christmas and one time we went. It was a bit of a disaster, I wasn't into parties and neither was my dad, he was a live cannon when we were out. I seem to remember Ardnish House was a bit of a museum piece. It must have been done up.'

'No, it hasn't,' said Georgia. 'I delivered pictures there last week, and it's awful. It was covered in dust and it's kitsch and ugly.'

'Sounds like the hotel last winter,' said Robyn.

'At least it had some inherent style,' said Georgia. She'd always liked the Glen Lodge Hotel. The building had charm, but Ardnish didn't. Georgia shuddered; the place reminded her of being shut in a tomb.

Robyn shook her head. 'I guess it won't appeal to your sister as much once she sees it.'

'Exactly that.' Georgia pointed her finger like a gun. 'And that's when shit hits the fan. She might be doing what she sees as a kindness just now, but as soon as she arrives and discovers the place is dreadful, she'll be off on her high horse. And you can guarantee it'll be my fault, somehow. She'll be miserable and so will everyone else, and she'll make damn sure I know about it. It'll be all over social media and everywhere she can think of, pulling me and the island into the muck.'

'You're so dramatic.' Carl smirked.

'I'm serious. This island has become part of me and if they end up hating it, it'll be like they're hating me too.' This time when she said *they*, she meant Tony. 'I'd want to take them on trips and show them everything beautiful on the island, but all they'll see is the inside of a gloomy old house.' If Tony was joining the house party, she couldn't sit by and let them rip the place to shreds. 'I know they'll hate it. Who wouldn't? It's ancient and decrepit. I can hear Tamsyn already, going on about how backwards it is here. Why couldn't they have booked a hotel? It's Tamsyn's bloody obsession with castles and the gentry.'

And it's about to backfire spectacularly – in my face!

'Why don't you volunteer to sort the place out?' said Carl.

'Are you serious?' said Georgia. 'It needs more than a string of bunting and a few throws.'

'Oh,' said Robyn. 'What a shame. Pity the owners didn't know about your design skills before. You did a great job on the hotel.'

'Yeah, I enjoyed that, but this place is beyond help.'

As Georgia drove home, the sun was setting. She headed north from Carl's beautiful seaside house in Carsaig to the village of Salen, tapping the steering wheel, her mind whirring around a plethora of crazy, reckless and entirely likely to fail ideas. But she couldn't shake Carl and Robyn's words. An iota of excited anticipation blossomed along with a tingle of fear. What if she did it? Did she have the nerve to approach Lord You-Don't-Have-Permission-To-Take-These-Photos and volunteer her services? It could go pear-shaped, but Georgia Rose wasn't a girl to shy from a challenge.

CHAPTER 8

Archie

Archie put the phone down, glaring at it for a moment. Why did he even have a phone like that? It had buttons and a cord, and it plugged into the wall. It was ancient, like everything else.

And now his mother had thrown the biggest spanner in the works so far. After insisting she'd never come back to the island and demanding he sell the place, she now wanted to come for Christmas. The one time she really couldn't. Archie hoped he'd done enough to fob her off. He'd already let it out to this damned house party, but he didn't want to let on. His mother might have a heart attack and he didn't want to be responsible for putting her in an early grave. He closed his eyes. It had been rash. The amount he'd have to spend to make the place fit meant he wouldn't break even, despite charging them an arm and a leg for it. And worse, he still hadn't made a proper start. After clearing out the rubbish and sending a van full of bags and boxes to an auction house, he now wandered around a considerably tidier house but without a clue what to do next. With all the clutter missing, it seemed even colder and emptier. Nothing he'd trained for in business had prepared him for this.

Another light bulb had blown in the dining room. He'd already changed half a dozen, but no matter how many he put in it didn't appear to brighten the place at all.

Standing atop the ladder, he scanned around. What the hell would the guests think? It was a Christmas booking; they'd want decorations. And what else? A rehash of the gaudy set-up from his childhood? Or maybe he could recreate the wonderful arrangements his grandmother made in Monarch's Lodge, but that was beyond him. She'd had flair and an eye for seeing beauty in nature. Archie didn't remember any tat in that house. He wasn't even sure she'd had tinsel. Everything had been natural and handmade, like a little craft shop or a Christmas market. Archie's mother hated it. 'Hideous and old fashioned.' She'd called it. 'The woman has far too much time on her hands. Honestly, if I had that much spare time, I wouldn't waste it on craft.'

Archie didn't like to point out she had time and she preferred to waste it doing very little of anything.

As he twisted the bulb into place, the chiming bell tinkled. The sound of it drove him mad. It was a flouncy melody which was fashionable in the era of *Terry and June*. He descended from the ladder, grabbing his iPad from the table. He needed to make a list of Christmas-related items to decorate the house with. Hopefully it was a delivery at the door. An industrial load of sheets, duvet covers, and towels was due to arrive. Perhaps throwing enough clean linen in the guests' eyes would dazzle them.

He pulled open the door without paying much attention, still thinking about what to add to the list. Looking up, he frowned. 'Eh, hello. Why are you here?'

A bright face twinkled back with possibly the biggest smile he'd seen on the island. Georgia Rose, the artist, photographer, and trespasser. Before she replied, a hundred answers had already zapped through his head in the flash of a second. Another trespass, something wrong with the pictures, forgot one of them?

She peered around. 'Can I come in? Would this be a good time to talk?'

If the wind decided to change, Archie might be stuck with a giant groove across his forehead. He consciously straightened his brow and stood tall. Georgia had a beguiling smile, one that invited him to grant her every request just so he could keep looking at it. But Archie had a long history of dealing with women like this. Was she just another gold-digger? Was she playing a game? Alarm bells were ringing; he couldn't stop the sound blaring in his ears. 'It rather depends on what you want to talk about.'

'It's a business proposal.'

His brow furrowed again as his mind worked to keep one step ahead. Permission to take more photographs on his land, perhaps? Or was whatever she was going to say just a cover? He adjusted his shirt collar. *Stop being so paranoid.* Letting out a little cough, he quashed the instinct to close the door in her face. 'Ok, but make it quick. I haven't got long.'

She followed him into the hallway, and he led her down the dank passageway into the office. It wasn't particularly tidy, but it was easily the warmest room in the house. Gesturing to the old swivel seat by the window, he sat in the leather chair opposite. Georgia slipped into the rattly seat and dragged it closer, placing her wrists on the desk, clasping her fingertips. She wore an eclectic combination of rings, including one that wound around her thumb like a snake.

'So, does this business involve you taking more photographs on my land, perchance?' Archie leaned back in his seat and tented his hands.

'It does not,' she said with a glint in her eye, like she was facing him down in a round of twenty questions. She waggled her eyebrow, waiting for his next guess.

'Well, you better enlighten me,' said Archie.

She held his gaze for a few seconds. Archie adjusted his collar. 'I've heard on the island grapevine you've rented this place out over the Christmas period,' said Georgia.

Archie folded his arms and lifted his brows. 'Where did you hear that?'

'Never mind. You know what this island is like, everybody knows everything five minutes after it happened.'

He shook his head with a benign pout and a miniscule shrug, as though none of it concerned him in the slightest.

Georgia stood her ground. 'I know it's true.'

'Even if it is, what does it have to do with you?'

'Now there's the thing. I couldn't help noticing, when I was delivering the photos, that this place is somewhat worse for wear. It's not exactly the grand kind of place you're advertising on the website. I had a look and frankly, the lack of interior shots was probably wise, but you'll be singing a different tune when your guests arrive. They'll thrash you on Trip Advisor and everywhere else. They'll probably want a refund and they might even report you to Trading Standards.'

Archie took a deep breath. 'All that might be true, but it doesn't explain anything. Again, I'll ask, what does it have to do with you?'

'Technically nothing.' Georgia picked at one of her nails. 'But the thing is, I'm an artist and a photographer and the winter is a pretty dire time for me money-wise. But I also have a lot of design experience. If you wanted to hire someone to get this place into shape… Well…' She waved her fingertips to the ceiling and beamed. 'Look no further.'

Archie moved his eyes slowly over her face. *Wow, she has some nerve.* But the worst of it was, he needed exactly what she was offering – assuming this was real. Alarm bells were still chiming. 'All right,' he said. 'If in theory, I wanted to hire someone like you to…' He waggled his hand about. 'To work whatever magic you mean to work. What kind of price are we talking? An hourly rate? Minimum wage? What?'

Georgia stroked a strand of her tousled blonde bob from her cheek. 'It's negotiable.'

'So negotiate.' He leaned forward, resting his arms on the desk.

'Maybe something up front and the rest on completion… When you're satisfied with the work.'

Archie chewed on his lower lip and nodded. 'And what if I'm never satisfied?'

She smirked. 'Yeah, ok, there's that possibility. So, I don't know. I can tell you what I get paid for photoshoots, but I haven't done a lot of paid design work. I did the Glen Lodge interior last winter.'

'Maybe I should check it out before we go any further.'

'Look on their website.'

Archie opened the browser on his laptop and found the website. He scanned through the pages with interest. It looked very chic, exactly what he wanted. 'How much did they pay you?'

'Maureen paid me five hundred pounds.'

'Is that all? I think you undersold yourself.'

Georgia gave a little laugh. 'Yeah, but she lets me do exhibitions and things there for nothing, so it was a bit of an arrangement.'

Leaning back, Archie inhaled slowly. 'And was the hotel bigger than here?'

'About the same, though I only did the guest areas, so probably not as many rooms as this.'

'In better or worse condition?'

'Better. It had all new fittings by the time I got in.'

'So we're talking around two thousand pounds?'

Georgia's eyes popped out of her head. 'We are?' She cleared her throat. 'Yes, we are.'

'Right.'

'But…' Georgia glanced around. 'You'll have to have a budget for the house too, you can't make this place guest friendly without spending some money on it.'

'So, the bottom line is, you want me to pay you to spend my money to make my house respectable for someone else to live in?'

'Pretty much.'

Archie shook his head. How bloody irritating, but possibly a godsend at the same time. All businesses ran at a loss in the beginning; he'd already considered the possibility he wouldn't make any money out of this booking. If he took her on, he could abdicate some responsibility and concentrate on his real job. The one which paid the bills and where he actually knew what he was doing. Plus he could devote more time to sorting Monarch's Lodge, getting it ready for possibly his most perfect Christmas in years.

'Why don't you think about it?' said Georgia.

'I am,' he said. 'I don't exactly have much time.' Should he do this? Or was it all a trick? He flicked open Google again and searched for interior design quotes. 'And you'd accept two thousand pounds?'

'Well, yes.'

'A retainer up front and then what? A weekly wage, an end salary?'

'Yes,' she quipped.

He pulled his head to the side. 'Which?'

'A weekly wage would suit me best.'

'All right. In principle, I accept your proposal, but I'm going to draw up a contract. There are several things we need to agree on and I want to check your credentials. I need to call the owner of this hotel.'

'Sure, no problem.' She grinned and looked like she might be dancing a jig inside her head. Part of him wanted to jump right in and join her in a rousing foxtrot. She'd be up for a shimmy. There was no hiding it, he could always tell the ones who would.

'But…' he said, and her expression dropped. 'This is going to be done above board and strictly professional. No taking liberties.'

She laughed, the sparkle returning. 'Yeah, it's ok, no photos. Though if you let me take some, you could put them on your website. And I could set you up on Instagram too.'

Archie allowed himself a smile. 'All right, that's delightful, I'm sure, but if you want to work for me, we'll do it properly. A lot of jobs on the island are done cash in hand and on a need-to-know basis, but I don't work like that. If you give me an email address, I'll draw up your contract and, assuming I get a good reference for you, we'll stick to it.'

'Aye aye, captain.' She saluted with a wink.

Archie let out a sigh and closed his eyes. He really hoped he was doing the right thing and he wasn't about to sign a blank cheque to a near stranger with an alluring smile. His ex with the broken-down car flickered through his mind and he swallowed a moment of doubt. He got to his feet and shook Georgia's hand. Her smile looked genuine. Please god, let it be real because this could be the miracle he'd been wishing for.

CHAPTER 9

Georgia

Georgia couldn't be one hundred per cent sure Archie wasn't watching from one of the sash windows, so she restrained herself from jumping and clicking her heels together as she nipped down the front steps to her van. As soon as she got in and started the engine, she burst out laughing. Not only would she make sure the place was perfect for Tony's arrival, but she was going to get paid for it.

'How much cash does this guy have?' She chuckled, momentarily thrilled by her own brilliance. It would have been an acceptable compromise to have done it voluntarily. She could have gone down the needing experience road or something similar. She was good at winging it. But to come out with the promise of two thousand pounds… 'This is beyond exciting.' As she drove off, she flicked on her Christmas CD and did a happy dance before belting out 'All I Want For Christmas' like a rock star… Until her engine died halfway up the drive.

'No, no, no!' She turned the keys for at least the fifteenth time. 'Do not do this to me. I don't need this now. Nooooooo!'

No amount of coaxing or forcing had any effect. Was there any point in opening the hood? *What exactly am I supposed to look for?* A nest of mice? 'And no reception. Of course, there's no reception.' She stamped her foot on the icy cold ground. This left only one course of action. Go back and beg to use the landline. She trudged down the drive, clapping her gloved hands together. Better it happened here than halfway home in the middle of nowhere.

She rang the bell and waited on the step. The wind gusted along the front of the house and the dormant ivy shuddered. Behind the mottled glass, the tall, broad-shouldered figure of Archie appeared. This place was too big and creepy for its own good. When Tony arrived, would he expect Georgia to stay here with him? She didn't fancy it. It must be spooky as hell after dark.

'You again?' Archie pulled open the creaky oak door.

'Yes, it is. You won't believe this, but my van's broken down on the drive. Can I use the phone, please? I'm not getting reception.'

Archie lowered his eyebrows, not attempting to hide his irritation. 'Really?'

'Yes. If you're any good with cars maybe you want to give it a go?'

'No.' He stepped back and let her in.

'I'm sorry, this is really frustrating. I love my van, but I guess it's of an age that things are bound to go wrong. I've been half-expecting it for a while.'

'No doubt.' He closed the door with a thud. She prayed when the house party arrived, he'd make himself scarce. Nobody wanted a sullen face like his turning up. 'It's in the office,' he said, pointing to the gloomy passageway.

'Thank you.' He didn't follow, and Georgia closed the office door to make the call. The recovery truck was out and about, it would be a three-hour wait. Her heart sank. She didn't suppose Archie would want her hanging about. *And I don't want to.* But she didn't have any other options.

He was lurking in the hallway on his iPad when she emerged.

'Oh, there you are. Guess what?' she said.

'What? He frowned.

'It'll be at least three hours. So… Can I wait here, please?' Georgia all but batted her eyelashes, trying to be appealing. She wouldn't put it past him to turf her out into the cold to wait.

'I'm sure you'll find somewhere that suits,' he said, wafting his hand around. 'And you'll be interested to know that just before you came back I was on the phone to the owner of the Glen Lodge Hotel.'

'Oh?'

'She speaks very highly of you.'

'So…'

'So you're officially hired.'

'Brilliant. How about I start now then?' she said brightly, hoping to turn his frown upside down. 'I could get started on the designs. If I make a list of things to order when I start properly, we'll have the stuff. I guess the sooner I get onto it the better. After all, you know what island deliveries can be like.'

'Yes, I do,' he conceded with a sigh. 'All right, fine, you get on with that. Use the laptop in here.' Without waiting for her to agree, he stepped past her into the office and opened it up, typing in a password. 'I'll leave you to it. I have a lot of work to do.'

'Ok.' She backed into the doorframe as he tried to make a sharp exit and was hit by a heady scent, an expensive, deep aroma. She let her eyelids drop, breathing in, trying to unlock the combination of fragrances. They embodied virtue and strength with cheeky hints of mischief and zing. He brushed past and her eyes sprang open.

Archie stopped opposite and folded his arms. 'You realise this is a strictly professional engagement?' His cheeks looked slightly red, but Georgia was sure it wasn't embarrassment. Anger, more like.

'Of course.' It was her turn to feel the heat. 'What else would it be?'

'Exactly. Nothing else. If your van has broken down then I'm sorry, but if this is some phoney attempt to get stranded, then...'

'Why would I do that?'

'Because, well, it's happened before and I don't want to... play games.'

Georgia gaped at him. *What?* Her eyes widened as she caught his train of thought careering straight out of his mismatched irises. *Does he think I'm coming on to him?* She put her hand to her mouth to stop a laugh escaping. 'Ok. I can put your mind at rest. I'm not here for any hidden reason. Why would I be? You're married. I'd have to be pretty brassy to do what I assume you're suggesting.'

'I'm not married,' said Archie.

'Engaged then, or whatever.'

'No.'

'I saw your girlfriend at my exhibition.'

He shook his head fractionally. 'No, you didn't because I don't have one.'

'Sorry, I thought the dark-haired lady...'

'Oh. That was Marcia. She's my mother's secretary.'

'Oh, oops.' Georgia shrugged. 'Well, it doesn't change anything. I'm not trying to hit on you.' It was a struggle not to giggle. Did he really think that? 'I'd prefer not to have a broken-down van. I came here about the house because, er, I need money.' A white lie, but partially true. What a high conceit he had of himself. To think she was there because she fancied him. Her eyes were laughing, she couldn't stop them. If she did, the frenzied giggles would burst from her mouth.

Archie's jaw tensed, and his face twitched. 'Good. So, you get on with whatever it is you need to do.'

'I'll have a look, but let's get this straight, I'm not here to take advantage of you. You might be used to women lining up for you, but I'm not that easily impressed.'

'Yeah, all right. Let's drop it now.'

'Maybe I should be the one checking your references.'

'All right.' He held up his hands. 'I think we've established where we stand. Now, I have to get on.' He adjusted his collar as he strode off. Georgia leaned out the door, admiring the way his crisp white shirt tapered into his slick navy trousers, showing off a trim backside. Actually, he was a bit of all right but that didn't mean anything. Georgia appreciated human beauty in many forms; it didn't follow she wanted to leap into bed with every handsome man she saw – far from it. Because of Tony, she was well-practised in abstinence.

'Bloody cheek.' After he closed the door at the end of the passageway, Georgia shut the office door and laughed. Seriously? Had that conversation just happened? Sitting in front of the laptop, she let her eyes snoop around the room. Despite this apparent female adoration, Lord I-Have-A-Great-Backside-And-Don't-I-Know-It preferred to stay in this ugly big house by himself. Why? Was she hiding from his admirers? He appeared more like the type to be lapping them up. He could run this place as his own love nest.

As the mistress of multitasking, Georgia was able to search for decorations, lights, mirrors, throws and an overabundance of decadence while still puzzling out Archie's self-obsession. She'd need to see the house properly before ordering but there were some Christmas must-haves she could start with. Maybe Archie had fallen foul to money grabbers in the past, but was he for real? What grounds did he have to accuse her of anything like that? Chuckling to herself, she added some smart cushions in grey tweed with a stag imprint to her basket.

It would take all her willpower not to tease him. In fact, she wanted to pretend she fancied him just to wind him up, but the thought of two grand dangled in front of her. And she was supposedly doing this for the man she was getting back together with. That notion knocked the wind from her sails.

Sitting in an office for several hours without moving wasn't something Georgia was used to; in fact, she couldn't. She didn't dare wander about either, Sir Women-Line-The-Streets-In-Wait-For-Me might not be thrilled to find her creeping around.

As she dropped a red tartan table runner into the basket, she considered her next move... Read the invoices on the desk? The door opened. Archie came in and Georgia leapt back into the seat. He narrowed his eyes, and she lifted her brows, drumming her fingertips and assuming an innocent air. *Check him out! The loose button, showing off that chest. How will I stop myself falling for his charms?* Georgia grinned as he balanced himself into a half-sitting position on a bookshelf. She eyed him from head to foot. Why was someone this good looking and well-off still single? There was something amiss here. Possibly his self-obsession? After giving him a second going over, she considered he was actually a fine specimen of a man. *Oh dear! I won't be able to behave myself, no matter how hard I try.*

Archie ran his hand round his neck. 'How's the list going?' he asked.

'Very good, would you like to see what I've got so far?'

'You've ordered stuff?' He sounded panicky.

'No, I need to look around the house first. I've just been adding to baskets. You need to hit the order button unless you want to give me free rein with your credit cards.' She gave him an irresistible smile.

'No, I bloody don't.' He pulled the dodgy old office seat round and sat beside her. She spun the leather chair, her legs a hair's breadth from his. He tensed, but his fragrance diverted her internal giggle. It was so intense and provocative.

'So what have we got?' He leaned over and clicked through the tabs. She should have moved out of his way, but she used the moment of proximity to inhale gently, though not being too obvious.

His curiously mismatched eyes scanned through the baskets. 'Quite the spending spree you've been on, isn't it?'

'Yes, but it's necessary and most of it you can use again, though the Christmas stuff only at Christmas, obviously.'

'Yes, I worked that out. I don't see myself needing about sixty metres of fairy lights for the rest of the year.' He drew back, then perhaps noticing how close he'd got, stood up. 'And is this all?'

'I doubt it. Can I have another look around? I'm doing this from memory. It would be better if I looked, then I can visualise it.'

'Be my guest,' he said, sarcasm clinging to every word.

Georgia made her way to the drawing room before she realised he hadn't come with her. The room was more like a poorly shoved together lounge in an outdated hotel than something high-end guests would appreciate. Would Archie mind if she moved some furniture about? She decided to risk it. She could always put it back if he was bothered.

The cleaners hadn't done a great job, one shove of the sofa and a rectangle of dust was revealed on the carpet. She kept on pushing and dragging things around until a funny tinkling bell distracted her. Was it a clock somewhere? She'd lost track of time, and the room didn't have a clock – mental note to add one to the basket. Her phone wasn't in her pocket either, she must have left it in the office.

'That's the tow truck,' said Archie.

Georgia jumped and spun around to see him standing in the doorframe. 'I didn't hear you come in. Was that chiming sound the doorbell?'

He nodded and folded his arms. 'This looks… interesting.'

'I'm not finished yet,' she said, 'but I can move it back if you don't like it.'

'No, you knock yourself out,' he said. 'But maybe get your van sorted first.'

'I will, well, I'll go and see what they can do. The thing is, I'm not sure how I'll get back here to work if they can't fix it.'

It was a genuine concern, but she looked up to see his head tilt and his fingertips digging into his upper arm as he held them across his body: his expression said he didn't believe a word of it.

'Ridiculous, isn't it?' She nodded at his unspoken sentiment. This wasn't a game, this was her life, full of crazy chaos. 'The next thing you know I'll be setting up camp here and we can only imagine where that might lead.' She tapped her nose and winked. A chortle desperately wanted to escape, but she bottled it, pinched her lips tightly together and passed him by. Crossing the hall, she ran straight for the door to meet the mechanic, hoping beyond hope she wouldn't have to fork out the two thousand-pound pay cheque she hadn't even received yet to get her engine up and running again.

CHAPTER 10

Archie

Heavy rain and wind battered the house for the next week. Archie liked to be out and about, especially with the dogs, but it was almost too miserable even for them. As they made their way along the heath towards the hill leading to the ridge that morning, icy blasts caught Archie in the face and the dogs leapt around in the spray from the sea. 'Let's get back,' he said. 'This is horrible.'

Stepping into the house these days was like entering some random place that reminded him both of Christmases as a small boy and the time he'd got stuck in a half-finished window display at the House of Fraser in Glasgow. After he'd knocked over about twenty boxes and two naked dummies in his attempt to get out, his mother had whipped him within an inch of his life and she'd never shown face in the shop since, despite it being thirty years ago. Neither had he. Far too traumatic. As he unwound his scarf and looked about at the piles of boxes, the half-hung evergreen garlands and the abandoned stepladder, Georgia skipped out of the drawing room. A crescendo of Christmas music blared from the open door.

'Oh, hello.'

'Hello,' Archie replied. The garage had fixed the dodgy starter in Georgia's van, thus avoiding the having-to-stay-the-night possibility that obviously amused her so much. Archie cursed himself. *Why couldn't I curb my tongue?*

I've become such a jerk – and a joke. But after being hit on by so many women who cared for nothing except the bulging wallet in his trousers, it got rather tedious.

The dogs leapt forward. The younger pointer jumped up on his powerful rear legs and licked Georgia on the nose. She squirmed and giggled. 'Dexter!' Archie barked. 'Down.'

Georgia hung a piece of tinsel around the dog's neck and smiled. 'Why did you call your dog after a serial killer? It's a tad alarming.'

'What are you talking about?'

'Seriously? You haven't watched *Dexter*? You haven't lived.'

'Evidently. It's already looking a lot brighter in here.' Archie tried his most convivial tone, blinking as he focused. Meeting her eye after his stupid comments the other day was uncomfortable; he'd opened himself up to no end of teasing. Playing along seemed the best way to go, keeping it light-hearted. Maybe she'd forget or think he'd been joking. He'd made her a contract with bland terms and conditions, avoiding his personal concerns as it had started to sound like a prenup and he'd fancied he could hear her giggling even when he was just thinking about it. He had to live a little and stop stressing. Georgia never stopped smiling and looked guileless. His gut was telling him it was ok this time. 'What are you doing today?' he asked as she dotted around, humming along to the tune wafting out the other room.

'I have a list of jobs, but one thing leads to another.' She pulled open a box and peered inside. 'Do you like whisky?'

'Yes. Why? Is there some in that box?' Had she uncovered the two stolen bottles he'd accused his ex of stealing?

'No, this is the first load of fabric, I think. I was asking because someone gave me a bottle last year but it's not to my taste.' She glanced up. 'You look like a connoisseur. I'll bring it with me next time.'

'Thanks. What brand is it?'

'One of the Islay ones with an unpronounceable name, Bunny-Haven or something like that.'

Archie grinned and looked away. He supposed it did sound like that, but he could almost see her imagining a little rabbit hopping into a house made from an empty bottle. 'Bunnahabhain. It's a good one. It means mouth of the river in Gaelic, nothing to do with rabbits.'

She threw her head to the side with a pout. 'Oh, Archie, you've spoiled it.'

'Sorry, I thought I might have. But you don't need to let on that you know. Just forget I told you.'

Her mock stern look morphed back into her smile at a new song from the drawing room. 'Oh, I love this song.' The jazzy opening to 'Man with the Bag' began. 'It always makes me want to dance.' Georgia threw up jazz hands and swayed, beaming. She looked momentarily stuck in her own little world. 'Wanna join in?' She laughed, clearly expecting him to say no. Something in her eyes was laced with flirtation. Was this her way of punishing him? He might be more cautious than he had been some years ago, but he was no stranger to this game.

His feet itched. He simultaneously wanted to say no and yes. No would avoid embarrassment, yes could be fun. If he thought about it too long the song would pass and so would the moment. It had been years since he'd had a good dance. He cast his scarf aside with what was possibly an unnecessarily theatrical flick, took hold of Georgia's hand and twirled her under his arm.

'Ooh! My god.' She squealed with laughter as Archie caught her from her spin and led her around the flagstone floor in his own version of Strictly. Exhilarating adrenaline burst through him and his cold limbs burned with energy. Georgia followed, wide-eyed, moving in perfect sync with him, her hips swaying, feet zipping.

'You can dance,' she said. Her grin was so wide Archie could have counted her perfectly white teeth, but that would be a terrible misuse of time right now. The cute little dress she was wearing flared out as she twirled around the entrance hall.

'So can you.' He smiled, and wow, he hadn't worked the muscles in his cheeks this hard for years. Smiling felt good, much better than digging into the old forehead with his frown.

Dexter barked and Duchess looked on with a disapproving eye, matching her name to a T.

Georgia skipped and swayed, and Archie became aware of his hand resting on her waist, his palms suddenly hot.

As the song ended, he held Georgia's arms wide. He couldn't stop smiling and she returned it.

'Well, well, well,' said Georgia. As soon as Archie let her go, he couldn't figure out where to look. All he wanted to do was stare into those liquid brown eyes, but that was totally inappropriate. 'Aren't you the man of hidden talents? Quite the Fred Astaire.'

'Hardly, but I used to enjoy a bit of ballroom dancing. I haven't done it for a long time.'

'Why not? You're good.'

'Dance partners are hard to come by.'

Georgia sized him up, and Archie adjusted his collar. 'Couldn't you just have paid someone?'

Archie rolled his eyes. 'Yes, I could, but I didn't. It's not the same.'

'Well, come and give me a whirl at my next break. I'm very reasonably priced, remember.'

'Are you? I thought you were extortionate.'

Georgia winked. 'You can have the dance for free then.'

'Such generosity. But I better get some work done.'

'Archie.'

When he looked back, she had a serious expression. 'Yes?'

'I just wondered, when the guests arrive, where are you going to go?'

'Hmm.' He rubbed his forehead. 'My plan was to move into Monarch's Lodge, I'm just not sure I'll be able to get it ready in time.'

'Monarch's what? Don't tell me you once had Bonnie Prince Charlie hiding in it or something.'

'Ha! No. It was named that because apparently a huge stag used to visit the garden every year. You know, the monarch of the glen, so called. Its head probably ended up mounted on the wall by my great-grandfather.'

'Ew, delightful. So where is this place?'

'Just over the hill, it's well hidden, but once you're there... Well... I tell you what, let me have an hour or so, then I'll walk you down and show you. It's a place that'll inspire your creative juices, I'm sure.'

'Great. Just give me a shout when you're ready.'

Archie opened the door to the passageway and let the dogs go through. They padded to the end room and he heard them heaving themselves into their beds and nibbling their toes. Archie settled in the office and knuckled down to some work. Oil sales were a complete brain drain after the buzz of the dance. Georgia was crazy and full of fun. As long as the joke wasn't on him. If it was just a game to pass a cold month in winter, he could handle it.

The business took longer than he'd planned, and it was almost two o'clock when he got up from his desk and stretched. After checking the dogs, he shut the door and made his way through the house. Although not all the deliveries had arrived, and he'd had to pay a ridiculous subsidy to get most of them so quickly, the difference in the rooms was remarkable. Lights in jars adorned the sideboard alongside his old candlesticks and some random jugs. It was a mismatched jumble of old and new, but somehow perfect. Along the front hung cream and fur stockings. If he'd set things up like that it would have looked like a bric-a-brac table but Georgia had it spot on. *Praise the day she came knocking on my door,* Archie thought with a rueful smile. All down the bannister on the grand staircase trailed faux greenery mixed with cones and baubles of gold and sparkling silver, and at the bottom a set of perfectly gift-wrapped boxes in co-ordinating wrapping paper.

A solo voice from the drawing room made him stop and he leaned closer to the door to listen. Georgia was crooning 'In the Bleak Midwinter'. Archie furrowed his brow as his ear rested on the oak panel. What a beautiful voice; she struck every note and the melancholy words drifted effortlessly. Rooted to the spot, he listened until she finished, then he opened the door.

'That was quite something,' he said. 'Not just a dancer, a singer too.'

'Oh, my god, were you listening?' Georgia peered up from the midst of a pile of fairy lights.

'I certainly was. Maybe when the guests arrive, you could give them an evening of entertainment.'

She pulled her head to the side. 'Very funny.'

'I mean it. You're very talented.'

She furrowed her brow. 'Are you being cheeky?'

He shook his head. 'No, really, I'm not. You can paint, sing, dance, take stunning photographs, and grab a random collection of objects, put them together and make a tired old house look like a castle.'

'Haha, thanks. And much as I'm loving the flattery, I'm not as posh as you, so I draw the limit at shows in drawing rooms. I wouldn't even do the pub karaoke… unless I was very drunk.'

He crossed the room. 'I suspect you underestimate yourself. Here.' He sat behind the piano, opened the lid, and spread his fingers over the keys. 'I'm a bit rusty but try this.'

He began the opening notes of 'Silent Night'.

'Seriously?' Georgia folded her arms. 'You play the piano? Oh dear.' She dropped her face into her hands. 'So, it's you who's the talented one. There's no way I'm singing along. Far too embarrassing.'

He kept his eyes on the keys, smiling, but didn't reply. Without looking up he was aware she'd gone back to sorting decorations and untangling fairy lights, but if he kept going, her curiosity would win out, wouldn't it? He finished the last chord before starting something new. 'How about this one?' He began the introduction to 'Oh Holy Night'. His favourite, mainly because it was his party piece. If he was in the mood, he could sing it reasonably well. And he was up for giving it a go, even though he hadn't practised for a long time. 'Sing along, come on,' he said before singing, accompanying his words with the opening bars. It was years since anyone had heard him. These days he saved it for the car, or when the house was empty. Hiding behind the piano gave him strength and he began softly but assuredly until he noticed Georgia had stood up and was staring at him. He faltered slightly but saved the note in time so it passed undetected.

'Ok, you can really sing.' She placed her hands on her hips and shook her head.

He continued, gesturing for her to join in as the notes soared from his chest. Thank Saint Nicholas they were so rounded with no practice or even a drop of alcohol.

Georgia held up her palms. 'No way. I couldn't get that high without shattering the windows,' she muttered. 'Not a look we want for the house party.'

As he finished off the last notes, he glanced up. Georgia was still watching, her lips parted slightly.

'That wasn't very nice,' she said.

'Charming,' he retorted.

'I don't mean the singing. The singing was sensational. That's the point. Asking me to sing along was cruel. Now I know you were taking the mickey. Did you just come in to show off?' Her smile seeped into his veins and made him grin too.

'Maybe.'

'Typical,' she muttered through her smirk, pulling a long line of fairy lights across the mantelpiece.

'It's true, I'm an awful man. But how about this? This is definitely you. Come on.' He ran his fingers up the keys, then tinkled, 'Jingle Bell Rock'. When she didn't start straight away, he began, but watched her with an I-dare-you smirk.

'Oh, Archie.' She shook her head. 'You really are a bad man.' Ticking her finger towards the window indicating for him to move along, she walked towards the piano. She gave her blonde bob a little flick and the loose waves danced. Archie shuffled to the edge of the stool and she sat beside him, taking up where he'd left off with, 'Giddy-up jingle horse, pick up your feet.'

His grin broadened. Her slim leg pressed against his thigh, making him twitch, but he continued. The room looked like a different place; sun poked through the windows, glinting on the newly polished surfaces. His fingers skimmed the keys and bounced up and down to the chirpy rhythm. He beamed at Georgia as they finished the song. This smiling thing was amazing, better than therapy. He finished and lifted his right hand with a flourish before the reality of where he was and what he was doing slapped him. What an entirely inappropriate interlude… Though rather a lot of fun.

'Very nice,' said Georgia, giving his knee a double pat and standing up. 'But I have work to do.'

He stared at the ivories then closed the lid with a slow thud. 'Yes. Sorry about that. I couldn't resist. The Christmas spirit finally found a way in. Your voice was the key, it was so enchanting.'

'Nothing like as good as yours.' With her back to him, she'd started to hang the string of lights. She didn't look round, but he had the impression she was laughing.

'I'll beg to disagree. Now, do you still want to see Monarch's Lodge?'

'Oh, sure. I forgot about that. As long as there's no more singing or dancing. Remember, I'm supposed to be behaving myself. You're making my life very difficult with all this flirtatious behaviour.'

Archie straightened his collar. 'Oh, god. I'm sorry. I didn't mean… anything. I don't quite know what happened.'

Georgia swivelled around very slowly, but before he could even see half her face, he guessed she was smiling. 'I'm joking. It's good to know you're not as stuffy as you look. In fact, randomly enough, in some ways, you're quite like me… Only with more money and a posher accent.'

'And not an artistic bone in my body.'

'I don't believe that for a second.' She stuck up the end of the lights and dusted off her hands. 'So, are you going to show me around this house then?'

'Follow me.'

With a twinkle in her eye, Georgia passed him and made her way into the hall. Archie watched her approach the antechamber, get her coat, and swing it on. She tied the belt around the scarlet fabric and glanced up, flashing him another wide grin. He took a deep breath. The house wasn't the only thing benefitting from her creative soul.

CHAPTER 11

Georgia

After seeing a different side to Archie, Georgia no longer dreaded her days at Ardnish. With the prospect of being swept off her feet into a ballroom dance or taking part in a Christmas sing-along, she turned up early every day. But Archie seemed to have scared himself off and she barely saw him over the next couple of days.

Perhaps he'd gone to Monarch's Lodge. Wow, Monarch's Lodge. Georgia almost wanted to ditch the main house and go help him. When she'd walked there with him, she hadn't been prepared for anything like it. It was the most dramatically stunning place she'd ever seen. Archie had asked her if she was ok; he'd never known her to be so quiet. She could have stood at the crest of the hill and looked at that view forever. If her house was the most boring place on the island, Monarch's Lodge was the polar opposite. Its dramatic cliffside location tickled every part of her with a desperate desire. Maybe if she decorated it for free, Archie would gift it to her. She giggled as she settled a new rug in place. Ok, silly idea, but it was Christmas, she was allowed a crazy wish or two.

After lunch, she took a walk, knowing her feet would carry her towards Monarch's Lodge. She wasn't even bothered if Archie caught her. Excuses tripped off her tongue and he didn't seem to mind if she had a skive here and there, which was good because making up excuses for other things had become something of a full-time job. Not with her family. Keeping what she was doing from them was easy. She wasn't even sure they knew what she did for a living. Last Christmas she'd overheard her mother telling some friends she was still on a gap year. At twenty-nine, she certainly wasn't but her mother couldn't get the idea this was her life, not just something she was playing at. But her friends had started to sit up and take notice. Beth had invited her round for a drink later, and Georgia suspected there might be an inquisition.

As she approached Monarch's Lodge, Archie came out, shirt sleeves rolled up, carrying the remnants of an old chest of drawers. 'Oh, baby Jesus,' muttered Georgia. *Just as well I'm spoken for and Archie's a posh twat, because if I was single and he wasn't so bloody rich, he'd be one hot Christmas dinner.* Already, he was right up there with black forest hot chocolate covered in cream. *If he starts chopping wood, I'm a goner.* Georgia stopped, but it was too late, he'd seen her.

He tossed the wood onto a pile outside the door, dusted off his hands, and waved. 'Come to help?' he asked.

'I will if you like, but there's still a lot to do at the main house.'

He folded his arms and gave her a look. 'So, why are you here then?'

'Being nosey.' Best excuse yet.

He smirked. 'Some of the stuff in here is beyond me. I think I need a joiner.'

'Oh, I know someone who would do it. You know Mike Robertson, the guy who lives in Gardener's Cottage?'

'Yes, but I've already employed him to work on the grounds, I can't ask him to do anything else.'

'Let me finish. He has a son who's training in joinery, Blair. I'll give him a call if you like? He'd love to do something like this.'

Archie raised an eyebrow. 'And is he a special friend of yours? Is that why you want me to employ him?'

'Well, he is super handsome and he looks like a Viking warrior, so there's every chance I fancy the pants off him. Why don't you give him a call? And we'll see if I ditch my attempts to get my hands on your hard cash and go for his tools instead.'

Archie poked his tongue into his cheek and looked away. 'Seriously?' He exhaled slowly. 'Right. You call him up and get him to come and see me.'

'Really? He'll be thrilled. So, what do you want me to do? Help here or go back to the house?'

Archie considered her. 'Much as I love your crazy company, it's probably better if the main house gets done. I'll just keep smashing shelves here and working on my muscles, in case my cash flow runs dry.'

'Rock on.' Georgia winked her satisfaction. 'I can't wait to see the results.'

As she walked back to the house, she chuckled and shook her head. All the innuendo was ridiculous, but she hadn't had so much fun for a long time. *Hang on!* She stopped walking. None of this was meant to be fun. She was doing it to make the place habitable for Tony. Every time she thought about him, her heart slumped. 'I can't do it,' she told an icy bush as she started walking again. All this time she'd waited for him, but now the hour was upon her, she wasn't sure it was what she wanted.

She might not be on a gap year career-wise, but this lengthy separation couldn't be good for any relationship. Busying herself back at the house, she squashed the thoughts of Tony, but she couldn't concentrate. As darkness crept in, she packed in and headed off towards Beth's farm a few miles north.

Once inside the cosy kitchen, Georgia settled her hands around a warm mug of hot chocolate and admitted where she'd been working. Letting the rich chocolate scent filter through her nostrils, she waited for Beth's response, quite sure it wouldn't be pretty. Beth wasn't Archie's greatest fan after their altercation over the logging road in the spring.

'How did you land a job there?'

'He needed a designer, and I needed money.' She left it at that. What would Beth think if Georgia fessed up to wanting to impress a boyfriend none of them even knew existed?

'So, did he advertise for staff? I can't believe he's even doing it up. Murray heard a rumour he was selling the place.' Beth sat opposite, wearing a slight frown.

'No, I don't think he's selling it. I just heard on the grapevine it wasn't in the best of nick and he was looking for someone to do it up a bit.'

'Not because your sister wants you to do it.' Beth looked puzzled. 'She's the one coming to stay, right?'

They were steering into dangerous waters. 'Yeah, but that's just a coincidence. Archie doesn't even know it's my sister that's booked it.' Yet another slight problem. Though hopefully when the guests arrived, he'd vanish to Monarch's Lodge.

'Archie? You call him that?'

Georgia grinned. 'Yup. I wind him up all the time.'

'And how does he take that? I've always found him a grumpy git and very touchy about his private property.'

'Don't I know it. But he's ok. He's grown on me.'

'Rather you than me. I'm still annoyed at the way he poked his nose in here and caused all sorts of problems.'

'Yeah. He's an odd man. Sometimes he's like that, snippy and up himself, then other times, he's the opposite. It's hard to make him out.'

'You're more charitable than me. What surprises me is that he's opening the house at all. You know what happened there?'

'No.' Georgia frowned.

'Hasn't he told you?'

'Told me what?' Georgia racked her brains. They'd talked, but not about anything serious. Their conversations had consisted mainly of fake flirting and fairy lights.

'Last Christmas, his brother… committed suicide in the house.' Beth let out a sigh. 'Archibald was left the whole estate. I assumed he'd sell it. I mean, you would, wouldn't you?'

Georgia tapped her mug as she digested the information. 'I don't know. Maybe not. Maybe that's why he doesn't want to sell it. It's connected to his brother.' Lifting her mug to her lips, Georgia stared into the middle distance. 'I didn't know. That's sad. This will be his first Christmas without him.'

'It is sad and I'm not sure this makes it any better, but the brother wasn't a nice man. He had a bad reputation around here.'

'That isn't saying much, is it? Archie gets a pretty bad rap himself, but he's not as awful as all that.'

'Yeah, that's true. Is he still working in the oil industry or did he give it up to come back here?'

'He said he had a real job, so I guess he hasn't given it up.'

'Before he inherited, people around here used to call him the bard.'

'Why?'

'He writes poetry, he used to do stints at Burn's Suppers and things. Years ago. He's older than me, so I kind of missed it, but they had big parties at Ardnish and he would do recitals. Then he disappeared for years, and I never heard anything about him until he turned up here in the spring, acting all pompous and too big for his boots.'

'Hmm.' Georgia considered. So much for no arty bones in his body. He wrote poetry instead. His endless hidden talents. 'He must have been pretty raw when he came back. That was just a few months after he'd inherited, he probably didn't know what he was doing.' Poor Archie. She could imagine him trying to do what he thought was right and getting it all wrong.

After talking some more, Beth had to go and feed the animals. Georgia left with her head full of new curiosities.

The following day, she wanted to quiz Archie on Beth's information, but she didn't have the nerve. Ever since their sing-song, he'd kept out of her way, and they only met if she sought him out or they happened to pass in the corridor.

At least now she was officially working, she didn't have to ring the silly doorbell every time she arrived. She was glad to get inside and shut the hefty door on the wild storm raging beyond.

The piano in the drawing room lay woefully quiet. Georgia ran her fingers over the closed lid and smiled. What a laugh their sing-song had been, but it was so ridiculous. Who just starts singing? And dancing! As the world's biggest *Buffy the Vampire Slayer* fan, she was irresistibly reminded of the episode where they burst into song. Here she was starring in her own *decorate the castle for Christmas* musical, though her duet partner had vanished.

She'd set up her sewing machine near the bay window in the drawing room and was humming along to 'Merry Christmas Everyone' while she stitched a pair of curtains when the needle snapped. 'Shit.'

Somewhere she'd seen a box of sewing things and shoved it under a table the other day. *In the hall!* She raised her finger in a eureka gesture.

A wet nose greeted her in the hallway and she patted the lithe side of one of the pointers. 'Are you Dexter? You're not thinking up some dastardly way to bump me off, are you?'

'He'll lick you to death,' said Archie, making Georgia jump as he sidled out from behind the ugly bust.

'Holy Father Christmas.' Georgia's hand leapt to her chest. 'He won't have to if you keep doing things like that. I nearly died of shock.'

'I'd appreciate it if you didn't.'

She side-eyed him as she raked under the table for the cardboard box. 'I'll try not to.'

'I was coming to find you. We need to talk.'

Uh-oh, why did that sound so formal and alarming. 'What about?' Georgia pulled out a pack of needles and did a happy dance inside her head. Thank goodness there were spares.

'I had a phone call this morning from a Mrs Tamsyn Montgomery.'

AKA my sister. Alarm bells started ringing in her inner ear.

'Are you all right?'

'What?' The shock on her face must have shown. 'Yes, fine. What did Mrs Whoever have to say?'

'She's the woman who's booked to stay here for Christmas. And now she wants to extend her stay, she'd like to have the place a week earlier.'

'She would? Why?'

Archie sighed. 'Apparently, her sister lives on the island and she wants to throw a big birthday bash for her.'

Georgia's eyes almost leapt from their sockets. 'What?'

'Indeed. Do you know who her sister is?'

Georgia's heart rate rocketed. 'Eh, should I?'

'No idea, I just thought you might. You know lots of people on the island. I hardly know anyone these days.'

'Oh, right.' Georgia rubbed her face. This was not good. She didn't want Tamsyn throwing a big party, she was happy with her friends. They were the ones she wanted to spend time with, not Tamsyn's friends and Gordon's stuffy relatives. This wasn't fair.

'Yes,' said Archie, dragging out the word and scratching his chin. 'It's a problem, isn't it?'

She glanced at him. 'It is, well… is it?'

'It's more money, so I couldn't really say no, but it means this place has to be ready a week sooner, and I don't know if we'll have all the deliveries by then.'

'Oh, bollocks.' Georgia slapped her palm into her forehead, switching her brain back on.

'Pardon you,' said Archie. 'But you're right. So…' He rubbed his hands together. 'Can you do it?'

She ambled towards him and leaned on the ugly statue. 'Do I get a raise?'

His mismatched eyes twinkled in the light from the old chandelier and he pulled his head to the side. 'For a week's less work?'

'Hmm. But I might have to do extra hours.'

'Let's see how that pans out, shall we?'

'Ok. But I need one concession.'

He folded his arms and raised his left eyebrow. 'And what's that?'

'Please, can you get rid of this utterly hideous statue?'

The corner of his lips curved up and he nodded. 'Your wish is my command.'

'If that's the case, I'll take the raise too, please.'

She returned to the dining room with her needles and her head in tatters. So Tamsyn was arranging a party for her. *A party I don't bloody want! I want to turn thirty quietly and gracefully, not with a house full of people I don't like.* How could she let her know while acting like she didn't know about it? If she messaged out of the blue, it would look odd. *Why is Tamsyn so pig-headed? I am quite happy with an evening in the pub with MY friends.* Their company was a hundred times more welcome than being surprised by Gordon's snooty relatives and Tamsyn strutting about telling everyone how much the caterers cost. Georgia slammed her foot down on the sewing machine and revved up a seam.

The clock struck eleven simultaneously with the weird doorbell making a bizarre combination of sounds. Georgia half expected a tattered cuckoo to follow it, popping out somewhere. Instead, Archie put his head around the door. 'You have more deliveries.'

'Great.' She headed for the hallway. 'And we need to get Christmas trees. I'd prefer real ones. I wonder if the shop has any.'

'Go and cut one from the forest,' he said. 'There's an axe in the end room.'

'Really?' She arched an eyebrow in disbelief.

'Of course.' This time the sarcasm was obvious. 'Just tell me when you're going to do it. I'll come and watch.'

She presented him with her best resting-bitch face. 'Never underestimate the power of the small woman.'

Pulling up her sleeve, she flexed her arm like a pint-sized Popeye.

'I don't, that's why I want to watch.'

'Oh, get lost.' She crossed the hall towards the door to collect the deliveries, and he snuck off down the passageway with a grin.

Later, as Georgia ate her packed lunch by the window in the drawing room, she watched Archie walking towards the heathland with the dogs along the path which ran directly from the edge of the garden. His head was bowed against the wind and the collar on his Barbour turned right up. Georgia was glad it was winter and the guests wouldn't want to spend much time outside. The area loosely termed garden was a run-down mess. The hedges looked like they hadn't been trimmed for a long time and the beds were a mix of barren soil and tangled wood. Georgia hadn't even dared set foot in it. Hopefully, everybody would be so enchanted by the views of the sea beyond they wouldn't look too closely at anything else. Archie's figure was now a dot climbing the steep path to the ridge where she'd spent an afternoon photographing the sea eagles. The two pin-prick dogs sniffed about and padded here and there.

What would he do if she actually took the axe and chopped down one of his trees? Not that she knew how, but how difficult could it be?

She returned to her sewing after lunch and had managed two curtains for the bay window in the drawing room when Archie appeared at the door and scanned around. If she hadn't seen him outside earlier, she'd never have known he'd left the house. He was perfectly groomed, as always. His oatmeal chunky knit looked extremely expensive and no doubt felt amazing. Would stroking it be a step too far? She could check out his muscles while she was at it.

'Here's something that might interest you,' he said, passing her a piece of paper with something printed on it. She blinked, dismissing the curiosity about what lay beneath the jumper, took the paper, and read.

'Oh, cool.' It was a flyer for a small Christmas tree farm on the island. 'That's near to where I stay, but I've never heard of it.'

'Where do you live?' he asked.

'In Salen, the boring bit with the ex-council houses.'

'Why is that boring?'

'Because it's about the only place on the island that doesn't have a view of sea, hills, forests or anything islandy.'

'Fair enough. But it can't be that far from the sea. Can't you just walk two minutes for your view?'

'That's not really the same, is it?'

'I suppose not. I'm spoiled here.' He conceded with a nod.

'You so are. And this is the right side of the island for watching the sunset. I don't even get that.'

'You should see them here in the autumn. Sometimes everything glows red. It really is like wearing rose-tinted glasses.'

'I know what you mean, I've sat all around the island watching them with my camera. I'd love to be able to sit in my own garden one day and do it.'

'Maybe one day,' he said, and his smile looked warm and genuine. 'But will this do for trees?' He tapped the paper in her hand.

'Definitely.'

'You probably don't want to go too early if you want it to last.'

'Archie, it's the first of December next week then we only have a week before they arrive.'

He looked slightly surprised but said, 'Good point, so when do you want to go?'

'Do you want to come with me?' Her eyes widened. It seemed obvious from the question he did. He was full of surprises.

'Of course. You'll need my credit card after all.'

She half rolled her eyes as she smiled. 'So I will. Or you could just hand it over.'

'Not a chance.' He ventured further into the room and skimmed around. 'This looks wonderful. You might have earned a Christmas bonus.'

'Dare I ask what that is?'

'I haven't decided yet.' He folded his arms and shook his head. 'You know, I should apologise for the state of the place. It sounds like a dreadful cop-out, but it wasn't actually me who let it get like this. I just couldn't find the will to do anything about it until now.'

'I'm sorry to hear that.' She wasn't sure whether to let on how much she knew about his brother.

'Having you turn up was like a gift. Albeit an expensive one.' He cast her a look and she grinned. 'But I honestly couldn't have done any of this without you.'

'Thanks, and actually I'm enjoying it.' Most of the time it didn't feel like work, not unless her real motives burst in uninvited. 'Oh, my god. Mistletoe,' she blurted out. If Tony planned to propose, he'd expect mistletoe on every doorway. Georgia rocked her head, weighing up the idea; omit the deadly plant for that very reason? Or would that be the one thing they missed if she forgot about it?

'Pardon?' Archie's brow furrowed.

Georgia got up from the sewing machine and paced towards him, pressing her hand to her forehead. 'Sorry, I didn't mean to say that. Something you said reminded me of something else that reminded me of something else that reminded me of mistletoe.'

'You've lost me completely.'

'That's ok. I can find you again later.' She grabbed his arm and he drew back. For a second she was distracted by the wonderfully soft bobbly wool of his jumper. The notion from earlier returned and developed. How would it be to slip her hand up his arm, trail it over his chest and slip it around his waist? For a dance? Or a hug? A grope? All three?

He frowned at her. 'What are you doing?'

'Sorry.' She let go. 'So, where can I get mistletoe?' If her wayward mind took over, it would insist on her testing the mistletoe as soon as they found it... and not with Tony.

'I think you've lost the plot.' Archie ran his fingers through his hair. 'What do you want mistletoe for?'

'Eh, isn't it obvious?'

He glanced at her. 'I'm not entirely sure it is. Do you think the guests want it hanging around? I certainly don't. I'm not stopping to kiss random strangers every time I come through a door.'

'No? Think of the fun you could have.'

He narrowed his eyes. 'Yes, Georgia, I'm thinking exactly that.'

'But seriously,' she continued with a cough. Shit, what was he thinking? They were steering into dangerous waters. 'Where can we get it? Does it grow on the estate?'

'No, of course it doesn't. It doesn't grow wild anywhere in Scotland.'

'Doesn't it?'

'No. Order it online or try a garden centre if you want it that badly. But it seems like a big waste of time to me.'

'Hmm.' She looked out the window. How had she missed that information all her life? But then again, maybe that should be the best piece of news she'd had all year. No mistletoe meant no stolen kisses... With anyone.

CHAPTER 12

Archie

Archie pulled the Barbarian pickup truck through the gates of the small tree plantation and rolled up the stony path between rows of fir trees whose crowns reached various heights. The path led to a field of evergreens diverse enough to satisfy the pickiest Christmas-tree shopper. Archie had never been anywhere like this. As a child, he hadn't considered the provenance of their tree. He arrived home from boarding school every year to find it already in situ and never questioned it. The one his grandmother had in Monarch's Lodge appeared in a similarly magical way and always looked much better than the gaudy thing in the main house.

Georgia's van was parked outside. Archie shook his head and smiled. That van was the second wackiest thing on the island... after its owner.

Inside the container-cum-shed which doubled as an office and a shop were a small desk, a few random chairs, and a coffee machine with an out-of-order sign sellotaped to its front. Georgia was deep in conversation with a grey-haired man when Archie stepped up behind her.

'Oh, there you are,' she said. 'I was just asking Gary here if he has mistletoe. And guess what?'

'He does?' said Archie, raising his eyebrows in sarcastic excitement as he prised off his leather gloves.

'Correct.' She beamed and clapped the arm of his navy wool coat.

'Aye, I have it here, it's not easy to grow in this climate but there's plenty to cut some sprigs from,' said Gary.

'Fabulous,' muttered Archie.

'Lots of kisses for you.' Gary smirked. 'The young lady wants loads of the stuff.'

Archie flicked Georgia a dirty look as she grinned at Gary's mistake.

'And what a lucky man I am,' said Archie. 'But we're actually here about a tree.'

'Three trees.' Georgia smiled.

Archie summoned a smile. There were just no words.

'Have a wander,' said Gary. 'Come back and let me know when you've chosen. I can cut them for you or you can do it yourself if you like.'

'It's your lucky day then,' Archie said to Georgia. 'She can't wait to get her hands on the axe,' he added to Gary.

'So true.' Georgia opened the side door. 'And he can't wait to watch me in action.'

Low mist hung around the trees as Archie followed Georgia into the plantation. The eerie scene reminded Archie of a poem he'd written as a boy about a Will-o'-the-wisp. It had been burned along with all the others in Laurence's purge. Laurence. The significance of the date punched Archie in the gut, bringing cold reality with it.

He cleared his throat. 'I don't trust this weather.' Screwing up his eyes, he peered at the grey sky, heavy and ominous. 'It looks still just now, but I know this island, and a storm is coming. I can feel it.'

'Excellent, I love a good storm.'

'Well, don't take too long choosing. I don't fancy cutting a tree in a rainstorm.'

'Some trees, not just one.' Georgia corrected with a twinkle in her eye.

'You don't seriously want three?'

'Yes, I do. We need one for the hallway now the ugly statue has gone. Where did you put that by the way? And how did you move it?'

'Never you mind.' But Archie nursed a secret desire to leap in the air and cheer. He hated the hideous statue, a relic of Laurence's obsession with fake grandeur and snobbery. It wasn't even stone, but an adobe copy, and bashing it to smithereens had been therapeutic, even if he had traumatised the dogs in the process. 'And where else do we supposedly require a tree?'

'One in the drawing room and one in the dining room… At the very least.'

'That's definitely enough.'

Georgia pulled an uncertain face.

'What?' he said. 'You think we need them in the bathroom or something?'

'No… Even though it would look impressive in the main en-suite. But there should maybe be little ones in the bedrooms and maybe one in the kitchen. It's a big house, we want to do this properly.'

'Seriously. I'm sure three will be fine.' He held his breath waiting for her to argue some more, but she didn't. Instead, she started deliberating which size would be best for each area.

Archie hung around like her pet dog, doing nothing but nodding. As she inspected a row of eight-foot trees that all looked identical, Archie clapped his hands to keep warm. Whatever she chose was fine; he was only there to hold the wallet, but she wasn't in any rush.

'Archie.' She beckoned him over.

'What?'

She indicated for him to lean right in. He did so, bending so his cheek was close to the pompom on her hat. 'Look at that.' Behind one of the trees was a rabbit staring up at them and just in front of it was a robin. 'How cute is that?'

Rabbits were generally considered vermin in his family but he could see what she meant. 'A Christmas visit to the Bunny-Haven?' He smirked.

'Shut up.' She gave him a prod. 'It just looks cute. That reminds me though, I have that whisky for you in the van.'

'You're a funny one.' He gave her a pat on the back and she strolled off, up and down the rows, checking the trees from every side. He craned his neck for a better view as he caught a flicker of her coat some way off. She was like Little Miss Christmas in her scarlet coat with the white buttons and long boots. Even her white hat with the giant pompom had a cheery elfishness about it. She was almost skipping with excitement. Every little thing made her happy, like rabbits and robins; she was a proper little Julie Andrews. If someone placed a sprig of mistletoe over the door of the cabin shop, Archie was in half a mind to kiss her under it just to see what it was like. A little kiss from someone as festive as her would brighten his day no end; a no strings attached, simple little kiss. If such a thing existed.

She was on her way back. Archie gave a little cough.

'Right, get the axe,' she said, 'I've chosen them… and hurry.'

'Why?'

'In case I change my mind.'

Archie's jaw dropped and he snapped it shut again. 'You actually want to cut it yourself?'

'Sure.'

'In that outfit?'

'Why not?' She looked down as though she'd forgotten what she was wearing. 'This came from a charity shop, it only cost six quid, not like the posh togs you're wearing. I'm just a poor lassie, not a noble yah like yourself.'

'A what?'

'Never mind, just fetcheth the axe, kind sir.'

He rolled his eyes. What a mischievous little elf.

Moments later he emerged from the shop with Gary who had donned a huge grey padded jacket and was carrying the equipment.

'You do realise it's a saw you need to cut a tree? I was joking about the axe,' said Archie.

'Oh, what?' Georgia threw out her hands in mock offence. 'I really wanted a go at chopping.'

'I'll give you a wood cutting demo at the house one day.'

'Will you?' Georgia's gaze lingered on him, travelling down his face, over his shoulders and his chest, before skipping to his arms. Archie's insides flipped: it felt like she was undressing him. 'I can't wait.' She waggled her eyebrows. 'Singer, dancer, poet, and lumberjack. Wow.' Raising her hand, she fanned herself. 'He's too hot to be true,' she told Gary.

Gary raised an eyebrow, looking uncertain whether to laugh or not.

'But before I spontaneously combust in the heat around here,' said Georgia, 'maybe you can show me how to cut the tree down.'

'Certainly,' Gary beamed, 'show me the one you're after.'

'Actually the three.' Georgia glanced back at Archie and winked, then lowering her voice, whispered, 'Maybe four.'

'Three,' Archie said. 'I'm not deaf.'

She tapped the side of her nose at Gary.

'Your mistletoe's inside. I've tied up some sprigs for you.'

'Excellent,' said Georgia with a little hand clap.

'Are you hoping for a proposal or something?' Gary said under his breath. Archie pulled a side pout and scanned the row of trees. Did the man think he couldn't hear that?

'Oh,' said Georgia. Maybe he imagined it, but it seemed like her cheeks flushed. 'Of course not.'

Gary scratched his thinning grey hair. 'Sorry, I didn't mean to speak out of turn.'

'Well, he's my boss,' said Georgia, twisting around and smiling at Archie. 'And lovely as he is, I'd rather he didn't propose under the mistletoe.'

'Oh. He's your boss?' said Gary. 'Sorry, I got the wrong end of the stick completely.' He bustled off to set up the tools.

'Now you've embarrassed him,' said Archie. 'I warned you about flirting right from the start.'

'Oh, that's right, I remember. And what a bad girl I am, flirting with the man who sweeps me into mad dances and invites me to sing with him at his piano. Imagine being so forward with such a well-behaved man. Shame on me.' She looked him up and down.

He aimed two fingers at her like a pistol. 'Touché.' He blew over the top of them. She chuckled. 'I think your tree is ready.' He indicated with his head.

She cast off her coat and flung it jauntily towards him. He caught it before it hit the ground. Looking like she meant business, she rolled up her sleeves and pumped her fist. A few drops of icy rain fell, but she didn't appear to notice as she took the saw from Gary. He leaned under the tree, pointing to the right place to cut.

Archie stood back and held her coat tight, unable to tear his eyes from her. What would it be like when Christmas was over and she was out of his life? A sharp pang needled him in the side, and irrational ideas of re-employing her in the future sprang to mind. Maybe she could help with renovating the other estate cottages. All thoughts were soon driven out however as he watched her sawing valiantly at the tree. She may be small and slim, but she was determined and nimble. Eventually, the bough creaked and fell sideways. Gary caught it and laid it on a tarpaulin.

'That was so prickly.' She shook herself and dusted off some needles. 'I'm all scratched. But I didn't want to ruin my six-quid jacket.' She winked at Archie.

He looked at the tree. 'Not bad going.'

'Says the master of lumberjacking.' Georgia held out the saw. 'Go on then, you show us how it's done, maestro. I can't wait to see these muscles in action.'

'You don't live on an island like this without chopping a few logs.' Handing Georgia back her coat, he took off his own. He wasn't sure he wanted his favourite sweater covered in needles either, so he hauled it off too. Stripped to his navy polo shirt, he dumped the coat and jumper on Georgia who almost disappeared under their bulk.

'Ooh, er.' She smirked broadly, fluttered her eyelashes, and dragged a hand from the clothing bundle to rest the back of it across her brow in a mock swoon. Archie picked up the saw, unable to help a smile leaking out. Whatever was going on – or not going on – this was a sprinkling of gold dust on an otherwise dull existence. Her glitter had brought some Christmas magic.

'Not bad, are they?' He flexed his usually well-hidden biceps. 'For a thirty-six-year-old who spends most of his life at a desk.' She burst out laughing and buried her head in the coats for a second.

He got to work on the tree. Not as easy as he'd hoped, but it came down nonetheless. 'There you go. I think we should leave the last one to the expert.' Archie passed the saw to Gary.

'No problem.' Gary nipped off ahead.

'Here's your jumper.' Georgia handed it to Archie. He was glad to have it back; gooseflesh had erupted over his bare arms in the chill air. 'So you can hide away the goods again. Who would have thought it? Archie Crichton-Leith, aka man of steel. Lovin' the muscles.' She squeezed his upper arm, eyeing his chest with interest.

'Thanks.' He smiled. How could he not? But was he falling down a trap again? It felt different from the other times… Or did he always say that? And really, what was he wanting to get out of this? What was she? A bit of flirting and fun – where was the harm?

The heavens opened like floodgates and rain gushed over them. 'Wait inside,' shouted Gary. As he was the only one with a sensible jacket and who knew how to bundle the trees, they dashed to the cabin without a second glance. Archie got there first, pushed open the side door and let Georgia through.

'I'm soaked.' She pulled off her soggy hat and shook it. 'Oh, this must be our mistletoe.' With a twinkle in her eye, she lifted a sprig from the counter.

'Yeah, don't go getting any ideas. You can put it up at the last minute.'

'Chicken.' She dangled it above her head. 'I dare you.'

For a split second, he considered, before buttoning up his long navy coat. 'No bloody way.'

'No?' She pushed out her lips in a huge pout.

'No.'

She chuckled, kissed her fingertips and blew over them, looking like Marilyn Monroe. With a shake of his head, Archie rubbed a view hole in the misted-up window. Despite her playful fun, a twinge of anxiety lingered around his midriff. Was he a joke to her? Were these moments of silliness just her laughing at him?

When Gary returned with the trees netted, Archie paid up and they wheeled the trees round to the cars. Georgia was so short there was no way she could help lift them on to the roof. He chortled and shook his head when she pulled a step ladder out from her van.

'Voilà.' She threw out her hands like she'd magicked it, then opened it out, dumped it in a puddle and propped it up by her van.

'You're unreal,' said Archie.

'I'll take two up here,' Georgia said to Gary, with a smirk at Archie. 'They could probably go inside, but I'd rather not mix needles with my art stuff, especially when it's so wet.'

'You'll never lift that,' said Archie, as Gary shouldered the tree in her direction.

Georgia side-eyed him and raised her Popeye arm. 'Watch me.'

'I am,' he said, and after a few interesting balances and lots of giggling, she had the two trees on the roof of her van.

'See, just leave it to the experts.' She brushed her hands together and winked at Archie.

After Gary manoeuvred the final tree into the back of the Barbarian, Archie shook his hand, eager to get out of the rain. 'Thanks.'

'No problem.'

'See you at the house,' shouted Georgia from the window of the van. 'Last one back has to play the piano naked.' With a muddy spin wheel, the van careered off up the path. Archie took a deep breath and rubbed the back of his neck.

'Good luck,' said Gary. 'Looks like you might need it.'

'Indeed, I might.'

CHAPTER 13

Georgia

Georgia was back at the house long before Archie. The door was unlocked, as was the case with almost every house on the island. After hauling the first tree into the drawing room, a snuffling at the door to the passage made her jump.

'Jeez.' She pulled back the door and the dogs came out. 'Honestly, why doesn't Archie lock up? It's such a ridiculously big house, what if someone sneaks in and hides somewhere?' Georgia shuddered. 'Oh, yes, you can look at me like that, Duchess,' she informed the dog, whose nose stuck out so straight she had a permanently snooty expression. 'Most native islanders laugh at my mainland ways, but I don't like the idea of someone creeping about in here, even if your serial killer son is on the lookout for them. I just wish Archie would hurry up.' She opened the door, ready to dash to the van for the second tree. 'And I'm sorry, doggies, I'm not letting you out, you'll have to wait. It'd be my luck the juiciest rabbit would run past and you two would hightail off after it. I don't fancy squaring that with his nibs.'

She darted outside and dragged the second tree from the top of the van. Rain battered her as she hauled it up the stairs and dumped it in the corner where the ugly bust used to stand. As she mulled over whether this was the best place for it, the outside door thudded open and Georgia spun around.

Another netted Christmas tree hit the rug and Archie's long navy coat disappeared out the front door again. Georgia followed. 'Where are you going?'

'Here's your Christmas bonus,' he said, unstrapping a fourth tree.

'You got another one.' Georgia bounced on the doorstep as the rain thundered down.

'Stand aside.' Archie passed by and a second tree fell on the rug. He shut the door with a thud and turned around, dripping all over the floor. 'It's a bit wet out there.'

Georgia laughed as he slicked back his hair, giving him a Cary Grant coming out the swimming pool kind of look. Wow, she paused for an internal swoon. Right now, she was ready to throw away the warnings, forget about Tony and jump him. Mistletoe be damned, it would just get in the way.

Archie stamped the mud off his boots before kicking them into the corner. 'Where are the other trees?'

'That one's there.' Georgia pointed at the obvious one in the corner. 'And I put the other one in the drawing room. This one can go in the dining room, and the extra one in the kitchen.'

'And do you need help with that?'

'Don't be silly.' She grabbed one of the net bags, ready to drag it through to the dining room. 'Have you forgotten my She-Ra powers?'

'How could I? But I will help. If only to preserve the carpet.'

They carried it into the dining room. 'So, do you want help with the decorating?' asked Archie, sinking his hands into his pockets.

'Not really, I have a plan, and I think we have enough decorations even with the extra tree.'

'Oh, right.' He took a couple of steps back and rubbed his hands together. 'Well, if I'm not needed here, I'm going to change. I should take the dogs out, but this coat isn't waterproof.'

'I can see that,' said Georgia, 'but will they want to go far in this?'

'Probably not.'

After he left, Georgia stared at the empty space where he'd been. Had she offended him? Maybe he wanted to help decorate the trees. It was his house after all.

She got the trees into their stands and set them in the right position – after much deliberating. The decorations could wait until Archie returned. If he wanted to help, he could. It was the fun part. Georgia rubbed away the condensation and peered out the window. It was getting dark despite it being only two o'clock. The sea was barely visible through the lashing rain and thick clouds.

A loud banging on the door made her heart stop. Who the hell? Hoping it was more deliveries, she bustled across the hall and pulled open the thick wooden doors. A young man wearing several layers smiled back at her. She'd recognise that hair anywhere. Who else had that fine a set of blond dreadlocks? 'Hi, Blair. What are you doing here?' She stepped back to let him in.

'I've been working at Monarch's Lodge.'

'You've started?'

'Yeah, after you called me the other day, I came over and chatted to the guy. He said I could crack right on – he wants it finished ASAP.'

'Wow, I didn't know. It's in such a weird place. When you're up here, you can't see it at all.'

'I only started a couple of days ago. Listen, is he here? Archibald.' He lowered his voice. 'Sorry, I can't say that name without laughing.'

'Yeah, it sounds like a Medieval monk or something. I call him Archie. He's never corrected me, so we'll stick with that, but no, he's not here. He was walking the dogs, I'll check out the front and see if he's on his way back.'

'Cool.' Blair discarded his boots and followed her into the drawing room. 'Wow, this is amazing. I don't know what it was like before, my dad said it was drab and hideous, but this looks great.'

'Thanks. It's been a lot of fun, but I'm a bit worried it won't be finished in time. The house party is coming next week.' A tremor of disquiet ran through her as she peeked out the window. Just one week before Tamsyn and co descended on the island.

'Yeah, that's why I need to speak to… Archie. I hope I'm allowed to call him that. He scares me a bit.'

'His bark is definitely worse than his bite.'

'Well, I don't think there's any chance I'll finish that place by next week. I might be able to have it watertight so he can get the heating guys in before Christmas, but it's way too much to do the whole thing on my own.'

'Oh dear.' The panic ricocheted around Georgia's stomach. She wasn't a worrier, but this was getting tense. 'So, he might have to stay in the house when the guests arrive.'

'That's up to him, I guess, but even getting the place watertight in this weather could be interesting.'

'Oh gosh, yes. It's dire. The guests won't want to set foot outside. Though maybe that's just as well, the garden isn't much.'

'You've done up this place so nicely, they won't need to go outside.'

'Let's hope, though they're probably expecting snow.'

'Ha, good luck with that.'

'Yeah, that's one miracle Archie will have to work on his own.'

Blair nodded. 'Snow is almost unheard of on Mull at Christmas, except on the mountain tops, because of the gulf stream and all that. I only remember maybe two Christmases in my whole life when we've had snow.'

Georgia sighed. 'Let's hope they're like me.' Though she knew they weren't. 'I enjoy a good storm. Have you heard of the Icelandic concept of *gluggavedur?*'

'Glug-a-what?'

'It means "window weather". The type of weather that's fun to watch while you're cosy inside.'

'Never heard of it.'

'I love it and its perfect for here. This place has an awesome view of storms and it might be even better at Monarch's Lodge, it's so exposed to the elements. It doesn't work at my house. It has a truly pathetic view unless I want to watch my neighbour's washing twisting round the lines.'

'Yeah, not so appealing.'

'Oh, god.' Georgia groaned, watching the wind bully the bushes and hustle the dead ivy. Tamsyn would hate it. Georgia could almost hear her moaning.

'Is everything ok?'

'Yes, fine.' The blurred figure of Archie and the dogs battling downhill caught her eye. 'That's Archie on his way back.'

'Oh, right. I'll grab my shoes and catch him at the door.'

'Cool. I'll nip down sometime and see how things are getting on at Monarch's Lodge.'

'Not today. I'm heading off after I've spoken to him. You should go too, it's treacherous out there. You don't want to wait until after dark.'

'I won't, another half hour or so and I'm done.'

As Georgia opened boxes of decorations, the outside door clunked open with a howl of wind. Archie and Blair's voices carried through, though she couldn't distinguish what they were saying. With a loud thud, the front door shut again. Georgia sat cross-legged on the floor, laying out the various red and gold glittering baubles. Archie spoke softly to the dogs somewhere and the door to the passageway clicked. She'd sneaked a peek into the dogs' room once or twice and it was like a palace with comfy beds, cushions, toys and a cosy radiator. Would they have to stay in the house next week too? Tamsyn hated the smell of wet dogs. Hopefully, Archie would padlock himself in his passageway and not leave it for the fortnight. The idea of him being in the house sent more sparks of panic flying through Georgia. What if she met him when she was visiting the house for the festivities? How would she explain why she was there?

'There you are,' said Archie, 'I saw your van. Why are you still here?'

Georgia checked her phone for the time. 'It's early yet.'

'But the weather. You should get away while it's still daylight. That road is prone to flooding, you might get cut off. The trees can wait.'

'Oh well, I have my essentials in the van. If I get stranded, I can sleep in it. I want to at least start the trees before I go. Do you want to help?' She sat up brightly, aware the way she was sitting probably made her look like the elf on the shelf. *If only I thought to put on stripy red tights.*

'I, em, yes. That would be nice.'

'Good. I've got traditional red and gold for in here. Silver for the dining room and rainbow for the entrance. Wait until you see the lights, they'll make an amazing first impression.'

Archie smiled and rubbed his hands together. 'Sounds wonderful.'

'Good.' Georgia leapt to her feet and lifted the first string of lights. 'If we start here.' She stretched towards the top of the tree, but even on tiptoes, she couldn't reach. 'I'll get a chair.'

'Allow me.' Archie took the string and draped it over the top, flicking her a wink.

'Nice. It's not my fault I'm vertically challenged.'

'I feel like we need music,' said Archie.

'You could play the piano, but you can't do that and decorate.'

'I'll do that after,' he said, 'as long as I can keep my clothes on.'

Georgia smirked and gave him the once-over. 'It's non-negotiable.'

'You are so naughty.' He opened a sideboard, beautifully decorated with baubles in jars and salvaged candlesticks, and pulled out an iPod dock resembling a retro radio.

'Whilst you are the pillar of society.'

'But of course, I have a reputation to preserve.'

'Yeah, the one where you tumble unsuspecting lady's maids into your bedchamber. That's fairly common for your kind, isn't it?'

'Something like that.' He fiddled with his iPhone until the sprightly opening bars of 'White Christmas' filled the room. 'That's better.'

A few moments later they were hanging baubles to Bing Crosby's crooning. A warm fuzzy feeling flooded every particle of Georgia's veins. She closed her eyes and smiled. 'This is just… I don't know… So much fun.'

Archie laughed. 'You really are Little Miss Christmas, aren't you? Were all your Christmases merry and bright as a child? Is this your gift to everyone else, spreading the cheer to Scrooges like me?'

Smiling at him from behind a golden bauble, she gave it a little flick so it swung. 'No, all my childhood Christmases were nightmares, or at least the ones I remember. And so were most of my adult ones.'

Archie frowned and narrowed his eyes. 'Are you serious? Are you ever serious?'

'Deadly. They were dire.' Georgia hung some more baubles, trying not to recall the ghosts of Christmas past, but images wafted in and out. Like when she got a game of Buckaroo while Tamsyn strutted about with a life-size pushchair, a hairdressing doll, and a make-up set. When she was told to give Tamsyn the full end of the cracker because apparently she'd won it fair and square, despite Tamsyn already having all the hats, jokes, and toys. How common was it for Tamsyn to be sitting at Christmas dinner wearing four paper crowns and eating with one hand so she could keep the other one firmly clamped on the plastic toys? Every bloody year!

'So why do you love Christmas so much?' asked Archie.

'Who said I did?'

'It's obvious.'

Georgia shrugged. 'I like the idea of it. I like warmth, happiness, fun, laughter, and love.' She waved her hand like Andre Previn conducting the New Year concert as she said each word. After she added her last bauble, she stepped back. 'I know it's a phoney ideal, but I can't help myself. My parents keep telling me I need to get my head out of the clouds, but I never listen. Every year I keep trying to make the magic happen, hoping this time it'll work.' She looked up at Archie, shuddering like she'd stripped off a layer of skin. Rubbing her hands up and down her arms, she cringed. Why had she exposed herself like that? She didn't usually share anything so personal.

Archie appeared thoughtful. 'But this magic you're making isn't for you, you'll be somewhere else. I hope you've spent some time organising an equally wonderful Christmas for yourself.'

Her cheeks tingled. Was now the time to confess? Or would it ruin everything completely? Sometimes the truth did that. 'I have plans, yes, but even if this makes just one person happy, then my work is done.'

He smiled. 'Very philosophical.'

'Yup, that's me, the idealist and the philosopher. Which is why I'm poor.'

Archie shook his head and placed his final decoration. 'If you're the philosopher, then you'll know money doesn't buy happiness. I can testify to that.'

Was he alluding to his brother? He'd never told her about it, but it was obviously common knowledge around the island. 'I'm sorry,' she said. 'I heard about your brother. My friend told me.'

'Yeah.' He sighed and rubbed his forehead. 'That was a mess. It certainly changed my life, though that wasn't exactly what I meant. I've had money all my life, I was born privileged, but I don't think I've ever been happy, not wholly.'

'That's a bit depressing.'

'Yes, it is. I apologise. I should stop talking. I'm not trying to bring doom and gloom to your parade. I tend to do that without meaning to.'

Georgia cocked her head and ran her teeth along her lower lip. Now she looked, she saw care lines in his face. He was young but carried worldly weights, the kind she shrugged off at every opportunity. Even if Tony swept in and whisked her off her feet, would she go? It was easier being free. The pang returned, the one which gnawed at her every time Tony entered her brain. Maybe she could disappear for the next three weeks, take her pay cheques and go live it up in a swanky hotel somewhere. 'Let's do the other trees,' she said, smile back in place. 'And you don't bring doom and gloom, not in my experience. You're the one who brings the music and dancing.'

Archie smiled but squinted out the window and the care lines increased. 'Let's not be too long. You really should go. It'll be dangerous after dark.'

Brushing off his concern, Georgia shimmied to the dining room. She'd lived on the island a while now and she'd driven in storms; there was no point worrying about them.

Just before four, they finished the final tree in the entrance hall. Music from the drawing room fluttered through, faint and cheering in the background.

'Isn't it amazing?' Georgia switched off the chandelier so the multi-coloured lights twinkled in the corner.

'Yes,' said Archie. 'It really is.'

Her arm brushed against his as they gazed at it. She glanced up to see him smiling.

He took her hand and spun her, then pulled her close, slowly leading her as Frank Sinatra serenaded them with 'A Christmas Waltz'. 'Your work is done.'

'Is it?' She laughed, forgetting herself in the dance, forgetting how close he was, and who he was. Right now, he was a smart guy with a hot body and top dancing moves. *Just check out those hips.* She'd be an idiot to waste this moment thinking about anything else.

'You've made me happy this afternoon, so you can leave knowing your Christmas goal is accomplished.' He twirled her again and she beamed as he reeled her in.

'You big softy,' she said, pressing her palm onto the solid curve of his pecs, safely hidden by another gloriously soft knit. 'You're not Scrooge at all. He couldn't dance.'

'Maybe not. Now, you better get going.' As abruptly as it had started, the dance ended, and Archie stepped back into the shadows. 'Email me when you're safely back. I worry about things like that.'

'Why don't you get into the real world and get messenger?'

'Because I don't like social media. Now, in the nicest possible way, please get out of my house.'

Retreating to the passageway, Georgia grabbed her coat from the hook, gave Archie a wave, and made a run for it. Coaxing the van up the hill, she was close to the main road. The wipers streaked, and she peered into the closing darkness. Her foot hit the brakes and she slammed to a halt in a huge puddle pooling on the surface. Not just a puddle, there was something else there too. Something very large, very solid, and completely impassable. Now she had a problem.

CHAPTER 14

Archie

The kitchen was cold and empty compared to the rest of the house. It was the only ground floor room Georgia hadn't yet worked her magic on. Archie usually enjoyed cooking, but tonight it felt like a chore. All day, he'd put off the inevitability of what would happen once he was alone. With the bad weather, it came sooner than he'd intended. Cutting trees and decorating them was a more than welcome distraction. Because now he was alone there was silence, time to think and dwell. And he didn't want to do that. Not today.

The bad news about the state of Monarch's Lodge wasn't unexpected, but it threw a Santa-sized hammer into the works. Just one drop in the ocean of thoughts waiting to cascade over him at any second. He let the dogs into the kitchen even though he was trying to get them out of the habit. Guests didn't want dogs under their feet when they were cooking, not to mention the hygiene concerns. But they were good company. If he wanted to eat scrambled eggs on toast, they wouldn't mind. Duchess would give him a disapproving look, but at least she couldn't comment.

As he whisked up the egg mixture, a loud hammering on the main door made him drop the bowl. He caught it just before it slipped over the edge. The tinkling doorbell followed, adding its ethereal sounds to the persistent knocking. Archie had locked the door, something he didn't bother with during the day, but at night he liked to baton the hatches, especially in this weather. The heavy pounding continued.

Dexter jumped up and barked. 'You tell them,' said Archie, as Dexter sank back into his basket to gnaw on a bone. 'I'm coming.' Archie dashed down the corridor, across the hall, and pulled back the hefty front door.

A soaked, dripping Georgia peered out from under her drenched hat. 'It's me again.'

'So I see. What happened? Come in.' He stepped back to let her in, then bolted up again.

'There's a fallen tree blocking the driveway, near the gate. I'm not sure who to call, but can I use the phone? I don't suppose anyone will be able to move it tonight unless Mike can work a chainsaw.'

'Even if he can, I'm not sure he'll want to go out in this.'

'Maybe I could hang here for a bit then kip in the van later.'

Archie shook his head. 'Georgia, this house has sixteen bedrooms. I'm sure one of them will suit your exacting needs. I'm aware you haven't done much decorating up there yet, but they have new linen.'

'Haha, yes, that's lovely, but you don't want me staying here. You said so.'

Archie ran his hand through his hair. 'Yes, I said that, but it was before I knew you. In fact, most of the things I said were thoughtless and insensitive.'

She nodded, pulling a side pout. 'Just a bit.'

'I know, I do things like that. It's a bad habit. I blame genetics.'

'Why?'

'Very few of the men in my family have been noted for their charity or kind hearts, let's put it that way.'

'You can break the mould then, can't you?'

'I'd like to, but people usually see my money and my family's reputation before the real me. But never mind that. Come through to the kitchen.' Seeing her made him want to swing her into a dance again. She had no idea know how much he needed company tonight. 'I'm making my gourmet dinner of scrambled eggs on toast. Come and join me.'

'What, no smoked salmon? That's a bit of a disappointment, I thought your type would always have that.'

He flicked her a sarcastic grin. 'But of course, I do, milady. I also have beans, for the plebs amongst us.'

'Haha, nice. But who the hell eats beans with scrambled eggs?'

'Your type, perhaps,' he threw back at her.

'Not me. I hate beans.'

'Salmon it is then,' he said, returning to the kitchen and adding more eggs to his mixture. 'Welcome to the upper class.'

'Yeah, right. That's somewhere I'll never be welcome.'

The dogs looked up and waggled their rears excitedly at Georgia's reappearance, though neither wanted to leave their bones long enough to make a grander gesture.

'Whose bones are they?' Georgia asked, removing her wet coat and hat, chucking them onto the coat stand and taking a seat at the table. 'I knew Dexter was suspect right from the start.'

Archie laughed as he stirred the eggs. 'My Aunt Betsy, she always was a terror.'

'Ooh, horror stories for a dark stormy night at Christmas. Fabulous.'

'Yeah, very.' He could tell her a real horror story, one which happened exactly one year ago. He doubted she'd find that fabulous.

'By the way, are dogs allowed in here?'

'Not really and once the guests are here, they'll be banished to their room.'

'And what will you do? I spoke to Blair, he didn't think Monarch's Lodge would be ready.'

'Lock myself in the passageway and leave them to it, I suppose. It has a door in the room I sleep in which leads outside. A highly inconvenient place for it, but it was originally a servant's area and not designed to be a bedroom. I suppose I'll have to deal with the dogs trailing in and out, and they'll probably end up in my bed. Best I keep out of the way though, it would be odd to interfere.'

'Good idea. It would be weird if the owner butted in.'

'I can work on Monarch's Lodge, even if I can't live there yet. That's my end goal, this house is too big and full of bad memories. But you should have seen Monarch's Lodge at Christmas when I was a child, you would have loved it. My grandmother was like you, she made magic with whatever she had. She made tree decorations out of anything: cones, twigs, twisted wire and beads, even knitting. The house smelled of baking and everything was warm and homely.'

'It sounds lovely. Do you have photos?'

'Yes, somewhere. I'll have a look later, I think I know where they are.'

'Did you spend Christmas there rather than here?'

'A bit of both. I liked to hide down there. My parents liked big lavish parties, and I… Well, it wasn't really my scene.'

'Even with your dancing skills?'

'That was before I learned to dance.' He'd only done that in a last gasp attempt to win the woman of his dreams, but it hadn't worked. Instead, she and Laurence had married and sailed off, leaving Archie with nothing but bitterness.

'Monarch's Lodge is much nicer than this scary big house. And you sleep downstairs?'

He nodded. 'I hardly ever go upstairs.'

'And I'm going to be sleeping up there on my own? I think I'd rather have my van,' she said with a shiver.

'Yes, it is a bit intimidating. Leave the lights on in the hall if you like.'

'How can you live here alone? I'd be terrified. I know other people live on the estate, but even so.'

'Only Mike. The other houses aren't fit for habitation, his house isn't great either. They're works in progress.'

'So, don't you freak out, being here alone?'

He laughed as he took the eggs off the stove. 'I'm a bit too old to be scared of things that go bump in the night.'

She pulled a face. 'I don't think you ever get too old for that, not in a house this big. Can I sleep on a sofa down here? Or in the dogs' room? Dexter hasn't bumped me off so far, so I can take that as a good thing.'

Archie laughed and shook his head. 'You can sleep in my room if you like. I'll have the sofa. That's the way it's meant to go, isn't it?' He flipped her a look.

'It depends on what you watch or read. There's another version where we're meant to end up sharing.' She eyed him from head to toe and back with a pronounced lift of her left eyebrow.

'In your dreams.'

'Or yours,' she quipped. With a smirk, Archie doled the eggs onto the hot buttered toast and arranged the salmon on top. Georgia was still smiling when he put the plate in front of her. 'Excellent presentation.'

'Thank you.' He took out a large bottle of champagne and uncorked it. 'Let's celebrate.'

She quirked an eyebrow as she took her glass. 'What are we celebrating?'

'Life.' He raised his glass.

'Works for me.' She took a sip and her eyelids fell for a moment. 'This is really good. You're far too sophisticated.'

'Well, I've got loads of the stuff, so you can work on refining your palate.' He tossed back his champers a little quicker than he meant to and poured another. 'You know,' he said, 'I wasn't going to mention this. In fact, I've been deliberately not thinking about it all day. But today is...' He took another sip and glanced at Georgia. She smiled at him, wide-eyed and expectant. 'It's the anniversary of the day my brother, you know... died.' He sighed.

'Oh, Archie.' She put her hands to her face. 'I'm sorry, and here's me joking about serial killers and horror stories. Oh, god, I'm such an insensitive idiot.'

'It's fine. I'd rather you were just normal. It's worse when people tiptoe around me, expecting me to shatter before their eyes.'

'But still, I feel terrible. Wouldn't you prefer to be alone? I'll go to the van.'

'No, please don't. I'd rather have company. Normally I'm fine, but the date just makes me remember.'

'Did it happen in the house?'

'In his bedroom.'

Her eyes widened. 'Oh god.'

'Yup.'

'Was he depressed, or ill?' She replaced her fork without eating a bite.

Archie finished his second flute of champagne. 'He must have been. We weren't close. We're not that kind of family. As boys we were horrible to each other. As adults, his lifestyle was poles apart from mine. He was a playboy and a gambler. To me, he seemed to have everything and then some. But it clearly wasn't enough.'

'Or maybe it was too much,' said Georgia, eating her forkful. 'All this is a big responsibility.'

'Don't I know it. But Laurence wasn't always a responsible man. He let this place go to the dogs. He only came back occasionally. My mother wanted him to get rid of it. She always maintained it was the weight of the place that sent my father to an early grave. After Laurence died last year, she's been determined I should sell it.'

'Why don't you?'

'Because it's my home, my ancestors built it. They had the land here before that. If I sell it, I lose all that. It might be insane, but part of me wants to keep it for the good of the island. If my rent-a-castle idea works, it puts money into the economy. If I can fix up the cottages on the estate, it makes local housing available. I don't want to charge high rents and line my pockets. Life's too short to be that selfish.'

'Wow, I didn't realise you were such a philanthropist. That's not your reputation, you know.'

'Of course I do.' He knocked back more champagne. 'I inherited my father and Laurence's reputations along with everything else. People expected me to behave in a certain way. They see what they want to see. This was thrown at me and I didn't know any other way. So, yes, I made an arse of myself with that road in the spring. I didn't stop to think, and I treated it like I was up against some business rivals instead of people I want to make peace with. Honestly, sometimes I think there's no escape from my destiny.'

'Which is?'

'To become my father? My brother? I don't know. That sounds very *Star Wars*, doesn't it?'

'A wee bit, but I get what you mean. I have a similar situation with my sister. She has everything, and everybody thinks she's Wonder Woman. I'm literally the poor relation next to her and I can do nothing right as far as my parents are concerned.' Georgia closed her eyes and pressed her lips together. 'There's nothing quite like sibling rivalry, is there?'

'Georgia, really? I'm sorry, you don't come over like someone who's had a troubled upbringing.'

She held up her hands. 'No point letting it ruin the here and now.'

'You really are a good philosopher.' He clinked glasses with her.

Sticking out her little finger, she sipped then placed the glass on the table and gave Archie a searching look. 'Why the hell aren't you married?'

'Pardon?'

'Just explain it? How can someone so rich, and so handsome...'

He burst out laughing.

She continued through a broad smirk. 'Who sings, dances, writes poems and puts on lumberjack displays not be married? It's impossible.'

'And yet, here's the living proof.'

'So, explain… You're also a priest?'

'Er, no.'

'Is it just the whole paranoia about women loving your money more than you?'

'Partly, yes.' He poured them both another glass. 'I met my ideal woman about twelve years ago. We were both young, but things were good.' He sipped some more, ignoring the bubbles tickling his nose. 'That was Louisa and, my goodness, she was beautiful. She still is. The problem was my brother liked her too. Well, most of the women my mother threw at him and me weren't much to look at, and when we were younger, we were very shallow. But Louisa.' He closed his eyes and took a deep breath. 'She was something. As Laurence, however, was the one with the money, the land and everything else, she chose him.'

Georgia sat back and laid down her fork. 'Wow, she doesn't sound very pleasant for all her good looks'

'Exactly. I told you I was shallow. At least I was spared. She and Laurence divorced a few years later.'

'And you still moon about her?'

Shaking his head, Archie choked on his drink. 'No, not at all. But it made me very cautious. It was clear she'd only wanted Laurence for the money. More and more I met women who were exactly the same… I've had cash stolen. My bank accounts were cleared out. That ex was caught. She served three months in jail for that but I'm sure she's still sitting on two extremely valuable bottles of whisky. I've given up trying to get them back. Even selling them on the black market, she'll make at least ten grand from them.'

'From whisky?' He nodded. 'Now I'm embarrassed I gave you that Bunny-Haven stuff. I bet it didn't cost a thousandth of that.'

'I don't mind, it's good stuff. I appreciate you thinking of me and at least I can drink it. But now you see the kind of thing I'm talking about. I've heard so many lies, I lost confidence in my own judgement. How could I tell who was real and who wasn't? I got paranoid. Now I just accept my own company and try not to worry about it.'

'Really?'

'Kind of, but my mother has other ideas. She always has some friend somewhere with an eligible daughter or two.' He raised his glass across the table, feeling lightheaded. 'That's why I made such a ridiculously inappropriate comment to you when you first came here. I could regale you all night with tales of the bizarre set-ups I've had after women discover I'm a single man of good fortune.'

'Ergo, you must be in want of a wife.'

'Very good. Correct line but wrong sentiment.'

'What? You'd prefer a husband?'

'Again, interesting concept, but wrong. I'll happily marry a woman of my choosing when I meet the right one. But I won't be coerced, pushed or forced into anything and I don't want somebody who loves my cash more than me.'

Georgia flicked him a wink. 'Damn right.'

'How have we got onto this?' He pushed the champagne away. It always loosened his tongue. 'I apologise, I must sound ludicrous.'

She laughed. 'Not really.'

'I should stop.' He stood up and cleared the plates. 'Do you fancy dessert?'

'Oh, sailor, I haven't even tackled the main course yet.' She burst out laughing.

'Enough of your sauce.' He peered back at her. She sure made him smile, even on a day like this.

'So, hit me. What do you have for dessert if isn't sauce?'

'What kind of sauce would you like? I see you as a strawberry. Sweet, cheery, bright.'

'Or juicy and a bit seedy.' She laughed. 'And what are you? Ketchup.'

He put his hands on his hips. 'Why?'

Georgia giggled. 'Ok, that was mean. You're more like chocolate. Rich and smooth.'

'Melt in your mouth and all that.'

'Ooh, Archie, are you propositioning me?'

'Sure, how about some ice-cream, and you can sample some of my chocolate sauce later?'

Georgia almost spat out her drink. 'Ok, is that code for something?'

'Of course not,' he said in his most serious tone before lifting a bottle of Sweet Freedom Chocolate Shot from the cupboard and waggling it.

'Just as well.' Georgia laid down her glass. 'Because you still haven't done your forfeit and if chocolate sauce gets thrown into the mix… Who knows what might happen?'

Archie set a bowl on the table in front of her, then sat down, placing the sauce bottle between them. 'Who knows indeed.'

CHAPTER 15

Georgia

Georgia jumped on the sofa and pulled out one of the furry blankets she'd put in a basket nearby. Good planning on her part. 'It's a bit chilly in here, just as well we're prepared.'

Archie threw some logs on the fire and stoked it up. 'We'll be toasting in a minute. Oh, that reminds me. You sit tight, I've got something to show you.'

'Should I be scared or excited?'

'Ha. Wait and see.'

She tossed back her head and grinned at the smooth cream ceiling. Her temples throbbed slightly. The champagne was good, and fast-moving. It had reached her brain at lightning speed without any detours. Her judgement was often cloudy; now it was non-existent. She didn't attempt to work out what Archie was doing but waited patiently, examining the intricacies of the plaster ceiling rose surrounding the chandelier.

Moments later, he returned, carrying a large leather-bound book.

'Ooh, what's this?'

'Photographs,' he said. 'There are some Christmas ones. I can show you what Monarch's Lodge used to look like. Just don't laugh at what I used to look like.'

'Sorry, can't guarantee that, especially if you're wearing lederhosen or something.'

'Why would I be? I wasn't brought up by German nuns.'

'No, but you went to boarding school and that's almost as bad.'

He shook his head and pulled open the book. 'Here we go. Is this where you start bashing my upbringing?'

'No, but did you enjoy it? I've never met anyone who did.'

'Not particularly, but that's by the by. It's water under the bridge now.'

Georgia sat up on her knees and crawled towards him until she was shoulder to shoulder with him. Wrapping the blanket back around herself, she curled up, leaning on his upper arm and peering down at the neatly laid out pages. 'Someone had very nice writing,' she said, observing the loopy script under the pictures.

'My grandmother. She made these books. We have a few of them, this is the most Christmassy one. That's the wreath she made for the front door.'

'Wow, impressive. I wish I'd seen that sooner, I would have tried that for here.'

'There's always next year.'

'Yeah, but I won't be here.'

Archie looked around for a second. 'Oh, no, I suppose you won't.'

'Unless you pay for my services.' She smirked.

'Maybe I'll do that.' He flipped the page over. 'And there's me.'

'Aww, look at you. So cute. And is that your brother?'

'Yup.'

'He's quite like you, but not as much as I expected.'

'We didn't look alike. I look like my father, while Laurence is much more like our mother.'

Georgia wondered if that meant his mother was short and a little plump, like the boy in the photos. Before voicing this, she was distracted by Christmas cuteness. 'Oh, wow. It's beautiful. Who took these pictures? They're really good.'

'My father. He didn't have a lot of plus points, but he was very good at photography.'

'Did he ever get a sea eagle, flying over the estate?'

'Ha! No. Though I have to tell you, you got off lightly with me; if my father had caught you, he'd have shot you, and I don't mean with his camera.'

'Wow, he sounds a real charmer.'

'Not half.'

'I like his pictures though. It was a lot harder before digital cameras, you didn't get so many chances.'

'True.'

'Aww, look at the tree, and those decorations. I love the little knitted ones, they're just the cutest.'

'I knew you'd like them,' said Archie, flipping another page. Georgia's eyes feasted on the festive delights and her mind took a wander down her own memory lane. They'd never had a real tree as children; her mum objected to the needles. She wasn't keen on homemade decorations either. Everything had to match her set of silver and purple baubles. Anything Tamsyn and Georgia made at school was hung up for an hour or so, then mysteriously disappeared overnight. Her mum didn't generally give an explanation but Georgia had liked to think a peculiar little elf had snuck down the chimney and taken them to decorate Santa's house; he would appreciate it at least.

'Looks like you had a beautiful time,' she said.

'Some of it. I guess it's not possible to have a lifetime of happy Christmases, but it wasn't all bad. That's my grandmother.'

Georgia looked at the woman he was pointing at. She had strong features not unlike Archie and a kind expression. 'I can see the family resemblance. She looks like someone with a lot a patience.'

'Yes, she was. It's a pity none of it passed to my father.'

'That's a pretty little necklace.' Georgia ran her finger over the delicate rose design around the woman's neck. 'I like roses. Because of my name I think.'

'Yes, that was her favourite piece. She loved roses too and my grandfather had that made for her early on.' He laid the book aside and twisted to face her, his eyebrow lifting as though he'd just realised how close she was, despite the fact she'd been leaning on him for the last ten minutes.

'It's all right, I won't make a grab for your wallet.'

He drew back with an expression of fake shock. 'No?'

'But tell me where you're going to leave it when you do your forfeit, just so I know.'

'Oh, ha bloody ha, but I'm not doing the forfeit, ok?'

She flopped back, laughing, giddy from an excess of expensive champagne. 'Pity.'

'Careful what you wish for.'

'And what do you think I'm wishing for?'

'Maybe it's best if I don't answer that.' He glanced at her. 'I don't mind playing a song or two, but my clothes are staying put. On second thought, it might be safer to watch a film.'

'Do you have Netflix? Or is the Wi-Fi too slow?'

'No, and I don't know, to answer your questions. But I have a DVD player and several DVDs. They're in the storeroom next to the office. I'll go and get some.'

'Ok, but make sure it's Christmassy; I don't like sci-fi, or horror, or gore.' He was on his way out when she added, 'Or anything with Jim Carrey.'

'Great, that narrows it down nicely then, as I think the only Christmas film I own is *The Grinch*.'

'Why does that not surprise me?' She giggled but didn't really suppose he'd be a fan of *Love Actually* or *The Holiday*. He looked like a classics type of guy. Maybe he'd have *It's A Wonderful Life* or *White Christmas*, either of them would do.

She checked her phone, knowing there would be nothing new except the time. Reception was non-existent and the Wi-Fi was often ropey. It was nearly eight, which surprised her. They must have chatted for ages over dinner, even though most of it was nonsensical banter. But it was the anniversary of Archie's brother's suicide. He was taking it well, or was it a cover? The amount of champagne he'd knocked back was possibly deadening the pain considerably. How awful. Despite the irritation Tamsyn threw at her, Georgia would be devastated if anything happened to her.

The wind roared past the window, creaking the frame and rattling the panes. Georgia shuddered, pulling the blanket tighter around herself. A door shut somewhere. The lights blinked, and she glanced up. No, they couldn't go out. She glared; maybe she could force them to stay on if she trained her thoughts on the winking bulbs. Three seconds later, she was plunged into darkness. *No!* Only the flickering firelight remained, casting dancing shadows across the rug.

A loud crash resonated from the hall. 'Bugger,' cried Archie. The dogs started barking.

'What is it?' Georgia cast off the blanket and stood up, fumbling her way through the room in the orange glow.

At the door it was faint and she could hardly see a thing. Opening it, she peered out. 'Archie? Are you there?'

'Yes. I tripped on the step in the hall in the dark. I've dropped the bloody DVDs.'

'Oh… just leave them,' she said. 'It's not as if we can watch them now anyway unless the power makes an amazingly speedy recovery and does that ever happen here?'

'Not in my experience,' said Archie.

One of the dogs was growling and giving a perfunctory bark or two.

'Dexter, shush. It's all right. Get back to your bed, go on.' Archie's voice was getting nearer.

Georgia hovered by the door, trying to accustom her eyes to the blackness. The heady scent of Archie's fragrance brought him closer and she realised he was almost beside her. She jumped as his hand landed on her shoulder. 'Jeez,' she said.

'You're very jumpy. Don't you like the dark?'

'Not particularly.'

'Well, you better move.'

'Why?'

'You're standing in the doorway, and I can't see if there's mistletoe or not.'

'There is.' She smiled. 'I dare you.' Standing stock-still, she waited. Would he?

A gentle peck landed on her cheek. 'That's all you're getting.'

'Seriously? You call that a kiss? Your dogs could do better.' She stepped out of the frame and stumbled over an end table she'd piled with Christmas magazines. They slid to the floor with a thump. 'Shit,' she said, as Archie let out a low laugh.

'Dear, dear,' he said, taking her by the wrist and leading her. 'Who'd have thought you'd be such a wuss in the dark?' She followed blindly. On her right, the fire blazed low and red.

'Where are we going?'

'Just here,' he said, letting her go.

She bumped into something large and solid, and fumbled about. 'Is this the piano?'

A few notes responded. 'Sit down.'

She hesitated. 'Archie, please tell me you have your clothes on.'

He burst out laughing and tinkled 'Rudolph the Red-Nosed Reindeer'.

'Is that some kind of code?' she asked, feeling her way to the seat. 'Are you sitting there with nothing on but a red nose and antlers?'

'What a vision,' he said over the music with a laugh in his voice. 'But you're the one who was desperate for me to do the forfeit.'

Hands flailing in front, Georgia landed them on his bristly hair.

'Careful, you might put my eye out.'

'It's dark so you can't see anyway,' she muttered, finally finding the seat and edging down. She placed her fingers on his arm and was relieved to feel his chunky knit sweater.

'Happy now?' he said, moving from Rudolph to 'Jingle Bells' in a swift movement.

'Almost.' She moved her hand to his leg and squeezed – jeans – phew.

'Oi,' he said, momentarily losing his place. 'Mind where you're grabbing.'

'Just looking for your wallet,' she quipped.

'Well, you very nearly found the crown jewels, so keep your hands to yourself.'

'Oh dear.' She covered her face. 'You're awful.' Laughing, she leaned on his arm as he jingled on.

'You're calling *me* awful?' he scoffed. 'Takes one to know one.'

'Exactly.'

She swung to the music, lightly tapping her foot, as carefree as Santa on Boxing Day. This was a moment to commit to memory and replay on dark days, something which couldn't be bought or manufactured. With a flourish, Archie rolled into 'The Holly and the Ivy'.

'Jeez, how can you play without seeing the keys?' asked Georgia. 'In fact, how can you play without music?'

'I can't even read music,' he said. 'I just feel and hear the notes. My mother hates it.'

'Why? It's an amazing talent.'

'She thinks it's a waste. If I'd learned to read music, I could have entertained her with great Beethoven concertos and overtures by Handel. Instead, I annoyed her by copying show tunes or film scores, like this…'

Sitting up straight, she listened as a few familiar notes played. She frowned, unable to place it until it burst into the full theme from *Jurassic Park*.

'Oh my god, that is brilliant.' She covered her mouth as the song played out in full glory. Maybe the darkness had heightened her sense of hearing because it was like magic, a brainwave which Archie seemed to pick up on as he moved seamlessly into the famous *Harry Potter* tune. 'Archie, this is so awesome. I don't know how anyone could not like this. Wow. Just wow.'

His shoulder butted against her and he jolted her about, reaching for keys, never hitting a wrong one or making a mistake as he progressed through the tunes. If the lights had been on, she would have shut her eyes, but in the darkness, she just listened in unadulterated bliss.

'Any requests?' he said, finishing up a medley of traditional carols.

'No, I'm just enjoying the free concert.'

'It's nearly done. Time for bed, I think. Or sofa for me.'

'Maybe we should both sleep in here. I'm not sure I want to be down that passageway on my own.'

'Fine,' he said. 'Or you can have the dogs in with you. They'll keep you warm and ward off evil spirits.'

'I'd be happy if they just bite intruders on the backside.'

'They might, if it was a very bony-bummed intruder.'

She giggled. 'I think I'll have the other sofa thanks.'

'Ok, as long as you're quiet. I don't want you talking to me all night.'

'Fine.'

'Now, last request?'

She sat up straight and considered. 'Ooh, let me think.' What to choose now the world was her oyster? 'How about good old "White Christmas"? You can sing it to me as well.'

Now her eyes were more accustomed to the dark, she could vaguely make him out.

'All right, your treat. Just let me get a drink of water. I have one over here.' He got to his feet. The scuffling as he moved about was the only sound except for the rhythmical ticking of the new clock. When he sat down, he smelled even more amazing than usual and she breathed deeply. Her cheek touched his shoulder and she jumped at the feel of bare skin.

'Oh my god, you took them off.'

He laughed so hard the stool shook and she wobbled off the edge. Maybe she should run away but instead, she gripped the side, not daring to look down even in the dark.

'That's what you wanted, remember.' His voice barely withheld a laugh. She slid her hand down to his leg to make sure – still jeans – thank goodness. 'Satisfied?'

'I'm not sure I can answer that truthfully.'

'Ok, hold on to that thought.' He cleared his throat. 'When this is done, that's my forfeit well and truly complete. Isn't it?'

'Definitely,' she said, but her heart was going for a speed record. It would be oh so ridiculously pleasurable to wrap her arms around his chest, but thoughts like that didn't belong in her head. Was this the sad, lonely singleton she'd become? Lusting after a man like him? Ok, yes, a very handsome, very fit man with a dry but fun sense of humour and a great talent, not to mention a pretty bank balance and a big house. *So WTF!* What wasn't to like?

Her mind started kicking and screaming, battering her brain – *do not say the name, just don't, don't mention the 'T' word. No, not now. Keep him out.*

Archie started to sing and Georgia's eyes closed, soothing away the irritating ideas of Tony. Who was Tony anyway? He didn't belong in her brain right now. Was it so wrong to let go to this moment? Archie's voice was like a rich toffee fudge cake and his own brand of warm chocolate sauce. Utterly sinful and addictive.

'… and may all your Christmases be white.' He rounded off the end note perfectly.

Georgia's eyes were still shut. Before she opened them, something gentle brushed her cheek. Archie's fingertips. Her eyelids sprang up. 'I don't have the mistletoe,' he whispered. 'But I'd really like to kiss you, and properly this time.'

'I thought you'd never ask.' She'd been waiting forever to hear those words, or so it seemed. Sliding up, she found his lips and sealed them with hers. He tilted his head slightly as she slung her hand round his bare shoulder and pulled him closer. He wrapped his arm around her, leaned over, and she fell back in a swoon.

He held her, supporting her head and twisting his fingers in her hair, all the while continuing the long languid kiss. The sensual curve of his lips on hers and the rub of his five-o'clock stubble on her chin sent a ripple of contentment through her veins. Closing her eyes, she parted her lips, taking him deeper. When her tongue touched his, a rush of blood and desire shot through her. Nerve ends tingled; her pulse soared. It had been such a long time since she'd kissed anyone, and this was divine, all-consuming. It could lead anywhere, and she wasn't going to be the one to stop it. While massaging his shoulder muscles, she smiled into the kiss and nibbled his lower lip, tasting the chocolate sauce. It couldn't get any better.

When they broke off, Georgia's breathing was all over the place. Archie held her back, and she didn't attempt to move – partly from enjoyment, partly for fear of falling off the stool completely.

'Did that just happen?' she whispered onto his lips, their noses rubbing together. She summoned every ounce of self-control because the urge to launch into another kiss was like the Hulk about to split out of his clothes. She clung to him in case she toppled backwards.

'I believe so,' said Archie, assisting her back into a sitting position. The world spun around her, her head was light and fuzzy, possibly from champagne, possibly from the kiss, possibly from being almost upside down...

Probably all three. 'After all, I can't have you thinking Dexter is a better kisser than me.'

She laughed, her lips feeling tender and swollen. 'I want it noted you started it.'

'Did I?' Archie said, the smile present in his voice. 'I asked, but technically you got to me first.' His hands dropped from her back and she returned to sitting unaided. Just beside him, no longer connected.

Ignoring the distracting sense of loss, she said, 'Enough of the technicalities. Just remember, this was your doing, so tomorrow, you can't sack me for any breach of contract.'

He laid his hand on her leg, making her jump. 'What happens at the piano stays at the piano.'

She bloody hoped so, because trying to make sense of this was going to take a long time. Alcohol and an overdose of music would have to suffice for the time being. Perhaps after a good sleep, they'd both come to their senses, but when they did, she wasn't sure she wanted to face the complicated and scary reality of what was going on or not going on in her life.

CHAPTER 16

Archie

When Archie's eyes opened, a twinkle of lights by the window caught his attention. If the tree was sparkling, it stood to reason the power was back on. Through the dull ache in his forehead, a wash of relief flowed over him. Until he realised he had no shirt on. 'Shit.' He dragged himself up, cringing at the pain in his head and struck by a panic he would find a naked Georgia lying beside him.

He scrabbled about in the dark, confirming he was alone. Finding his phone, he checked the time. Three o'clock. Resting his head back, he sighed into the darkness. No sleeping now. Not with this headache and the memories of his utter stupidity the night before. Maybe a Christmas miracle had put Georgia to sleep on the other sofa because he'd happily have had her beside him. Her soft breathing filled the still air. The cover of darkness was fine, but the morning after was creeping ever closer. How the hell was he going to explain himself? Closing his eyes, he tried to force himself back to sleep.

It must have eventually worked because when he came to again, the room was lighter. He squinted across to where Georgia had sat up, her eyes barely open. 'Morning,' she croaked. 'You look like how I feel.' She raised the heels of her hands and massaged her temples. 'How much champagne did we put away last night, and what the hell was in it? You posh guys don't half know how to knock a girl out.'

'Don't we just.' He peered at her without making it too obvious. 'I should apologise for my behaviour, I—'

'No.' Georgia held up her hand. 'Don't. What you said last night is absolutely right.'

'What the hell did I say? I'm not sure I remember the finer details with much accuracy.'

'What happens at the piano stays at the piano. That's good enough for me. We were both willing participants under the influence of some very fine champagne, and I think we can leave it at that.'

He nodded. Yes, she was right. 'At least the power's back on.'

'Is it?'

'The tree lights are on, so I assume so.'

'Oh good. That's quick for here.' She stretched. 'And that means I'm here nice and early, so I can crack on with work, assuming I can stand up.'

'I should let the dogs out,' said Archie. 'I'm surprised they're not scratching at the door. It's not too dark to leave you alone, is it?'

'What do you mean?'

'In case you're still terrified of things lurking in the shadows.'

She gave him what he supposed was meant to be a stern look, but it obviously hurt her head, so she stopped. 'Right, I should take a shower, but first I need to nip out and get some clean clothes from the van. Who knows what I have? It might be an interesting look.'

'No doubt.' She had a way of looking good in anything. Archie stood up, taking the blanket with him. He didn't feel up to exposing his bare chest in the daylight. As he passed by, her eyes bored into him and she smiled. This was bordering on dangerous territory again. Had his champagne-fuelled game played into her hands? Georgia was a smart and talented woman; all this could be a double bluff. The jokes and assertions of not being interested in him could be part of her master plan. Was he falling into a very clever trap? Because it was working and he was falling. She'd given him no reason to doubt her, so was it safe to trust her? Or to trust his own judgement?

After a scalding shower – he couldn't face a cold one however much his hangover demanded it – he walked the dogs towards the ridge, the wind buffeting him hard. Harmless flirting was one thing, but they'd crossed a line last night. How they'd avoided crossing another one was anyone's guess, the added soporific effect of excessive alcohol perhaps. That kiss had lit a fire inside, igniting emotions Archie had supressed for years. But what the hell should he do? Ignore them? Act on them? 'Oh, for Christ's sake,' he muttered. He hadn't been brought up to act on sentiment. But Georgia... Funny, helpful, clever, cheerful, exciting and wonderful Georgia aroused so much in him but nothing he could confess. She'd laugh him off the planet if he suggested something more serious unless it was part of her endgame, which made the whole situation a minefield, and Archie didn't know where to start.

Could he dismiss these ideas? It was just one kiss, and one kiss under the influence. The fact these feelings had been growing ever since they'd met was a coincidence. It happened when two people were forced together and Georgia, being as she was, made herself easily likeable.

Back in the kitchen and out of the driving wind, Archie glimpsed a flicker of red before he pushed the door fully open. Georgia was dotting about in a scarlet skater dress. She looked like an extra from *White Christmas* in the remastered colour version.

'Excuse the outfit,' she said, 'I'm not even sure why this was in the van, but it seems quite fitting. Christmassy and all that.' She gave a twirl.

'Very you,' said Archie. 'And very pretty.' This was going to be downright bloody impossible. He let out a sigh as he refilled the kettle. 'I need to head out and look at the tree situation. You won't be able to leave until it gets moved.'

'I'm not going anywhere, I have work to do. I'm starting in here today. This room needs a lot of work. The guests will be cooking here.'

'Well, I have to find someone to move the tree. I'm no great shakes with things like that. I have a chainsaw and if Mike can work it, he might do it.'

Georgia's dress swirled around as she dropped into a chair at the kitchen table. 'You should ask Beth McGregor at Creagach Farm, she's hot stuff with a chainsaw.'

'Yes, I know her, vaguely, but she's not my number one fan. She subscribes to a similar opinion as you.'

'What do you mean?' Georgia propped her chin on her hands and eyed him. 'She thinks you're a good candidate for the December photo in the naked pianists' calendar too, does she?'

'Oh, shut up. I mean, you both think I'm a rich, privileged arsehole.'

Georgia pouted and raised a playful eyebrow. 'You do seem pretty rich to me and you were born that way so I think that makes you privileged, but I never said you were an arsehole… Or maybe I did, but anyway, Beth is a great person once you get to know her, and I'm sure she would do it. I'll ask her if you like.'

'Not yet.' Archie took a swig of coffee. 'Let me try Mike first.' He forced down his coffee and the only food he could face – dry toast – and headed out.

Having to find someone to remove a tree was a welcome distraction because putting distance between him and Georgia was imperative. Once she was gone, he could go back to being normal and fine. Less than a week to go. A warzone erupted inside him between the desire to see her again and the need to keep her far away.

As he trundled the Barbarian up the main track, he swung around dodging puddles until he reached the fork in the path where the right turn led towards Gardener's Cottage. He looked towards the main gate and saw the tree tangled across the road. It heartened him because it verified Georgia's story and he so wanted to believe she was genuine. A little wisp of hope flickered, but he couldn't be sure she felt the same. God, it was so difficult. He didn't want to ruin what they had with some stupid move.

Parked behind the tree was a small white transit van, and Archie remembered Blair was due down at Monarch's Lodge. He drove up to meet him.

'Good morning,' he said as he jumped out the Barbarian. Blair glanced up and tightened the band in his blond dreadlocks. Archie frowned and just stopped himself from shaking his head. Maybe it was a sign of getting old, or maybe he really was dull because he couldn't work out why any guy would do their hair like that. He couldn't forget Georgia's comments about how handsome and sexy she thought Blair. In fact, he couldn't be sure they weren't seeing each other. 'You any good with a chainsaw?' he asked.

'Yeah, I can handle one, but I don't own one.'

'I do, so you're in luck. It's in one of the outbuildings. Having said that, I doubt it's been used for years, so it might not work, but let's give it a go.'

'Yeah, yeah, definitely.'

'I was on my way to ask your dad.'

'I'll walk down and see if I can get him to help. The more people we have to move it, the better.'

Archie agreed and went to dig out the chainsaw from an outbuilding he wasn't even sure was safe to enter. It was so typical of the whole estate. The amount of work needing to be done filled Archie with a moment of panic so great his head spun in a dizzy mess. Was this how it had been for Laurence?

Standing tall, Archie took a deep breath. No, he couldn't succumb to thoughts like that. He'd made a commitment to the estate and more, to the island. His job in the oil industry had been profitable and he wasn't wholly ready to give it up, not yet, but it was an ever-changing and volatile sector. If he could secure the estate as a viable commodity, he would change direction and make this his chief concern. This lifestyle was much more suited to his personality, and Mull was his perfect place to settle.

As he dragged the chainsaw box to the Barbarian, a vision of Georgia danced into his head. A strange path, paved with glitter and lined with fairy lights, opened out before him. One where he and Georgia were together, dancing and singing whenever they liked. Nothing fazed Georgia, she knew who to call and how to make things work, and if they didn't, she laughed them off and found an alternative.

Archie craved some of her crazy enthusiasm in his life, and not just for Christmas. But it brought him back to the same conundrum. Was it even possible to bring about something like that? His first task was to discover if the feelings were mutual without sounding crazy.

After an hour of Blair manically sawing and Mike and Archie heavy lifting, they cleared the fallen tree. There was enough cut wood to keep the home fires burning for several days, and Archie had filled the back of the Barbarian when Mike returned on his second trip with his trailer attached. Another load filled and Archie peeled back his collar, flapping it a little. The cool air snapped at his neck and down into his chest as it met the thin layer of sweat he'd worked up. His stomach flipped at the idea of going home. Part of him wanted to see Georgia, but the other part suggested keeping his distance would be more sensible, so he followed Blair through the incoming mist to Monarch's Lodge. Maybe if he helped out there, there was still the tiniest sliver of hope it might be habitable in time for Christmas.

CHAPTER 17

Georgia

Kitchens were always tricky to update, and this one was particularly bad. Pressing her fingertips to her forehead, Georgia scanned the outdated and ugly units. Even attempting to get some country chic out of this would be next to impossible, at least not without new cupboard doors or paint, and there wasn't time for either.

'Ok.' She pulled in a breath and slowly released it. No point stressing about things she couldn't control, she just had to work with what she had. After scribbling down a few ideas, she pulled open a cupboard. 'Right, that's a whole lot of junk.' Tidying it up would be a good place to start and hidden gems often turned up. She had a fimbling-feeling something unexpected was going to come to light. Perhaps a set of vintage doors hidden behind the ugly eighties frontage.

After hauling out the contents of every cupboard and piling it on the table and the floor, she'd given up hope of finding anything useful and wished she hadn't started, but the thought of Tamsyn opening a cupboard and finding the contents of a vintage store, rather than gorgeous shiny antique cooking pots, filled her with dread. Not that she'd want to use them, but they'd have to be there, preferably arranged by size.

A gentle tinkling on the bell sounded. Georgia pulled her head out from the inside of a cupboard and wiped her haphazard hair from her face. How long had she been doing this? She had no idea what time it was. She checked her phone and was shocked to see it was ten past one. The bell sounded again, followed by a sharp knocking. Where was Archie? Supposing it was more deliveries, Georgia headed to the door and pulled it open with a flamboyant motion.

As she came eye to eye with a furry leopard print hat, Georgia's brow creased. She scanned downwards over a wrinkled forehead onto a huge fur jacket that matched the hat.

'Who are you?' said the coat's occupant, her eyes flashing. 'Where's Archibald?'

Before Georgia had a chance to reply, another woman with long black hair teetered up the stairs, adjusting the collar of a thick black coat. 'Just go in,' she said. 'There's no need to ring. He never locks it.'

'I always like to ring, especially when he doesn't know we're coming,' said furry hat.

Another car pulled up behind a large black Mercedes, and two more women got out. One was tall and elegant, ageless with her long caramel curls. Georgia thought she was maybe a few years older than her while the other woman looked much younger.

The black-haired woman had reached the top of the front stairs. She stopped dead as she gaped at Georgia. 'Who are you?' she demanded in a whip crack of a voice with a heavy, Glaswegian accent.

'I'm Georgia Rose,' she replied, looking around with a flutter of anxiety. She'd seen this woman at her photography show, and assumed she was Archie's wife. Marcia? Was that the name? Archie had told her she was his mother's secretary. The penny slowly dropped as she squinted back at the older woman. 'Are you Archie's mum?'

'I'm Archibald's mother,' she said, picking at something on her coat. 'Now, let me in. I've never heard of you. Are you a cleaner?'

Marcia inspected Georgia closely, her eyes snakelike. 'You're that artist, aren't you? The one Archie caught trespassing.'

'Well, yes. But I'm—'

'You're a what?' said his mother, her pencilled eyebrow raised high on her tanned and severely creased forehead as she examined Georgia's outfit.

'The designer,' said Georgia, 'I'm doing up the house for the guests. They're arriving next week.'

'That's us here now,' said his mother, pulling off a pair of leather gloves. 'Louisa, darling, bring Yvonne inside quickly. The wind is horrific.'

The four women strolled into the entrance hall. Marcia closed the front door with a resonating thud.

'Well, well, well,' said the elegant woman, twirling a lock of caramel hair. 'What a transformation. The last time I saw this place it was barely fit for canine habitation, never mind humans.'

'You can leave.' Archibald's mother squinted at Georgia with an irritated pout. 'Oh, where's the bust? Laurence's bust. He paid a lot of money for that.'

'So he did,' said the Mistress-of-Elegance. 'He always did waste his money,' she muttered aside to the younger woman.

'Eh… Archie moved it,' said Georgia, standing stock-still. Had Archie's mother just told her to leave? And where was she supposed to go? She had to find Archie, and fast.

'Please go now. We've had an absolute nightmare of a trip and I need to relax; I don't want all and sundry hanging around while I'm busy.'

Busy relaxing? Georgia smirked. *Seriously.* 'I'm working here. Archie is paying me; I can't just leave.'

'Paying you?' said Marcia.

'Will you stop addressing my son as Archie, it's far too familiar from an employee. Mr Crichton-Leith, if you please. And I'm not concerned if he's paying you or not, I don't want an audience. You can finish off whatever it is you're doing some other time.'

Georgia glanced around hoping for someone to jump out and yell, surprise! This had to be a wind-up? And if not, what was she meant to do?

'I'll get my things,' she said, passing the mother and heading down the passageway. She didn't have anything there, but maybe she could call Archie on the landline. He might be somewhere with a signal. She crossed her fingers as she keyed in the number on the ancient phone.

It rang off. What now? Why would the idiot not sign up to messenger? Though the probability of him being in a Wi-Fi zone was equally low. 'Shit! The kitchen!' His mother looked like someone who drank a lot of wine and coffee when she relaxed. No doubt they'd be heading for the kettle or the fridge at that moment. Georgia almost leapt over the desk in her haste to get out of the room and down the corridor. She bolted out the door and ran bang into Archie.

'Oh, Archie.' She grabbed his upper arms. 'Thank god you're here.'

He grasped her elbows. 'Why? The new sofa and chairs arrived at Monarch's Lodge, I was getting them in, then I saw Marcia's car. What's she doing here?'

'It's not her,' said Georgia. 'Well, it is, but it's worse.'

'Archibald!'

Archie jumped and spun around, Georgia released him with the speed of light. 'Mother? What are you doing here?'

'Surprise!' She peered in the end of the passageway.

Archie stiffened and flexed his neck before walking towards her. 'Surprise, yes, but why?'

'Oh, Archibald,' she said as he stepped into the entrance hall. 'That's not much of a welcome for your old mater.' She pulled him into a cursory hug like she was fawning over a favourite pet.

'Mother, why are you here?'

'We had this arranged weeks ago. You knew I was coming. I would have been here sooner, but the boats were cancelled for this bad weather. Wait until you see who's here.'

'Who?' The deep furrow in his forehead was back. Georgia saw it, even from her hiding place in the passageway. She wasn't sure what to do, but she had to get out and block anyone from getting into the kitchen.

'Come with me.' Mrs Crichton-Leith took Archie by the hand and led him across the flagstone floor and up the step towards the drawing room. Georgia followed stealthily. Once they were inside, she would make a run for the kitchen.

'Let's get this straight, Mother. We talked about your coming and I said not this time, it would have to be next year. I have a house party coming next week. You can't stay here.'

'Oh fiddlesticks. It's not like I'm a stranger to house parties.'

'No, Mother, it isn't that kind of party. I'm serious. I cannot—' The drawing room doors flew open and Archie's jaw dropped. Georgia stopped just in time, lingering close to her multi-coloured Christmas tree. 'Louisa? What are you...' Archie's voice trailed away.

Louisa? Georgia stared at the caramel-haired woman. This was his brother's ex-wife? Ok, his family were even more twisted than hers. Why was she here?

'Hello, Archie. I've brought someone for you to meet. My cousin Yvonne.'

'She's the daughter of Lord and Lady Wormit,' said his mother.

Georgia couldn't hold in her laugh. Wormit? *Seriously?*

'I thought I told you to leave.'

Georgia held her hand over her mouth, realising she'd been caught. Mrs Crichton-Leith was staring daggers at her.

'Mother, please, you can't tell her to leave.'

Mrs Crichton-Leith arched her eyebrow. 'Archibald.' She pulled him to the side and turned her back as though this would block her words. 'This woman claims to be your designer. I can see from her dress what kind of designs she has on you. Now, I'm not judging, you're a single man and I know that comes with... Well...' She lowered her voice. 'Certain desires,' she hissed. 'But please get rid of her. We don't need that sort around here.'

Heat bloomed on Georgia's face, making her cheeks burn. It took every ounce of restraint not to tell the snooty old bitch where to go.

'Mother,' said Archie through gritted teeth. His eyes darted into the drawing room where Louisa picked at a nail like she was trying not to laugh, and young Yvonne looked on like a frightened rabbit. 'That was rather offensive. Georgia is here to do a job and I need her to keep doing it. Now, if you would come with me, we can discuss this in private.' He glanced at Georgia with a half exasperated, half apologetic expression that morphed into a wonky eye roll. 'I'm sorry. You can get back to work, I'll sort this out.'

She waited until he'd stepped into the drawing room before she saluted him and said, 'Aye aye, your lordship. That'll be me well and truly dismissed.'

Like Cinderella in rags, Georgia traipsed back to the kitchen, wondering what was going on at the ball and which delightful princess Prince Charming would choose. Clearing out cupboards had lost its fun. Pots and pans clattered to the floor, and Georgia only just avoided smashing a nicely painted Christmas plate with holly and snowflakes. Thank goodness she saved it in time. It was the only pretty thing she'd found so far.

The new arrivals changed everything. A bitter sense of apathy spread through her veins. For a day or two, she'd felt special, even if it had been nonsense. It wasn't every day a girl was swept off her feet, sung to, and kissed at the piano. She touched her lips. All day, she'd deliberately pushed the thought away, but that had been some kiss, so tender, yet passionate. And yes, she wanted to do it again, but that couldn't happen now; she was back to being the nobody at the bottom of the heap. Another pan dropped and reverberated around the kitchen. She had to get used to this. Come next week when Tamsyn and co descended, things would get a lot worse. She'd sooner face the music and dance with Archie than see Tony again, but dancing while this crew was in the house wasn't going to happen.

Heaving a pot to the ground, she stared around. 'What the hell am I doing here? What the hell am I doing with my whole damn stupid life?'

In the drawing room were four women who all had some claim on Archie. His mother for one, but the other three… Were they suitors? The brother's ex-wife, the secretary hoping for the rags-to-riches tale, and poor young Miss Wormit. Was she a young heiress about to be thrown at Archie's feet? And who would he choose? 'My money's on Louisa,' muttered Georgia, throwing another copper pot to the floor. 'He's always fancied her, and she looks like a glamour model. Lucky cow.'

As the clanging pot stopped spinning, the door opened, and Archie peeked around. For a second, Georgia imagined picking up the pot and knocking him round the head with it. It might appease her irritation in the short term, but she didn't want to cause him any lasting damage. 'Can I come in?' His face was pinker than usual.

Georgia looked up from the midst of the clutter. Shit, what a mess. It was worse than the bric-a-brac section of a poorly sourced thrift shop, a dusty collection of lace, brass, copper and some mottled green glass bowls. 'It's your house. You can do what you like. I'm putting this stuff back in the cupboards, then I'm going.'

'Please, Georgia.' He clicked the door shut behind him. 'Please don't leave. I need you here. My mother is… Well, you saw.' He sighed and ran his fingers through his hair. 'And as for the others, don't get me started.'

'It's fine. I'll come back tomorrow, but I think it's better if I finish up here for the day.'

'All right, but don't put any of this stuff back.'

'Why not? They'll want to come in here.'

'No. I've persuaded them to go out for dinner. Leave this, I want to go through it with you, then we can throw out the useless junk. I'm sorry about the state of the place. It's awful.'

'Never mind. We'll get it sorted.'

With a brief smile and a nod, he left. So that was that. Georgia left the piles of junk as he'd instructed and grabbed her coat and hat. Twenty-four hours ago, things had been so different. Now they were as they should be, but everything felt wrong.

Instead of taking the quick way home, she turned north towards Calgary. This way took her past Creagach Farm. While umming and ahing about whether to stop, she spotted Beth's quad at a bend in the road close to the farm. She slammed on the brakes and pulled in behind it. In the dim afternoon light, she saw Beth clomping down the hill with her two collies.

Sitting quite still, she waited until there was a knock on the window. 'Hi,' said Beth. 'What are you up to?'

'Are you busy? I know you always are, but are you too busy to talk?'

'I've finished up here, so I'm good to talk. What about?'

'Can we go for a walk?'

'Sure,' said Beth.

Georgia got out of the van and retrieved her welly boots. Wearing them with her red coat, she was aware how Mrs Claus-like she must look. Beth just smirked at the combo and the two of them crossed the road and jumped down from the verge onto the grassy headland below. Over a few low scrubby bushes was a path. Below was a deep gully and beyond that, the sea spritzed and foamed around the rocks. Around the bluffs to the south Ardnish, and further around the corner was the main house and the beautiful Monarch's Lodge.

'Is everything ok?' asked Beth. 'Bloody Crichton-Leith hasn't been giving you grief, has he?'

'Not really. He's ok. In fact, he's sorry about how he behaved with the road. He's not a bad guy.'

Beth snorted. 'Pfft. Has he put some kind of spell on you?'

'Maybe, he is a bit of a charmer, but no, that's not what I want to talk about.'

'What then?'

'I need to confess something, and I don't know who to tell. I think out of all my friends you're the one least likely to judge me.'

Beth slowed her pace and frowned. 'Have you robbed the house or something?'

'No, nothing like that.' Georgia took a deep cleansing breath and Beth watched with a slight frown. 'When I was seventeen, I met a guy called Tony Stuart. He's my brother-in-law's cousin. He was a cool, funny guy, and we dated for a bit. Then we kind of stopped at university when it got tricky. I was in art school in Glasgow and he was in Aberdeen so it wasn't the easiest commute, but when we finished up, we got back together. We were together for six years, plus when we were teenagers.'

'Wow, you kept this quiet.'

'Yeah.' She ran her hand through her hair. 'And that's not all.'

'Ok, carry on.'

'One day, Tony told me he'd got a job in London. He hadn't even told me about the interview, nothing. I was… well, shocked.'

'I bet,' said Beth.

'But I went along with the idea. You know me, I'm usually game for most things. But Tony said no. He wanted to go alone, have a break, not forever, just a year or two for us to have some time alone before things got serious. He said it was part of a master plan and it was for the best.'

'Wow, ok.'

'Yup. Ridiculous, isn't it? It doesn't end there. I was shell-shocked. I'd never imagined my life any other way than with Tony. And my family liked him, even though they didn't approve of anything else I ever did. Tony could always placate them and laugh off the fact I never had a proper job, dressed like their worst nightmare and didn't want to join the pony club. When I let him go, it was on the understanding that one day he'd come back.'

'You agreed to that?'

'Yup. And in the beginning, he'd call and message me. But I'm not a sitting around and waiting kind of person, and after a few weeks, I did something insane.'

'What?'

'I bought a van, painted it pink, decorated it and moved here.'

'So, that's why you're here.'

'Years before, I'd visited Mull with Tony and some friends on an island-hop. I had fond memories of it. I chose somewhere I thought I could be happy.'

'And you are, aren't you?'

'Yes. Really happy. I didn't expect to like it so much. I've thrown my heart and soul at this place.'

'I know you have, but has something changed?'

'Tony's coming back.'

Beth looked down on Georgia with a pitied expression. 'And you're leaving to get back together with him?'

'I heard, by accident, he's coming here to propose in some grand gesture this Christmas.'

'Oh.'

'But… I don't want to leave. I don't want to marry Tony. I came here to wait it out, but that's not what's happened. I've built a better life here and it isn't one I want to give up.'

'Good. I'm glad to hear it because if this was anyone else telling this story to you, you would tell them to hop off the bus and stop waiting for some idiot who dumped you to show up and expect you to pick up the pieces like he never left.'

Georgia covered her mouth, feeling a well of tears and laughter. 'That's what I needed to hear.'

Beth slung her arm around Georgia's shoulder as they walked. 'He sounds like a twat, and you're too good for that. You deserve someone much better. Though it explains why you weren't interested in anyone else. We did wonder, though no one liked to ask.'

'Oh dear, I didn't want to hide anything, it just wasn't something I wanted to share. I didn't see myself as being single or available.'

'Luckily for me.'

'No, Beth. Murray only ever had eyes for you. I wouldn't even have tried.'

Beth grinned. 'Good.'

'I just wonder what I should do if Tony shows up. Do you think I should message him and tell him I know about it, and don't want him here?'

'You could do or let him come.'

'Really?'

'Yeah, why not? Then find a nice prickly bit of holly and burst that smug bubble of his. Fancy thinking he can expect you to wait for him indefinitely.'

'I've been such an idiot.'

'We're all idiots when it comes to love. I certainly was. I suppose you clung to the idea of him.'

'Yes.' It'd been easier that way. She'd never had to think or worry about the future, knowing it had an outcome her family would approve of. Now that outcome had been blown right out the water, but Georgia didn't feel grief, far from it. Relief washed over her like the cleansing waves below, sparkling orange in the low winter sunset.

CHAPTER 18

Archie

Lavinia Crichton-Leith had made herself at home before Archie had time to consider how to get rid of her.

She wasn't even out of bed the following morning when Georgia arrived. Archie had been up since five, walking the dogs, sorting the kitchen, and trying to figure out what the hell he was going to do with four stubborn women.

'Oh.' Georgia stopped dead as she opened the door and her eyes fell on him. 'You're here already.'

'I am. You're very early too.' He checked the clock; it was heading for eight.

'I wanted to crack on. I don't think it's a good idea for me to be here when the house is so busy.'

'Please don't be put off by them. I'm trying to get them out; they can't stay here. I need to get that message through to my mother.' He dropped onto his knees amidst a sea of copper cooking pots and started piling them up. 'But I'm all she has now. I don't think she wants to spend Christmas alone… if I can just persuade her to book into a hotel.'

'That sounds sensible.' Georgia unwound her scarf, hung it and the coat on the rack, then joined Archie on the floor. 'These pots are actually fine, if I shine them up a bit they'll look like new. Otherwise, you'll need a whole new set of cooking utensils before next week.'

Settling his gaze on her, Archie sighed. 'I have to thank you for everything you've done here.'

'You're paying me, remember, so there's no need.'

'You've done over and above what I've paid you for.' Archie mirrored the little grin growing on Georgia. 'And yes, I'll give you a raise.'

The grin blossomed, but Georgia shook her head. 'That won't be necessary.'

'I appreciate this. I didn't know where to start, I couldn't even have guided you. You've taken the bull by the horns and made something amazing out of a junk hole, and I really don't want my mother and these women to spoil it.'

'Why did your mother bring the others?' asked Georgia, sorting a selection of pots and setting them to one side.

'The usual reason. Yvonne is an heiress, so my mother instantly thinks the poor girl will want to marry me. She's only twenty-one. Twenty-one,' he repeated. 'I'm thirty-bloody-six, I'd finished school before she even started.'

Georgia chuckled and grabbed a cloth from behind her. 'I've known people who wouldn't object to an age gap like that. I think it's ok as long as both parties like each other and are consenting.'

'Well, this party isn't. I'm sure she's a lovely girl, but she's not for me.'

'Is that because of Louisa?'

'You're a sharp one, aren't you? You worked out who she was.'

'Of course,' said Georgia, polishing one of the pots. 'I guess she's not here to marry you off to her cousin, not if she can have you for herself.'

'Hmm.'

'Is that even legal?'

'How do you mean?'

'To marry your brother's widow?'

Archie raised his eyebrows. 'I think historically it was illegal, but it wouldn't hold in this case anyway. Louisa and Laurence were divorced for years, he had another wife after that and he divorced her too. So technically, she's not his widow. None of which matters anyway because I don't want to marry her.'

'She's very attractive.' Georgia laid the shiny pot to one side and picked up another.

'Yes, she is. And I told you, there was a time when I was very shallow and would have been easily swayed by that, but not any more. I wouldn't touch her with a ten-foot pole these days and I want her out of the house.'

'If you used a ten-foot pole, you could prod her out with it.'

Archie let out a laugh, releasing a build-up of nervous tension. 'You do make me laugh. All you need is some tinsel in your hair and you could be the Christmas fairy.'

Georgia stood up and lifted the two shiny pots onto the table. When she took her place on the floor again, she had a silver tinsel halo wrapped around her head. 'Will this do?'

'More than.' Archie gazed deep into her dark brown eyes, glittering with the reflected sparkle of the tinsel. Her blonde bob bounced with haphazard waves that, despite being at odds with each other, still worked perfectly together. Louisa may have a perfect elegance, but here sat a true beauty. Georgia shone from within. She was blessed with a pretty face, but moreover, a kind heart and a loving soul. Impulsively, Archie stretched out and took her hand. 'I'm so glad you came here.'

'Archie.' Georgia glanced at his grip. 'Are you ok?'

'I want to get rid of them all, but I don't know how. It's going to mess everything up.' He raked his fingers through his hair.

With her hand still in his, Georgia shuffled forward on her knees. Her eye contact was blazing. She pulled her hand away and coiled her arms around him, gently patting his back. 'You can do it,' she said.

Do what? He wasn't sure he could do anything right now, other than hold her close. The warmth of the embrace spread through every vein, reaching his extremities like a soothing balm. Yes, he could do it. Whatever *it* was. He could do anything. Keeping her firmly in his grip, he was aware she had an equally tight hold on him, every curve of her body pressed against him. They were almost crushing each other when Georgia raised her head from its position on his shoulder and placed a gentle but meaningful kiss on his cheek. Archie leaned into it and closed his eyes. Now was a moment for control. She was being kind, infusing him with strength, and he had to accept that. But how easy it would be to kiss her back.

He leaned in a little, and the tips of their noses brushed. A centimetre more and he could claim those lips. Their eyes locked, but neither spoke. If he kissed her now, he couldn't blame alcohol or anything else except the raw desire buried deep within. A kiss now would come straight from his soul and be searching for hers. Her dark eyes twinkled and the doors of her pupils widened, inviting him in. Her sparkling pink lips parted. His breathing grew terse.

The sharp click of the door shattered the moment and Georgia let go so fast Archie toppled over. He fiddled with his shirt at his waistband and Georgia's head was down while she polished the pots again. Thank god for the table, blocking the view. Archie peeked up to see who had come in. Both Louisa and Yvonne entered.

'What is going on here?' asked Louisa, surveying what must look like fallout from an explosion in an antique shop and taking a seat. Her long legs stretched too close for comfort and Archie moved out of their way. Maybe ten years ago that view would have had a different effect on him, but now all he wanted was for Louisa to use those glamorous pins to get back out of the room and leave him alone with Georgia.

'We're clearing out,' said Archie. 'Next week is a big week for me, as I've already told you.'

'And who are you again?' Louisa asked Georgia.

'Just Georgia.'

'She's my designer,' said Archie, 'and my friend. Georgia, this is Louisa, and this is Yvonne.'

Georgia's big smile returned and looked impressively genuine. 'Hi, nice to meet you both.'

'The house is looking lovely,' said Louisa. 'You've done a great job.'

'Thank you,' said Georgia.

She still had tinsel in her hair, but such was the beauty of Georgia, he knew she wouldn't care. 'Yes, she's a worker of magic,' said Archie, sending her an appreciative nod.

Louisa pulled up her perfectly shaped eyebrows in a know-it-all way. *Yes, yes, so what if you suspect me of falling for my employee, suspect away, because it's true and if you would bugger off, I could get back to giving her my undivided attention.* Archie tried to impart the sentiment to Louisa with a fake grin plastered across his face, though he wasn't sure if Georgia really wanted his attention. A hug was one thing, an intense look another, a kiss, well... Did any of that mean she craved his affection as much as he wanted to give it to her?

'I feel so bad about this,' said Yvonne. 'I thought you knew we were coming. I would never have come if I'd known. This is such bad timing.'

'It's fine,' said Louisa with a dismissive flap of her hand.

'Actually, she's right.' Archie jumped to his feet. 'The best thing you could do is find a hotel to stay in if you're dead set on remaining here. And if you can persuade my mother to join you, then even better.'

But Lavinia Crichton-Leith was not to be put off. Not after the effort she'd put into getting here and doing Archie what she viewed as a service, bringing him a potential bride. What she didn't grasp was Louisa's ulterior motive. Archie was damned if he would let himself be alone with her even for five minutes.

He would have hidden in Monarch's Lodge, but he also wanted to keep the women away from Georgia. She needed space to finish, and he didn't want them insulting her to the point where she left.

Archie decided to make them breakfast and serve it in the dining room in a bid to remove them from the kitchen.

'You should put on your tails,' quipped Georgia. 'You'd make a hot waiter.'

'Ha! You think? Is that more of your sauce?'

'Yeah, maybe we shouldn't go there again.'

'No,' said Archie. She was probably right. 'We should act with decorum.'

'Exactly, so make sure you keep your shirt on when you're serving up.'

'Noted,' he said, filling the teapot with boiling water.

Georgia sniggered. 'I don't suppose your mother would appreciate it.'

'Definitely not.'

With two trays laden with food, Archie headed for the dining room. His mother and Marcia had joined Louisa and Yvonne.

'The house is looking very nice, Archibald,' his mother commented, her eyes travelling over the crisp white tablecloth running the length of the table and the giant foliage centrepiece wrapped around a set of old candlesticks, polished to look brand new. Archie's insides warmed at how hard Georgia had worked to repurpose these old things and woven them together to make new beauty. 'Did you do it all for me?'

He rolled his eyes. 'No, Mother. In four days, I have a large house party arriving.'

'I know, and I thought we'd settled that. We can join them. They'll all be our sort. I'm glad you've come round to the idea of entertaining, it's the only thing this house is fit for.'

'No. They're not my guests. They're paying for the privilege. I won't be joining them and neither will you. You need to find some other accommodation and quickly.'

'Oh fiddlesticks,' she muttered. 'Paying to stay here? What nonsense. Who are they?'

'How should I know? They're people I've never met.'

'You've never met them? It all sounds very odd to me. What do you make of this?' She glanced at Marcia.

'It's a good idea in principle, but I don't think it'll make enough money in the long run.'

'So, he'd be better selling?'

'Mother, I'm in the room, and I'm not selling. I'll decide whether it's viable.' Marcia obviously didn't realise how much people were prepared to pay for the hire of a place like this. 'So, decide where you're going. I can't have you in the bedrooms after tonight because they'll need to be cleaned before the guests arrive. You can have my room in the office wing.'

'Office wing? Is that what you call that dusty old corridor?'

'Yes. If that doesn't suit, I can set you up in Monarch's Lodge for a day or two, but no more.'

'Monarch's Lodge!' His mother gaped as if he'd offered her a stable with some cattle and a manger.

'I've been working on it. It's not perfect, but it's almost ready for me to stay in. I'll see if I can get some beds and you can have it.'

'That's quite ridiculous. Monarch's Lodge is vile, it doesn't deserve such an illustrious name.'

Mother's go-to position. She'd always scoffed at it. Despite it being a five-bedroom house, with three public rooms, a gorgeous country kitchen, and a view to die for, it would never be a proper house in her eyes. She'd taken great pleasure in banishing her mother-in-law to it, not appreciating how happy she'd been there and what a wonderful home she'd made it. After she died, twelve years ago, the place had barely been touched until Archie had started this year. 'Well, I like it.' If he told her his long-term plan was to move in there, she'd probably die of shock, and while that would solve his immediate problem, it wasn't particularly charitable.

His mother shuddered. 'It's bleak and horrible.' Archie bit his tongue. His mother used that phrase about most things on the island. Why she ever came back was a mystery. 'You're too stubborn to do what's right. If you're not selling it, I'd rather you didn't rent it out to some common people.'

'Please, Mother, that's rather crass.' He adjusted his cuffs, trying not to make eye contact with anyone. He could sense Louisa's smirk and Yvonne's desire to open a trapdoor and disappear through it.

'Pfft. Can I see the guest list? If they're people of quality, I'm likely to know them.'

'Absolutely not.'

'I demand to see it.'

'No,' Archie snapped. 'Marcia, I wonder if you could look into some suitable hotels today, please.'

'I er.' She glanced at Lavinia.

'I think not.' Lavinia picked up her knife and began buttering her toast.

Archie returned to the kitchen. 'After I've cleared up, you can put any number of heavy objects over the door to stop them coming in,' he told Georgia.

'I think I will.'

'Please do, you have my express permission to do anything you like to keep them out, you can nail the door shut if you need to. I'm going to try to get them to go somewhere, but my mother is a stubborn woman.'

After a quick trip to Monarch's Lodge to check in with Blair's progress, Archie returned to the house, hoping to persuade the women to go out for lunch. Even if he had to go with them, it seemed better than having them here, making a mess of everything Georgia had worked on over the last few weeks.

Entering the drawing room, he saw his mother with a piece of paper in her hand and an elegant pair of glasses perched on her nose.

'What are you reading?' he asked.

'Oh, hello, Archibald. Marcia very kindly got me a printout of your guest list.'

'She did what?' Archie stepped towards her and made to snatch the paper from his mother, but she pulled it away. He'd forgotten he'd given Marcia computer access on her last visit, but what a liberty, browsing his private documents.

'On my orders,' said his mother. 'And this is very interesting. There's a name on here I recognise. A Mrs Elspeth Montgomery.' She looked up with a bright expression. 'I might give her a call.'

'What about?' Archie flung up his hands. 'Don't you dare tell her to cancel, this is important to me, Mother.'

She tapped her nose and stood up. 'Wouldn't dream of it.' She sashayed out of the room, waving the piece of paper.

Moments later, Archie stepped into the kitchen and shut the door, glad Georgia hadn't barricaded it. He flopped against it, letting out a furious tirade before Georgia had even looked round. His gaze travelled around the room and his jaw dropped as he observed the transformation. How was it possible this was the same room as before? With the clear surfaces and shiny copper pots everywhere, it was like something from a storybook. Faux foliage, twisted ivy vines and baubles adorned the alcove housing the Aga.

Georgia was busy on the final tree. 'She's doing what?' she said.

'She's contacting someone on the guest list.'

Georgia's eyes flashed red. 'Who?'

He shrugged. 'No idea.'

'You better stop her. Do you really want her gatecrashing their parties and family moments? That won't earn you good reviews. You'll be slated.'

He ran his hands down his face. 'Don't I know it? I just don't know what I have to do to make her listen.'

'Go and disconnect the phone then, and quickly before she gets through to anyone.'

But it was no use. His mother had already got through to her contact and judging from her wide grin, she'd had the desired result.

'Mrs Montgomery is delighted I will be here.' She adjusted some of the baubles on the Christmas tree at the window in the drawing room. 'She's glad there will be some decent company. It's her son and his wife who have organised the trip. Apparently, the daughter-in-law's family are dire. She has a total wastrel of a sister who lives somewhere near here. Mrs Montgomery says the girl roams around the countryside like a gypsy. So, she's very pleased I'll be here to smooth things over.'

Archie took a deep breath and balled his fists. Could things get any worse?

CHAPTER 19

Georgia

Ardnish was decked out like a Christmas castle and Georgia's work was almost done. The four new arrivals made her want nothing more than to make herself scarce, but her desire to discover what Archie was doing with them when the guests arrived kept her hanging around. Where was Archie? After their near kiss in the kitchen, she'd barely clapped eyes on him the next day. Maybe it was for the best. Every time she got close to him these days, she wanted to get her hands on him, or her lips, or any part of her anatomy really, and she didn't have the willpower to stop.

On her way home, she called on Autumn. Although Beth was the best listener, Autumn was good when it came to talking about the others. Georgia didn't like to bitch, but something was bothering her. 'I'm not going to turn thirty every year,' she told Autumn. 'So I don't get why none of them want to do anything. They never have plans, but come my birthday, no one is free. It's bloody annoying. Now I'll have to suffer Tamsyn's silly surprise, the one she hasn't officially told me about.'

No one had told her if Tony's coming was real or not either. One message, one phone call, that was all it would take. She could find out, but something stopped her. The hope – or was it denial – that Tony had no real intention of coming. Messaging him now might open the can of worms she was so keen to keep the lid on. Maybe if she wished hard enough, he'd get the vibe and stay away. Though it didn't solve the problem in the long run. Still, Georgia was quick enough to lift the doormat and sweep the whole thing under it.

'I have a definite excuse,' said Autumn. 'I'm working.'

'Yeah, and that's fine, but I'm not being funny, I love Beth, she's an amazing friend, but she's only been out about three times this year. How can one of those few times coincide with my birthday?'

'It does seem a bit strange,' said Autumn.

'It makes me feel rubbish. They've all met people this year, and I feel like the last single woman on the planet.'

'Of course you're not,' said Autumn. 'It's just a busy time for people.'

All true. And Georgia wasn't a brooder, but things kept coming into her head and wouldn't go away. She could barely shut her eyes at night, in her freezing cold house, when normally she went out like a light. The day before Tamsyn's arrival, she returned to Ardnish to check everything was in order. The sight of Archie at the gate, winding lights around a tree in his shirt sleeves, caused an eruption of goosebumps. Not only did he look as sexy as ever, but it was such a relief to see him. She'd missed him and the banter. Stopping the van, she eased down the window. A blast of cold air hit her. 'How can you stand it out here with no jacket? Have you lost your mind?'

Abandoning the string of lights, he came over. His auburn tinged hair flapped around in the wind and he repeatedly ran his fingers through it. Leaning in the window, he smiled and Georgia wanted to lean up and kiss those inviting lips. His warm fragrance made her skin do a tingly dance and when she glimpsed his forearms resting on the window edge, she bit her lip, hoping to hold back the flood of inappropriate ideas.

'Hello,' he said. 'What brings you here?'

'I thought I'd just kick back and watch the show,' she said, waggling her eyebrows and giving him an obvious once-over.

He rested his head to the side and pushed out an I-should-have-guessed pout. 'Sure. Do you want me to take this off too?' He tugged at his top button.

Hell yes. She almost opened the door and dragged him in. 'Sure, but your mother might be at the window with binoculars and I can't guarantee I'll be able to keep my hands to myself.'

'Me neither.' He grinned.

Georgia's stomach flipped like she'd gone over the edge of a rollercoaster and she gave a little cough. 'So, er, I thought I'd check everything is good to go for the guests. Is that ok?'

'Of course. Tell you what, let me get these lights up, then I'll come with you.'

'Ok, but shirt off.'

'Ha. Nice try.' He returned to hanging the lights.

Georgia hadn't mastered the art of a tidy car, and right now there were more pressing matters to attend to, such as ogling Archie's backside. When he was finished, he rolled down his sleeves and jumped in. 'Excuse the mess,' said Georgia.

'Mess?' He shook his head. 'You've just spent a month tidying my mess. This is nothing in comparison.'

'Fair point.' The wind buffeted the van as she crawled down the drive. It was a relief to park in the lee of the building.

'This looks so much better. It's still imposing but much more welcoming. You really are a marvel.'

'I don't follow. I haven't done anything out here.'

'The wreath, it's so beautiful. You're so talented.'

'Oh, stop it, Archie. You're making me blush.'

'I'm serious. Tell you what, once you're done inspecting, come and see Monarch's Lodge.'

'Is it ready?'

'Almost.'

'Wow, brilliant.' She adjusted the collar of her jacket and swallowed. Did that mean he'd succeeded in getting rid of the other women? Their cars weren't there, and Archie appeared cheerful, so she assumed he'd worked his magic. After spending twenty minutes, checking everything was in order and seeing no evidence of anyone in the public rooms, Georgia left satisfied.

Outside, the track rose in a rolling mound over a hill which descended to Monarch's Lodge. Archie was waiting on the crest, the dogs roaming around him. His hands were deep in the pockets of his navy wool coat and it flapped in the wind in swashbuckling style.

Georgia bowed her head against mighty gusts as she made her way to meet him. At the top, she scanned over a sight of rugged beauty. The stunning Monarch's Lodge was painted white and sat in its own garden on a flat area close to jagged rocks and surrounded by imposing cliffs and ledges. The sea whipped up below. 'Can the sea ever get to the lodge?' she asked.

'No, it's too high. It looks closer than it is. If you're at the end of the garden, you can catch the spray, but that's it.'

'It's so beautiful.' She glimpsed Archie and found him looking back. 'Come on.' And linking her arm with his, she started down the hill. 'I know I'm not good at being serious, but I think we make a pretty good team.'

'Indeed. I provide the cash, you do the hard labour.'

'Exactly.' She elbowed him but didn't release him. He was far too nice and warm to do that. 'And I like your company.'

'I do too. I mean your company, not mine.'

'I know what you mean.' She prodded him. 'And I like the dancing, and singing, and ogling you with your shirt off.'

'You really are incorrigible, aren't you?'

'Yup, and shameless.'

'Listen, Georgia, I want to tell you something…'

He stopped at the sound of someone whistling 'When Santa Got Stuck up the Chimney'. Down below, Blair pulled a length of wood from his van and nodded to them. Georgia hastily let go of Archie and waved at Blair. 'What were you saying?' she asked as Blair headed into the lodge.

'Oh… I er, the house, you'll see a big change in it,' said Archie. His cheeks looked slightly pinker than usual. 'It isn't anywhere near finished, but Blair's a bit of a miracle worker… Like you.'

Georgia smiled. 'I thought he'd be good.'

'Well, if you're looking for work after Christmas, there's plenty here.'

'Shall I come knocking again?'

'Please do.' He pushed open the door.

'Oh, my goodness.' After the gloomy, unloved air of her first visit, the place was airy and fresh. The walls and floors were bare, but the blank canvas was exactly what Georgia adored and her mind raced with ideas.

'The only furniture I have is the sofa and chairs, I wonder what you'll make of them.' Archie opened the living room door and let her in.

'Oh, they're amazing… They look like…'

'Ones you were looking at on my computer.'

'How did you know?'

'Cookies, I suppose, though not the nice chocolate chip ones.'

Georgia chuckled. 'They're so perfect in here. I'd love to finish off this place if you'd let me.'

'Let you? I'll pay you.'

She smiled, but for some reason, she didn't want his money any more. It was like something dirty or cursed. She wanted to do it as his friend. 'I can see it now, a new fire surround, Blair might be able to make one. And a wide grey rug with an antique coffee table, and over here—'

'Hey, guys.' Blair poked his head around the door, stopping Georgia mid-flow.

'Hi, Blair,' said Georgia. 'This looks awesome. I love this house so much and now it's just perfect. I might have another little job for you.'

'Little,' Archie scoffed. 'I'm not sure your view on sizes is quite the same as a normal person.'

'Oh, wheesht.' Walking through the rooms, she almost cried. How could a place do that? Her own house made her want to cry too, but not for the right reasons. 'This is like my dream house.' She gazed out the window towards the rolling sea.

'Maybe I'll gift it to you if you overhaul the other estate cottages,' said Archie.

'Don't joke, I might hold you to it.'

'I'm a witness,' said Blair.

'Are you two ganging up on me?' asked Archie.

'Aww, no, we wouldn't.' Georgia patted his arm. 'You're my favourite guys in the whole wide world.'

'Haha, classic,' said Blair. 'You're too funny.'

Archie sat on the ledge of the bay window but didn't say anything. Georgia winked at Blair.

'I better get back to my jobs,' he said.

'I'll come and help you later,' said Archie. 'I have a few things to sort out first.'

'Cool.' Blair gave Georgia a little wave and left.

'Are you ok?' asked Georgia, watching Archie as he fidgeted by the window.

'My mother has persuaded the guests to let her stay in the main house with them.'

'What? I thought you'd stopped her?'

'I tried. Louisa and Yvonne have gone to a hotel, and Marcia's gone back to Bearsden, but apparently Mother is friends with one of the guests or knows them through mutual connections. She tells me they're thrilled she's going to be there.'

'Why?'

'They don't approve of their son's wife and her family.'

The warmth drained through Georgia and out from her feet. She wrapped her arms around herself and gripped tight. He must mean Tamsyn... *and me.*

'Do you remember I told you they're having some kind of birthday party?'

'Oh, yes, that.'

'This friend of Mother's wants to cancel it.'

That was good news. Georgia's ear pricked up. 'Oh?'

'Apparently, it's for some down-and-out relative they all hate. Though it seems bloody stupid to me having a party for someone no one likes. I suppose they feel sorry for her.'

'Is that what they said?' Georgia stared in disbelief. Archie looked out the window, his gaze far away.

'Something like that. I just want to hide down here.'

'Then do it,' she urged. He needed to be out of the way. She didn't want him to see just how much the family hated the down-and-out birthday girl. At a pinch, she could fool his mother. The woman had barely noticed her. If she plastered herself with make-up and wore completely different clothes, she could probably get away with it, but not Archie.

'I'll try. But I know my mother, she'll drag me into the thick of it. She's probably hoping one of them has a spare sister or someone she can marry me off to if I don't go for Yvonne.'

Georgia frowned as she watched his silhouette in the window. Behind him, at the end of the long garden, the sea raged up the rock side in furious swirls. 'Poor Yvonne, I'd hate it if that was my life, just waiting around for a guy.' She snorted at the irony of her words.

Archie faced her. 'Truly, it's unfair. People shouldn't be commodities. That's what I feel like when my mother does this kind of thing. I want to be able to choose for myself.'

'I guess with your money, you can choose whoever you want. Who would refuse the chance to get their hands on your wallet?'

'Of course.' He looked away, sadness gleaming in his eyes.

'I'm sorry.' Georgia walked over, sat beside him, and rubbed her palm down his thigh. 'I didn't mean to make light of it. You're right, you should be able to choose for yourself and it must be horrible not knowing if someone likes you for yourself or your bank balance. I guess I'm jealous. I've never had a lot of money.'

'And corny as it may seem, I have to say you're rich in so many other ways.'

'Thanks, though sometimes I just wish I could pay the bills.'

Archie placed his hand over hers and looked at her with those terrifyingly beautiful, mismatched eyes; the left one wasn't wholly brown, a tiny greyish green sliver matched the right. Both of them held deep wide pupils. 'Hopefully this Christmas that won't be a problem.'

As she gazed back, she realised they were back in the position they'd been a couple of mornings ago, teetering on the verge of something. As if Archie had some magnetic force surrounding him, Georgia was drawn closer, and this time she needed it to happen, even if Blair walked in or knocked down a wall.

'Archie,' she whispered, the tip of her nose touching his. 'Do you know what I want to do?'

'Go for a sleigh ride? Rock around the Christmas tree? Walk in a winter wonderland?'

'No.' She half-closed her eyes. 'Well, yes. But it's cold outside.' She flicked her eyes to his.

His hand jumped from hers, grasped her firmly on the cheekbone and their lips met. This was what she was talking about. It started as a lingering but hard kiss. Georgia's arms snaked around Archie and her hands splayed across his back. His fingers slipped into her hair and she wanted to rip off her jacket and straddle him. Her breathing grew ragged until she pulled back, but he didn't stop, showering her with a series of pecks. She smiled as she collected herself, then joined in until it developed into a prolonged and sensual kiss. The Christmas stars aligned above them, and Georgia couldn't imagine what might be more blissfully indulgent than this. Eventually, Archie broke away, closed his eyes and drew back his head, before he gently pressed his lips on her forehead. 'Thank you,' he whispered.

'For what?'

'That was beautiful.'

As his hands slipped from her, she looked him in the eye and nodded. 'It was.'

'We're good together.'

'In many ways.'

He took a deliberate breath and tapped his knees. 'Georgia, I… I shouldn't hang about. I should get back.' He stood, observing her with a slightly uncertain expression. 'I should write your final pay cheque. It includes your bonus.'

'What? Oh… yes.' He might as well have thrown a bucket of icy water over her. She followed him with her head hanging low.

Sleet joined forces with the battering winds, nipping at her face as they hurried back up the track. The restless sea crunched and heaved on the rocks behind.

Georgia waited in the entrance while Archie disappeared to write her cheque. The multicoloured lights twinkled around as a pang of loss ballooned in Georgia's chest. Even though she would see this house again, and sooner than she wanted to, it wouldn't be the same. How could it be? All the singing, dancing, laughter and stolen kisses were already a thing of memory.

'Here you go.' Archie reappeared and handed her an envelope. 'I'll be in touch in the new year.'

'Yeah.'

'If you want me to.'

'Yes, of course I do.' She smiled, or tried to. Normally it was so easy, but this was hard.

'Have a good Christmas.' He hovered for a second or two. Would he hug her? Should she hug him? Could they trust each other to keep it at just that?

'You too.'

'And thank you, for everything.' He placed his hands behind his back, perhaps to stop himself doing anything else.

'You're welcome.' She waved the envelope at him. Should she say more? What? The words didn't want to be found, no matter how hard she tried.

She left, threw the envelope onto the passenger seat and started the engine. She couldn't even bring herself to listen to her Christmas music.

When she got home several messages flashed up. First Carl, all apologetic that no one had seemed excited about her birthday, then Tamsyn.

TAMSYN: I was hoping to make it over for your birthday, but we might have to delay. Sorry! X

Georgia raised an eyebrow. Was this true? A last-minute cancellation for the surprise party she wasn't supposed to know about. She pressed her fingers to her forehead and sighed. This was all getting too complicated. Another message from Carl pinged in.

CARL: Robyn and I will come for you at six-thirty on Wednesday. We have a birthday surprise. Wear your best outfit, we're going somewhere fancy!

Great! She shoved the phone away. After days of nothing, now it was all happening. At least that was Tamsyn out of the equation, for now anyway. Was it enough to hope Tony was also gone? Maybe the simplest thing would be to go into hiding and not emerge until January.

CHAPTER 20

Archie

Voices rang out from every alcove. Archie was glad he'd got rid of the ugly bust, it would have been knocked to the floor within seconds of the guests arriving. Two girls and a boy aged between two and six hurtled around the hall, and Archie found himself clinging to the Christmas tree as it swayed ominously.

'It's snowing,' one of them shrieked.

A few flakes swirled round in the wind behind the other new arrivals as they piled in, wrapped up heavily and carrying cases and bags.

'Hi, I'm Tamsyn,' said a fair-haired woman with large brown eyes. She looked inexplicably familiar. Archie shook her hand and introduced himself.

'Archibald Crichton-Leith. I'll show you around, then I'll make myself scarce.'

'Not at all.' She beamed. 'We're delighted to meet you. This is Gordon, my husband, my parents are back here and the children are somewhere about. Gordon's family will be here tomorrow.'

Archie scanned around and almost had his arm taken off as Gordon shook it, before he spotted Tamsyn's parents looking lost.

'Can I help you with anything?' he asked.

'My mother, Ellen,' said Tamsyn.

'Well, Mrs, er, Ellen,' Archie said, tapping his foot on the floor. It made him cringe addressing an older woman he'd just met by her first name. Grinning and bearing it, he asked again. 'Is there anything I can do to help?'

'Oh, maybe, yes,' replied Ellen. 'Tamsyn always finds these wonderful houses. Beautiful place. It's just the weather, terribly stormy outside, isn't it? I don't sleep well when it's too windy.'

Archie smiled and hoped that was enough empathy. 'Sorry, I can't even put your mind at rest; the island is windy at least eighty per cent of the time, but I look at it as being normal. I find it more disconcerting if it's quiet outside, lack of wind is always suspicious.'

Ellen stared at him and pinched her lips, not appearing in the least placated. In fact, she glanced at her husband with a petrified expression. 'Oh, Norman, that doesn't sound good.'

'I'm sure it'll be fine,' said Norman.

'Er, yes.' Archie coughed, adjusting his tie. 'Shall I take your case upstairs?'

He'd hoped to slip out but there was no way of doing it subtly. Tamsyn and Gordon kept him talking, and Archie found himself giving them a full history of the estate.

'Oh, yah,' said Tamsyn. 'So like Gordon's family, they've had the farm for forever and a day, very long history.'

When his mother showed up, Archie almost kissed her. She could take over. While the family seemed pleasant enough, this wasn't the kind of thing Archie was made for. And he certainly hadn't planned it to be like this. Maybe he should hire an agent to settle in new guests in the future so he could hide.

Lavinia Crichton-Leith peered down her long slender nose at the guests when she discovered the acquaintance she was waiting for wasn't arriving until the following day.

'My mother-in-law, yah,' said Tamsyn. 'Wonderful woman. She had five children and still has the most phenomenal figure, a true marvel. But, Mrs Crichton-Leith, you have a wonderful house here. I was just telling Archibald, such a charming man, about Gordon's family home.'

Archie backed out of the room as his mother started talking. She was a refined woman who knew how to behave in company, even if it wasn't the company she craved. He closed the doors behind him, turned around and staggered back in shock. Louisa stood before him, picking on a nail. 'Explain yourself,' said Archie. 'What are you doing here?'

'Your mother called. Apparently, the guests are here and she wanted backup.'

'You must be joking,' said Archie. 'This is my house, these are my guests, we don't require anyone else.' He glanced around. 'Especially not you.'

'That's a bit rude.'

'No, it isn't. You're not welcome here. You cheated on my brother and it's lucky for you my mother doesn't know.'

Laurence had found out, divorced Louisa, and everything had gone downhill for Laurence from then on. Maybe that had been the start of his troubles. 'You need to leave.'

'I would, but I have Yvonne here.'

'Where is she?'

'In the loo. Don't think she's feeling too jolly. Thing is, Archie.' Louisa scanned around. 'She's too young for you. A bit naïve if you get my drift. With you being single and me being single… Don't you think we'd be much better suited?'

'Oh yes, I do.' He looked her in the eye.

'Excellent.'

'Except, I don't like you.'

'That's a bit harsh.' Her eyes flashed.

'It's the truth.'

Yvonne came out of the cloakroom at the side of the hall, doubled over, her face grey.

'Are you all right?' asked Archie.

'I've been sick.'

'Then go back to the hotel and rest,' said Archie. 'You better take her, Louisa. I don't want anyone here catching a bug for Christmas.'

With a furious glare, Louisa helped Yvonne out to the car. Archie spent the next twenty minutes sterilising the cloakroom, just in case. When he came out, the drawing room door was ajar and Christmas music filtered out. 'The Man with the Bag'. The empty entrance hall where he'd danced with Georgia flickered out of focus and the memories drifted around like a red mist, clouding his gaze. Blinking, he was dazzled by the multicoloured lights on the tree. What would Georgia make of this lot? He considered phoning her, but what for? Just to hear her voice, was the only answer he could find. He resisted.

More guests arrived the following day, and Lavinia greeted Elspeth Montgomery like a long-lost friend.

'This is another of my sons, Kenneth,' said Elspeth, 'and his wife Flora. I have four sons and a daughter, but they're not all here. This was a logistical enough nightmare. My daughter is here though, Erin.'

Archie had palpitations at their introduction when he realised Erin was a young and possibly single daughter.

The cogs in his mother's mind were ticking over audibly. She was rubbing her hands together, ready to grill the poor girl.

A smart and slick young man with a city air about him arrived later in the day, announcing himself as Tony Stuart. He fixed his cufflinks as he entered the drawing room, and Archie relaxed when he saw him greeting Erin with a huge bear hug. Phew. Presumably he was her partner. Archie was saved.

The following day he made it to Monarch's Lodge and almost leapt for joy when Blair met him at the door, saying, 'It's pretty much ready for you to move in. With you helping out, it's really sped things on.'

'I'll make a handyman yet,' said Archie.

'You will, and you've still got time to nip to the mainland and get a bunch of furniture before Christmas.'

'I might do that. We have so much furniture in the outbuildings it seems ridiculous buying new stuff, but I honestly don't know if any of it is fit for purpose anymore.'

'Yeah, best get something new. If you find any bits worth saving later on, I'm happy to fix them up, or Georgia might work her magic on them.' Blair's look was a little too probing, and Archie wondered if he'd spied them kissing at the window. Maybe he'd nipped out to his van and happened to peek in. Shit. Just the way rumours started.

'Yes, I might ask her. Don't hang about if this snow gets heavier. I know it's rare for snow to lie here, but this sleety rain can be almost as bad to drive in.'

'Thanks,' said Blair. 'Did you see yesterday when it gave way to a proper snow fall for about ten minutes? The kids were running about going daft. It's neat for them.'

'They're on a Christmas break, they expect to be building snowmen every day.'

'Ha, yeah. Poor things.'

Archie tipped him a salute and made his way back to the house with the dogs. He came in through the passageway bedroom door and let the dogs into their room. From the end of the corridor, he overheard a debate in the entrance hall about the birthday party planned for that evening. He wasn't familiar enough with any of the guests to know who was talking, but there seemed to be two camps developing. One desperately trying to make it happen and one that clearly had very little interest. His mother's voice resonated loudly. 'It seems like a waste of time if the woman doesn't even want a party. Why are you bothering with all the fuss?'

Archie unlocked the door and stepped out, hoping to divert his mother. Why was she getting so involved? Tamsyn and her mother were sticking '30' posters and balloons around the hall, mixing them up with the Christmas decorations. Georgia would have a fit, they were ruining her Christmas perfection.

Lavinia spied him and took hold of Elspeth Montgomery, leading her away from Archie into the drawing room.

'They don't approve of my sister,' Tamsyn said to Archie. 'But it's still her birthday and god knows I feel we have to do something. She's gone to the wilderness, it's time to bring her back.'

'Does she know about this?' asked Archie. He was so intrigued about the mystery guest now, he almost wanted to gatecrash the party just to see what she looked like, though Georgia had warned him explicitly not to.

'I thought she might have got wind of it, but I fobbed her off by messaging her and saying we defo weren't going to make it for her birthday. What she doesn't know is that I found out the names of some of her friends. That's the problem with her posting so much on social media, she's easy to stalk. Anyway, they're bringing her. She thinks they're taking her somewhere else, but they're going to bring her here and *surprise!*' Tamsyn threw up her hands.

Archie frowned, a vision passed before him of an alternative looking person, perhaps with bright green hair, thinking she was being taken to an underground rave only to be dragged across the island in a furious snowstorm and bundled into an old mansion house.

Tony and Erin came into the hall, pink-cheeked like they'd been out walking. Tony gave Archie a brief smile and Archie raised his eyebrows in return.

'Oh, Archie,' said Tamsyn, 'apparently you're a wonderful pianist.'

Archie was distracted by Tony messing up his hair in the hall mirror and Erin giggling.

'I can play, yes.'

'Fabulous. Erin plays wonderfully and she's a beautiful singer, aren't you? You should duet one evening.'

'Eh, no,' said Erin. 'Not tonight, that birthday party is on.' She rolled her eyes as though it was something she couldn't be bothered with.

'Now, now,' said Tony. 'Don't be mean. After tonight she'll be my fiancée.'

'More fool you,' muttered Erin.

'I thought they were a couple,' Archie muttered, looking between Tony and Erin.

'Cousins.' Tamsyn beamed, dumping a pile of birthday decorations in front of her mother.

Ellen frowned at them before glancing up at Tony. 'Are you sure you want to marry her? It's been a while,' she said.

'She's been waiting for me.' He smiled at his reflection, and Archie expected to see a little glint of light on his teeth like a toothpaste commercial. 'Now's the right time.'

'I hope so.' Ellen sighed. 'I do worry about her. Since you and her chose to live apart, she seems to have made some very odd choices. Coming to live here was the strangest. I can't quite understand why she'd want to. It's a terribly remote kind of place.'

'Oh, it's so exciting, darling,' said Tamsyn, clapping her hands. 'This, if nothing else, will get her back on the straight and narrow.'

Archie left them to their discussion, planning to return to his office and not leave the wing except to walk the dogs. He meant to stay well away from the party, but just before seven a hammering resonated from the locked door at the end of the passageway. His mother was outside looking cross. 'Archie, come with me.'

'Why?'

'This birthday party thing has been terribly badly organised. If they're arranging a surprise, they should do it properly. Someone should play 'Happy Birthday' on the piano when the woman arrives. You're the only one who can.'

'Why don't you get Erin to do it? Someone told me she could play.'

'She's classically trained, darling. You're the one who can beat out the simple tunes.'

He exhaled sharply. 'Fine. I'll do it, then I'm leaving. This party has nothing to do with us. I rented this place out as a private let, it doesn't feel right butting into their business all the time.'

'Oh, you do talk nonsense. All I'm asking is five minutes. What an anti-social man you are, so unlike Laurence.'

So unlike indeed. He wasn't anti-social, not with people he knew and in parties he was actually invited to. This was downright awkward. As he walked into the drawing room a few people jumped and someone yelled, 'Happy birthday, oops!'

He rolled his eyes and made his way to the piano but was distracted by some faces in the room. He frowned as he scanned around. A couple of familiar people nodded at him. One of them was Murray Henderson, the man he'd butted heads with over the logging road in the spring; his arm was around Beth McGregor.

'Mother, why are they here?' he muttered in her ear before he sat down.

'Who?'

'Beth McGregor from Creagach Farm and Murray Henderson.'

'Friends of the birthday girl, I expect.'

'Really?' He took his seat behind the grand piano and a pair of warm hands landed on his shoulders. He looked around and came face to face with Tamsyn. Sliding sideways, he tried to break from her grip. The familiarity of her look was potent. Why did she remind him of Georgia? Something about her eyes and her expression. Archie kicked himself as she smiled at him. He was so ridiculously smitten he was seeing her everywhere.

'Thank you so much for doing this. My sister will love it. She used to enjoy a sing-song before she went AWOL.'

'No problem,' said Archie, putting his head down.

'Your mother says you can play in the dark. I hope that's true because I'm going to put the lights out.'

'Yes, that's fine.'

Tamsyn beamed, and moments later plunged them into darkness. The children squealed and someone 'Oohed'.

The last time he'd sat here in the dark, magic had happened. This just felt downright insane.

'She's coming,' someone whispered.

'Start playing, start the music,' muttered Tamsyn.

With a flourish he began a jaunty 'Happy Birthday'. As he neared the end, the lights burst on and he glimpsed a woman with pinned-up blonde hair, blindfolded. She was flanked by a tall couple, both smiling broadly. He didn't need the big reveal to see who it was. Autopilot took him to the end of the song and a huge 'HAPPY BIRTHDAY' resonated around the room as the mask was whipped off. Georgia's focus was fixed forward. She looked incredible, her make-up flawless with smoky eyes and sparkly lips. Her outfit was a stunning silver sequinned dress which showed off her curves perfectly. Archie gaped. Why hadn't she told him? All those weeks? Was this her reason for showing up in the first place? So she could make the place immaculate for her own party, her own family? He'd paid her to set it up for their holiday. He'd fallen straight into her honey trap while desperately trying to convince himself she wasn't like all the others.

As he pushed the seat back quietly, hoping to sneak out, her family greeted her. Tony waded forward and embraced Georgia like a long-lost lover. Archie's heart flipped over as he remembered the conversation in the hall earlier. He was her boyfriend.

He stopped at the door and glanced back before spying the mistletoe above his head. Stretching up, he ripped it down. The sneaky little madam, she really was expecting a proposal this Christmas, and she'd prepared it perfectly. No wonder she'd been so desperate for him to stay away.

His chest crumbled under the weight of Georgia's deceit. How could she?

CHAPTER 21

Georgia

Sequins dug into Georgia's skin as Tony held her close. She couldn't breathe. The room was burning hot and now the piano music had stopped, all she could hear was deafening shouts and laughing.

'Can you let me go?' she said, pulling back with force.

'Georgia.' Tony released her and took a backward step, looking her over from head to foot. 'You look amazing.'

'Er, thanks…' She felt a little unsteady on her feet. Her eyes roamed towards the piano. She was acutely aware of who had been tinkling the ivories in the dark, but he wasn't there now. Eyes were on her. She saw her island friends looking aghast. Beth had warned her what was planned and Georgia had realised Tamsyn's text was a ruse. She'd started on the wine long before Carl and Robyn had turned up. Now she looked like a proper little liar: only Beth knew about Tony and here he was hugging her like the long-lost lover he was.

'Happy birthday, darling,' said Tamsyn. 'How's this for a surprise? This is the castle.'

'What? Oh, yes. It looks nice.'

'It's terribly windy upstairs though,' said her mum, making her way over to hug her. 'I haven't slept a wink since we arrived. I'm glad you won't be living here much longer. It's been too long in the wilderness.'

'How do you mean?' Georgia's throat had dried up and her cheeks burned.

'Over to you, Tony darling,' said Tamsyn.

He grinned and looked away. 'Ha, very subtle. Come with me, Georgia?' He cocked his head towards the door and although it was a request, he didn't look ready to accept no for an answer. Well, he never did, did he?

As Georgia followed him through the crowd, she saw Beth not far off. Beth gave a little shake of her head, her brow furrowed in an expression of deep concern. Georgia flicked up her thumb. She had this.

'So, I er…' Tony stopped at the door and Georgia noticed the mistletoe had fallen down, or been pulled off, judging by the tiny straggly bits which were left behind. 'You and me. Things haven't exactly been traditional. I've had a lot to think about—'

Georgia held up her hand. 'Let me stop you there. I'm going to make this easier for you.'

'No, no, no,' he laughed, 'I'm not breaking up with you. For a while I wasn't sure and I wanted distance to get clarity, but life hasn't been half as much fun without you. What I want is…' He looked around as if steeling himself for something, then he moved in such a way Georgia was sure he was about to go down on one knee. She grabbed his shoulders.

'Don't. The distance has given me clarity too. I came here because I was devastated. I'm not a texts and messages kind of girl. I like real human contact. Long distance was never going to work, so I chose somewhere quiet to hide. But you know what?'

'I know, it didn't work. I mean a place like this, it just isn't you.'

'Wrong, Tony.' She stared him down, hating his smug expression. Did he assume she couldn't be happy without him? 'Mull is me. I love it here. I love the life I have here. I'm not leaving.'

'Oh, come on.'

'You know what, I wish I'd done this two years ago.'

'Done what?'

'Told you that it's over. The past two years while I was "waiting" haven't been wasted, I've built a beautiful life here and this is where I'm staying.'

He scoffed and rolled his tongue inside his mouth. 'So, you met someone else? I knew you wouldn't be faithful.'

'Actually I have been.' Did a few kisses with Archie count? 'I didn't see anyone else. I fell in love with the island.'

'And it'll always be here.' He gritted his teeth. 'I was going to propose, you know? But you've rather killed the moment.'

'Then save it. I'm sure you'll find someone a lot more worthy.'

'You realise,' he said, his jaw set, 'I did this as much to appease our families as anything. They're worried about you and so am I.'

'Too late, Tony. You weren't worried about hurting me two years ago. Go and be free.'

'Whatever.' He stormed out the door and Georgia watched him, not turning away until she felt a tap on her shoulder.

'Where's Tony going?' Tamsyn squinted out the door as she proffered a glass of champagne to Georgia. Georgia took it and downed it.

'He's leaving.'

'But didn't he…'

'I said no. I don't want to marry him, ok?' Georgia glanced around, hoping to see more champagne somewhere. Instead, her gaze landed on Mrs Crichton-Leith. The woman's eyes narrowed and she gave a brief headshake. So much for staying incognito.

'You don't? But why… Oh Lord, this is deplorable. Where's Gordon? I need him to go after Tony.'

'Leave him.' But it was too late, Tamsyn had bustled off and Georgia's head was pounding. She spotted Beth and tried to get to her, but people were everywhere: Her mum asking her how it went, Gordon's annoying little sister, Erin, demanding to know if she had any dress ideas yet and who would be a bridesmaid. When she finally got to Beth, she almost cried.

'Are you ok?' Beth asked.

'I need to get out of here.'

'Where's the man… Has he left?'

'I told him to go.'

'Good.' Beth clapped her shoulder.

'But I can't stand all the questions and the stares, it's awful. And I have to explain… to Carl and Kirsten. They've been my friends ever since I came here and I never told them.'

'They'll be ok about it,' said Beth. 'Honestly, don't worry.'

'I need a drink… I don't know how else I'm going to make it through the night.'

*

Georgia woke in a fog. Where was she? She rolled over and closed her horribly dry mouth. Lovely soft pillows.

'Water,' she mumbled, fumbling about and miraculously finding a glass. With shaky fingers, she grappled for it. Who had left it there? Through a brain fog, she vaguely remembered Beth helping her up some stairs. Her mind slowly cranked into action until the shooting pain in her forehead stopped the train of thought.

'Oh god.' She held her head and groaned. 'The party.' Somehow she'd found the strength to fess up to her friends, but her family were furious. Where was Tony now? What were they saying about her? If she kept her eyes closed, it might go away, but no. With a wave of nausea, Georgia ran to the bathroom and slowly died by the toilet.

It took all morning for her to gather the strength to leave the room. Even opening the curtains took all her willpower. The light hurt her eyes and she massaged her temples as she squinted into the grounds. The low sunlight lit up a frosty scene. From this angle Monarch's Lodge was visible, nestled in its haven amongst the rocks. A lone figure was in the garden. Archie? He was lifting something. Maybe he hadn't recognised her last night. She hadn't seen him at the party after the piano playing at the start. Oh, what bliss it would be if he wasn't aware anything had happened. If she could just keep it that way.

*

'Georgia, you look dreadful,' said her mother, her eyes popping. It was true, Georgia knew it. She fumbled her way around the kitchen. Had she seen any kind of painkillers in her clear out?

'Thanks.' Georgia raided the cupboard for the first aid kit, dragged it out and pressed out two tablets, almost dropping them.

'Such a pity about Tony. He's such a good man. Won't you reconsider?'

'No.' Why did they keep banging on about how great he was? Didn't they realise how much he'd hurt her?

'Such a shame.' Her mother shook her head with a sigh. 'At least we can enjoy the house. Staying here for a while might help. It's magnificent, and so very like Tamsyn to find it, she's clever that way. And fancy the owner already knowing them, what a coincidence.'

Even through her thumping headache, Georgia couldn't help point out the mistakes, though her mother wouldn't care. But the constant gushing about Tony and Tamsyn made her skin crawl and rage bubble up inside. Years of unfairness and misplaced attention.

'I won't change my mind about Tony, we're finished. And Tamsyn doesn't know the owner. It was the owner's mother who happened to know Gordon's mother vaguely. It's not like they were bosom buddies.' She downed the tablets with her hot coffee, scalding her mouth. 'All these people are just ordinary folk. Who cares if they have some pathetic connection to the aristocracy? None of that matters.'

'You sound terribly jealous,' said Ellen with a simpering little laugh. 'If you'd accepted Tony, you'd have the connection too. It's a small world and if you move in the right circles you're bound to connect with the right sort.'

'Oh, for crying out loud!' Georgia's mug dropped from her hand and shattered on the kitchen floor, spraying hot coffee everywhere.

'Goodness gracious.' Her mother jumped back. 'Did you throw that?'

She had; she was furious. Her head hurt and she wanted to scream or cry or both. 'No, of course I didn't,' she lied. 'It slipped. But will you please stop going on about Tamsyn and these bloody yahs? I'm sick of the lot of them and I am never going to marry Tony or any of them!'

'Georgia! What a way to speak to me.'

The door opened and Mrs Crichton-Leith walked in, her slender nose high in the air as she scanned the scene. Her eyes inevitably fell onto the pool on the floor.

'My daughter,' said Ellen, 'she's so clumsy. She'll clear it up, don't worry.' Her voice sounded shaky, like she might burst into tears.

My fault, my stupid fault. Georgia grabbed a dishcloth and looked around, catching her mother running out, holding her hand to her chest. Mrs Crichton-Leith narrowed her eyes and placed her hands firmly on her hips. 'What is your game, young lady?'

Georgia furrowed her brow. 'Charades?' she suggested.

'You may think I'm some stupid old woman, but I'm not. The other day you were here under the pretence of being a designer. Now it seems the only designs you had were on my son. So, why in all that time you were working for him did you not mention it was your family who had booked in here? That this party was for you? I don't know why it didn't occur to you to mention it, unless of course you were up to something much more underhand.'

'That's between me and him.'

'Oh, no, no. You don't get away with that. I already asked him, and he is as ignorant about the whole thing as I am. In fact, he's very hurt. I could tell. He obviously had no idea. It looks to me very much like you've defrauded him.'

'What?'

'From where I'm standing, I see you having a wonderful party, a few weeks living in a well-decorated house, which you haven't paid a penny for but have actually been paid a pretty sum to do up. So, why did you volunteer to do that?'

'It was business.'

'Hardly. You saw my son had money and took advantage, as so many young women have in the past.'

'No, that's not what happened.' The nausea grew, but this time it had nothing to do with the drinking and everything to do with her own conduct, if she'd just told the truth. She'd seen a chance to make money and taken it, but it was wrong. The final cheque was still in the van, she'd never had time to cash it and she mustn't. She wanted to go and rip it to shreds; it hadn't been about the money. Maybe the teensiest bit in the beginning, but as time had gone on, it wasn't that at all.

'It's exactly what happened. Elspeth Montgomery told me about you. You're nothing but a waste of space who wanders around like a nomad, scrounging wherever you can. And now you've abused my son in a disgraceful manner. Archie was always the weak one, he didn't see you for what you were. You're a low bred excuse for a human being; you're lucky to have relations in such fortunate places. In time, they might be able to pull you from the gutter. But until then you can wallow down there with the rats. And don't bother thinking about making any more trouble. Once Christmas is over, you'll never set foot in this house again. Ever!'

With a sweeping movement, she left the room. Georgia stood stock-still, her heart drumming, her ears ringing. What had she done? No. No. No. She covered her face and let the bitter tears flow. What a stupid, stupid idiot she'd been.

CHAPTER 22

Archie

Archie had taken the bull by the horns and made up his mind to move into Monarch's Lodge. He assumed Georgia would be staying with her family and didn't want to bump into her. The office wing was too close for comfort, and with Blair giving him the go ahead on the lodge, the timing couldn't have been more perfect. Except he had no furniture.

'Don't you want to be with the guests?' asked Blair when Archie turned up that afternoon.

'No, it's a family party and nothing to do with me.'

'So, what's the plan?'

'I found some bits of furniture in one of the storehouses. Could you help me move them down here? I'll clean them up after. When better for a cleaning spree than December the twenty-second?'

'Ha, too right. Sure, I'll help. Will they fit in my van?'

'Between that and the Barbarian, I think we'll manage.'

So, while everyone in the main house was settling down to watch Christmas movies and do some last-minute wrapping, Archie and Blair ferried various items of furniture to Monarch's Lodge. A gorgeous oak table and chairs, an old dresser, a writing desk. Archie recognised a lot of the furniture his grandmother had had. How it had ended up bundled in a storeroom, he wasn't sure. It was possible Laurence had meant to send it to auction and never got round to it. Thank heavens.

He pulled open the drop-down front of the writing desk and a twinge of sadness swept over him. Some of his grandmother's things were still in it, like she'd just got up and walked away for a few minutes. They were all dusty but so familiar. In amongst the pencil boxes and notebooks was a small red velvet box. Archie picked it up and blew off the dust. It was like a ring box. He flipped it open and frowned. How was this in here?

'So, is this all you need?' asked Blair, breaking Archie's train of thought. He shoved the box in his pocket.

'For now,' said Archie. 'I don't have any beds, though at a push, I could sleep on the new sofa.'

'Have you got anything in the main house we could use?'

'The bed from the passageway might do at a pinch, but it'll be some job getting it out.' Archie raked his hair. 'You know what?' A moment of recklessness seized him. 'I think I'll go and buy a new one.'

'Today?'

'If I leave now, I'll make the last ferry. Could I borrow your van? I don't think it'll fit in the Barbarian.'

'Sure, though I'll need to get you put on the insurance.'

'I'm fully comp, that should cover me. You can have the Barbarian, and I wonder, would you mind looking after my dogs?'

'Sure, no worries. I love dogs.'

'That's great, thanks.'

They walked up together, checked the insurance was ok, and Archie explained the dogs' routine to Blair. Was this just madness? Oh, what the hell? It was nearly

Christmas; he could buy himself an early Christmas present. He was a free man – he could come and go as he pleased – he didn't answer to anyone.

With this resolved, he left the house and headed straight for Blair's van. As he trundled up the driveway an unmistakable pink van was coming in the opposite direction. Shit. Hopefully, she'd think it was Blair and keep going. As she got closer, he saw her winding down the window and leaning out. Too late. Her eyes flashed with shock as he pulled level.

'Oh, it's you,' she said. 'Where's Blair?'

'He's back at Monarch's Lodge. I'm just borrowing this.'

'Right,' she said. 'Well, it's you I came to see.'

'Oh?' Wasn't she staying here for the week with her family anyway?

'I came to give you this.' She held an envelope out the window. The one he put her pay cheque in with a sizeable Christmas bonus. It was unopened.

'Why?'

'Because I don't want it.'

He raised an eyebrow slowly. 'Why not?'

'Because I didn't earn it.'

'You admit you came here on false pretence.'

'Yes.' She dropped her hand and looked away.

'How could you?'

'Please don't. I've already had all this from your mother. When I first came here, my objective was to make sure the place looked good so my family wouldn't tear my life to shreds. If they hadn't liked the place, it would have been my fault. I would have done it for free, I will still.' She proffered the envelope again, but he didn't take it. 'I didn't expect you and me to get close.'

He scoffed and turned away.

'Yes, I know,' she said, 'ridiculous, isn't it? How can there ever be anything between the likes of you and me? You're right to sneer.'

'That's not what I meant.' He blinked and his jaw stiffened. 'I trusted you. I enjoyed your company. I felt a real affection for you, but you were playing me. You've got a boyfriend, one who's planning on proposing. Maybe he already has. Should I be congratulating you?'

She sighed, shaking her head. 'It isn't like that.'

'Don't make it any worse. I heard him talking about it myself. I'd like to say I'm not stupid, but I am. I walked right into your little game and fell hook, line and sinker. You did a great job with the double bluff, you had me fooled all the way.'

Her cheeks were pink, but her remaining complexion was pale and drained. All the vibrance had gone. Without her smile and the sparkling eyes, she was a shadow of the glittering girl he'd danced with in the hall and sung to by the piano. It had all been a lie. 'I'm sorry,' she said, leaning over and flinging the envelope onto his lap. She closed the window and drove onwards. The van trundled slowly down the hill in a less than spectacular exit. Archie stared at the envelope. He was in half a mind to go after her, but what was the point? She probably had a meeting with her fiancé planned and he had his own mission. He needed to do something to keep his mind off her.

As he drove around the headland, he passed Creagach Farm and saw Beth McGregor standing at the gate talking to Murray Henderson. Memories of their dreadful clash in the spring burst into Archie's head and he stopped the van abruptly.

'Excuse me.' He jumped out. Murray folded his arms, looking unimpressed. Then Archie noticed Beth had a large mallet and a glint in her eye that told him she knew how to use it. 'Listen, Murray, Beth, I need to apologise.'

'Oh, yeah?' said Beth.

'The way I behaved earlier in the year. It wasn't worthy of me. I was new to all this and I did what I thought people in my position should do rather than what was right. I hope in the future we can work together.'

'Hmm,' said Beth.

'Let's hope,' said Murray. 'The works I'm carrying out on the woodland area come close to your land, so we can chat about it in the new year.'

'Absolutely,' said Archie. 'I want to make Ardnish part of the community, not some big house where the islanders gossip about an out of touch landowner.'

Beth held her hand to her mouth as if to cover a grin.

'That was a good party at yours the other night,' said Murray.

'The house looked great,' said Beth, recovering herself.

'Georgia's doing,' said Archie.

'I know,' Beth said. 'She did a great job.'

'Though mostly for her own benefit,' he muttered.

'Not really.'

'I know all about it,' said Archie. 'And I'm aware she's your friend, so I won't say anything.'

'Probably best,' said Beth. 'But don't go thinking she did it for her own benefit. She did it for the money, yes, but things aren't easy with her family. It's complicated.'

'But I assume she got the proposal she was after.'

'Er, no,' said Beth. 'You were there. Didn't you see?'

'I must have missed it.'

'She didn't accept. They'd been separated for two years. You don't seriously think she did it for a proposal?'

'Whatever it was, she certainly had her own agenda.'

'At the beginning maybe.'

'How do you mean?' said Archie.

'I think latterly she did it for a different reason, but you should ask her about that. It's not up to me to tell you.'

None of it made sense. Why was he trying to figure it out, when he should just let go? 'Listen, I need to be off. I have a boat to catch.'

'You aren't going mainland shopping, are you?' asked Murray.

'Well, yes, kind of,' he said. 'I'm going to buy some furniture.'

'Furniture,' said Murray. 'Wow. Are you coming back tomorrow? Only I wonder if you could pick something up for us.'

'I'll be back on Christmas Eve, hopefully. What is it you need?'

'A parcel has been delivered to the Oban office. If I get the delivery card, would you mind collecting it?'

'Sure, no problem.'

This extra mission gave him the need to come back, otherwise, there wasn't really any rush. He could spend Christmas at his Edinburgh apartment and no one would care. Except maybe his mother, as he'd agreed to spend Christmas with her. At least he had Monarch's Lodge and with some nice new furniture, he could hide away until Christmas blew over on the breeze, hopefully taking all memories of Georgia with it.

CHAPTER 23

Georgia

If Georgia owned a sledgehammer, she'd have used it on her boiler. The house was colder inside than it was out. During the day it was ok – she could go out. Armed with her camera, she made a last-ditch attempt at some festive photos. What else was there to do? Cramming her Instagram feed with festive island shots might entice someone into buying even just one picture.

Her big plan had backfired spectacularly, but money was only a small part of the problem. She didn't dare spend the previous pay cheques in case she had to pay it all back now she'd been caught. Inside her ribcage, her heart was still beating, but it was like a broken toy. It didn't feel like Christmas any more. She didn't have a tree in her house and there didn't seem any point as she was due to spend Christmas Day at Ardnish.

She groaned. Just great. More time with her family, Mrs Crichton-Leith and Tamsyn's in-laws was not what she wanted right now. Though they had a working heating system which might be the clincher. What she craved was a large helping of Archie and if he was served with chocolate sauce and whipped cream then all the better. But those three ships had gone sailing, not to be seen on Christmas Day or any other morning.

Another icy night, however, wasn't something she could stand. She had to at least attempt to get the wretched boiler working. As her kicks were doing nothing but hurting her toes, she'd given up and called Beth – the heating engineer hadn't arrived from the first time she'd called, so was there any hope he'd arrive two days before Christmas?

'I'll come round shortly,' said Beth, 'I'm at the ferry with Murray picking up his parents. They'll be with us.' Beth's voice dropped. 'Apologies in advance.'

'Oh help,' said Georgia. 'My house is a mess.'

'I'll tell Murray to take them on a walk to the pier.'

'Will they like that?'

'Oh, sure, it'll be all his mum's Christmas wishes come true.'

Georgia heard the sarcasm, remembering Mrs Henderson was rotund and preferred to stay sedentary.

When they showed up, Beth looked like she'd stuck her finger in a socket. Mrs Henderson waddled in after her.

'Are you coming for a walk with me and dad?' asked Murray.

'Of course not, I'm far too exhausted from travelling.' She batted away the idea, marched into Georgia's living room and sat down. 'Nice place, shame about the view.'

'Don't I know it,' Georgia said.

'Jeez, it's perishing in here,' Murray said, rubbing his arms.

'Language, Murray,' snapped Mrs Henderson.

He threw up his hands. 'Jeez? Since when did that become a swear word?'

Murray's mum tutted, and his dad frowned.

'Is there any point in mentioning you could put on a jumper?' asked Georgia.

'Nope.' He grinned.

'Murray's never worn sensible clothing,' said his mother. 'I tried and failed to get him to wear a jacket all through school.'

'And apparently, I haven't changed.'

Mrs Henderson rolled her head around to look over the back of the chair. 'Murray, you should be the one fixing the thing. Beth shouldn't do it, it's man's work.'

Beth rolled her eyes at Georgia and they headed for the boiler cupboard.

'Mum, I don't know one end of a boiler from the other,' Murray said as they left the room.

'I might not be able to fix it,' said Beth.

'I know, but at least I feel like I've done something about it. I've hardly been here and I'm due back at Ardnish for Christmas Day.'

'Why don't you go and stay there for the next two weeks? That was a nice room you had.'

Georgia covered her eyes. 'Yeah, the room's nice but the company leaves a lot to be desired.'

'You could hide.'

'My family think I'm unhinged and I don't know why, but whenever I'm with them, I'm on edge and I become this monster.'

Beth eased her hand right back into the cupboard. 'Yeah, they have a weird effect on you.'

'I snap at them, I drop stuff, or worse, I throw it. Ugh.'

'Well,' said Beth. 'I've got this to put up with for Christmas.' She jabbed her head in the direction of the living room as Mrs Henderson laughed.

'I should introduce her to my mother, or better still Mrs Crichton-Leith.'

'Match made in heaven,' agreed Beth, fumbling around for something behind the boiler. 'Archibald

Crichton-Leith stopped by ours yesterday,' she said, still fishing about in the cupboard. 'He gave us an apology for all the crap with the road. He's odd. I can't make him out.'

'That's men for you.' Georgia sighed.

'Ha, yeah. He's a strange character though. I mean, who goes to buy furniture this close to Christmas?'

'What?'

'I know.' Beth laughed. 'That's what he said. He's buying furniture and not coming back until Christmas Eve. Maybe he's going to shove it down someone's chimney.'

'Maybe. I bet he's getting it for Monarch's Lodge, but it's a bit risky leaving it that late.'

'He's cross with you.'

'Yeah, I know.'

'When he comes back, I think you need to go and sort things out. I thought you and him had…'

'What?'

'Made friends, you know.'

'Yes… We did.' Georgia bit her lip, thinking. 'Listen, I just had an idea.' Her heart pounded an erratic rhythm.

'What is it?'

'An utterly mad and totally bonkers idea, but I have to try.' Christmas craziness seized her and despite knowing she had as much chance of succeeding with it as her mum did at making her eat sprouts, she was going for it.

'I have no idea what you're talking about.' Beth gave the boiler a last whack and stepped back rubbing her hands. 'I think that's it.'

'You are amazing.' Georgia put her arms around Beth's neck and kissed her on the cheek.

'Ok. Have you gone mad?'

'Actually, I think I have.'

'Well, before you go too crazy, I think your New Year's resolution should be to get a new boiler.'

'That's a good one, but you know what? I need a new house and I fancy somewhere with a sea view.'

'I think that would suit you better.' Beth patted Georgia on the shoulder before rounding up Murray and his parents. They left with *Merry Christmases* all round.

Georgia got her coat and hat, jumped in her van, and headed a couple of miles down the road to the Christmas tree farm. It was late to be doing this, very late, but she needed a Christmas tree and one way or another she was going to get one – even if it meant cutting one from the Ardnish Estate – though hopefully it wouldn't come to that.

An hour later she pulled up at Monarch's Lodge and clapped when she saw the Barbarian, knowing Blair must be there. She ran inside and called him.

'Hi,' he said, peering around the corner with a screwdriver in his hand. Duchess and Dexter padded out to meet her, looking like they'd made themselves at home with their beds in a pup-palace room off the kitchen.

'I need your help,' she said.

'With what?'

'I want to have this place decorated by Christmas Eve. I know exactly how I want it to look, but I also don't want you to tell anyone, and I mean anyone.' She stared pointedly at him.

'Ok…Christmas Eve, as in tomorrow.' He frowned. 'Why?'

'Because…' Georgia flexed her hands. 'I love Archie.'

'You what? Have you completely lost the plot?' asked Blair, his expression caught between shock, horror, and amusement.

'Yes, I think I have, but I don't care. I just know how I feel.'

'Wow. So what are you planning? Jumping out on him in a sexy Santa dress?'

'No, a bit more subtle. I'm going to make it look the way it did when he was a child.'

'You call that subtle?'

'Hmm, maybe not. But listen to this. He showed me photos of some decorations his grandmother made, I think I can replicate them, even though I don't know how many I'll manage and maybe not the knitted ones... I'm not great at knitting and definitely not that fast.'

'He found a box of his grandmother's decorations in one of the storerooms. I'm sure that's what he said.'

'Oh my god, Blair. Are you serious? Do you remember where?'

'I think so.'

'Please go and find that box, right now.'

Looking bemused, Blair downed tools and did as she instructed, while Georgia set to work on the tree. All the remnants of things she'd used at the main house were stashed in the van with plenty of leftovers to rig up some quick curtains. When Blair returned, she had everything laid out.

'Good god,' he muttered. 'What is all this?'

'I'll explain in a minute, first, will you put up some curtain poles and help me arrange the vintage furniture that's stashed in there?'

'Fine,' he said, gaping at her like she might need her head examined, but lifting the curtain pole.

'I'll go clean these decorations while you do that.'

She worked all day and although the boiler was working at her house, Georgia was barely home before she was out again. She'd arrived back after eleven in pitch black and left the following morning at six, then worked away at Monarch's Lodge until Blair showed up at eight.

'Have you been here all night?'

'No, but I want to get this finished.'

'It looks amazing. What are you doing now?'

Sitting at the newly installed table, surrounded by cut up bits of plants, ribbon, and wire, Georgia smiled. 'Making a special wreath.'

'Wow. So, you and Archie? What's that all about?'

She let out a little laugh and threw up her palms. 'I don't know.'

'I assume he likes you in the same kind of way?'

'I think so, but we're not good at being serious except when we're fighting.'

'I saw you and him the other day, getting it on at the window. I wondered what was going on.'

'Oh god.' Georgia slapped her forehead. 'You saw that?'

'Very intense. I hope it works out for you.'

'If I pull off this little surprise, we can take it from there, that'll be enough for me.'

Blair took out his tools and together they worked quietly until the sun came up and pale light shone in the windows, gleaming on the newly polished surfaces. Although still sparse, it had a much more homely feel.

'Wow,' Blair said as Georgia flicked on the tree lights. 'This looks amazing.'

Georgia smiled at the homemade decorations and her heart swelled at the idea of bringing them back to life. 'Blair, you should go. It's Christmas Eve, go and see your dad or have a drink with your friends. You've done enough here.' She embraced him and patted his bearlike back. 'Thanks for all your help and leave the dogs here, I'll make sure Archie gets them.'

'Good luck with this.' He stepped back and shook his head. 'And everything.'

'Thanks, Blair, and merry Christmas.'

As he drove away, Georgia followed him out and hung the wreath on the front door. It was close enough to the photo Archie had shown her of his grandmother's wreath. The lantern-style light above the door worked, so he'd see it even in the dark. Stepping back, Georgia admired the house, looking splendid in its Christmas finery, the most romantically placed Christmas house imaginable with its cliffside garden and ocean backdrop.

With that done, only one thing remained to clear up before the showdown with Archie. Back in the van, she drove the short distance to the main house and leapt out. Time to go find Mrs Crichton-Leith.

It didn't take long. Good or bad? Georgia wasn't sure. Mrs Crichton-Leith wasn't alone. Tamsyn and her mother-in-law Elspeth Montgomery both peered through narrowed eyes as Georgia approached.

'You're back,' said Tamsyn.

Elspeth shook her head and tutted. 'A bit late. Tony has left the island.' She didn't look at Georgia as she spoke. 'He's quite put out. We all are. He's quite a favourite nephew of mine, always has been and we stood by his choice in spite of...' She half glanced at Georgia.

Keeping her smile intact was difficult but Georgia held onto it. 'I wonder if I could speak to you.' She addressed Mrs Crichton-Leith, who put her hand to her chest looking politely surprised. 'Alone.'

Tamsyn coughed and blinked very pointedly as if trying to scold Georgia. *Seriously?*

'Certainly,' said Mrs Crichton-Leith, getting to her feet with a serene air. She left the room first and made her way along the corridor. 'Where would you like this discussion to take place?'

'I don't mind,' said Georgia.

'My husband's study is locked and sadly the morning room has been taken over as a downstairs bedroom, so it doesn't leave many options.'

Georgia held on to her eye roll. There were several other rooms. 'How about the kitchen? We can get a coffee?'

'As you wish.' Mrs Crichton-Leith led the way. When they reached the end of the corridor, she pushed open the kitchen door and sat down at the large table. Georgia made sure the door was tightly shut. 'What's this all about?'

Georgia sat opposite, crossed her legs and rubbed her knee. 'I feel like I need to make some defence for myself.'

'Indeed. Go ahead.'

'My family and I don't always get on. They see me as a wastrel and all sorts of other things like that. And maybe I am. I know I don't like being trapped and I'm not great at sticking to things, but since I've been here, on Mull, I've found my place.'

'I'm sure that's all lovely but it doesn't explain your behaviour to my son.'

'I'm getting to that. When I discovered my family were coming here, I thought it would be a disaster. I knew this house wasn't in good nick and I wanted them to be amazed by everything here so they could really understand why I love it. In the summer that's easy. I could have taken them all around and shown them every beauty spot, but at this time of year all they were really going to see was the inside of this house. I needed to make it work. I approached Archie with a business proposal and he agreed.

I didn't think he'd be here when the guests arrived, so I didn't let on it was my family. I knew he'd be annoyed. It was a mistake and I'm going to make it up to him.'

'How? By paying back his money?'

'I've already given him this week's cheque back. I don't want another penny from him. But that's not it. I've decorated Monarch's Lodge for him. The way he loved it as a child. It's ready. I just want him to be happy.'

Mrs Crichton-Leith raised an eyebrow. 'That sounds almost like there's something else going on. So you are after him, just as I thought.'

'No, not like that. I care about Archie, a lot. But I don't care about his money. I like the fact that he can sing and dance, make me laugh and that he lets me be me. He doesn't want me to be someone else. He lets me wear tinsel in my hair and chop trees in a Santa coat.'

'Oh dear. You have got it bad. But my son is from a respected family. Even if he feels similarly.' She waved her hand. 'You can't expect anything from him, not in the long term.'

Georgia smiled. 'That's ok. I don't really do long-term planning. If I can make him happy for one day this Christmas, that's good enough for me. I just want you to know that I haven't done any of this to dupe him or coerce him out of money. I didn't expect to… fall for him.' She bit her bottom lip. 'And I definitely didn't want to hurt him.'

Georgia looked at her hand as she felt something on it. Her brow furrowed when she saw the wrinkled and heavily jewelled hand of Mrs Crichton-Leith resting on top of her own. 'All right, I understand better now. And some of what he said makes more sense. I apologise for speaking to you the way I did before.'

'Thank you.'

'My son is all I have left of my family now and sometimes… I'm protective. You understand. But it's his life and goodness knows he's had to put up with enough from me. If this is what is really going to make him happy, then fine.'

Georgia's mouth fell open. She closed it just before Mrs Crichton-Leith looked at her.

'So, for this plan to work, do you need me to do anything?'

Hardly able to believe her ears, Georgia stared at the steely eyes and long regal nose of Mrs Crichton-Leith. Was it safe to trust her?

CHAPTER 24

Archie

As the van tyres hit land, Archie breathed a sigh of relief. He had possibly caught the last ferry onto the island that Christmas Eve. Even as he thought it, the ship lurched and he saw, in his rear-view mirror, the officials hold up their hands to stop the next car driving off until the swell calmed.

He made his way across the island. It was late in the afternoon but it had felt like dusk since midday; heavy grey clouds closed in and a sleety shower began as he crossed the high pass. He steadied the van. Christmas carols from Classic FM were cheering and he sang along. Once he got back, he would spend Christmas Eve decking the bed with mattresses. He turned up the radio. *Just stop thinking about Georgia and focus on the things within my control!* As he'd forced himself to face his demons and return here after Laurence had died.

His mother had left a voicemail from the landline, asking him to call in before he went to Monarch's Lodge. He supposed it was her way of showing concern. Although he was due to dine there, perhaps he could persuade her to join him at the lodge. They could skip festivities in the main house and have a quiet family Christmas together, leaving the guests to have the party they paid for. But it wasn't his mother's style. She liked to be in the thick of a gathering.

After dropping off Murray and Beth's parcel and wishing them merry Christmas, Archie continued the few miles south to Ardnish. As he pulled up, his heart hiccupped when he spotted the floral van, its pink hues dulled by the fast-approaching darkness. So Georgia was inside, perhaps enjoying the Christmas she'd designed for herself. No. He had to stop, give her some slack. If anyone knew how families could drive a person mad, it was him.

The house looked stunning, better than ever. Children laughing over the sound of gentle carols brought a lump to his throat. If only Christmas was really this magical. Georgia's multicoloured tree twinkled at the side of the hall.

He scanned the drawing room before entering. Gordon had a large whisky and was deep in conversation with his father and another man – Archie couldn't recall his name. Two of the children were stealing chocolates from a box on a table next to them, which was causing all the hilarity. Their father looked too inebriated to notice.

Lavinia Crichton-Leith rolled around lazily and waved Archie over. She was alone, which was surprising: she'd been glued to Gordon's mother since their arrival.

'How are things going here?' he asked.

'Oh fine.' She sighed.

'That doesn't sound so good.'

'They're a bit tedious,' she muttered. 'No conversation unless you want to hear endless tales of their own brilliance.'

'Hmm.'

'Those children will make themselves sick and their father hasn't the wits to stop them.'

'Hush, Mother.'

'Are you looking for someone?' She raised her eyebrow and sat up a little straighter.

'No…' Though he couldn't help glancing around. If Georgia appeared, should he talk or would she ignore him?

'Your designer came to speak to me earlier.'

'Georgia?'

'Yes. We had a frank chat and I must say I found it rather refreshing.'

'Pardon?' Had he heard right?

'That sister of hers is a real pain. And as for that engagement fiasco… Well, I don't think I'm popular any more.'

'Why?'

'Because I won't join in with the verbal abuse of Georgia. Honestly, they think they're royalty, this lot, and when it comes down to it, she's a lot more pleasant than any of them.'

Archie wasn't sure his ears were working properly.

'Where is she?' he asked.

'About somewhere.'

'I just wish she'd told me it was her family who were coming. I don't get why it was such a big deal.'

'Because she'd talked you into a business arrangement and she knew you'd react as you did whenever she told you.'

'I'm not sure that's true, Mother.' He flicked the back of his sleeve. 'I'd like to think even if I was annoyed, I would have understood her motives.'

'Perhaps. But something unexpected happened which hampered your judgement… and hers.'

'What are you talking about?'

'You started to care about each other.' Mrs Crichton-Leith's gaze slipped into the middle distance and she appeared momentarily lost. 'You got emotionally involved, both of you.'

Archie let out a sigh and pinched the bridge of his nose. 'Wow. Have you been on the phone to your therapist to get this or did you come up with it yourself?'

'I'm not as cold as you think. And it's always easier to see the bigger picture when you're not in it. So, for that reason, I'm going to step out of this one. You can do what you like with this house. I shouldn't have interfered. I see now you're much more capable than I ever imagined, and what you've achieved here is wonderful. I only wish the first guests had been more deserving.'

'Thank you.'

'But.' She laid her hand on his knee. 'You achieved this with the help of someone very special. Don't let that go.'

Archie looked at his feet and shook his head. 'Really, Mother? Are you suggesting we get together?'

'Absolutely. I think you've found someone perfect, and you did it without my help.'

Totally bemused, Archie mouthed his surprised thanks. 'Listen, are you sure you want to stay here? I can still get you a hotel if you'd rather?'

'No, I'll brave it. Did you get the furniture?'

'Yes, I need to make the bed… literally. I'd invite you to stay but I know you don't like it and I only bought one bed. The van wasn't big enough for any more.'

'That's all right, but I think you should go there now.'

'So why did you call me here?'

'I just wanted to see you smile, I've forgotten to appreciate the smaller things in life.'

Archie kissed the back of his mother's hand, his brow furrowing but with a more pleasant confusion than usual. 'All right, see you later.'

The house rang with excitement from the children. They charged down the corridors, screaming about Santa, and Archie heard Tamsyn yelling from the kitchen for them all to be quiet. He wondered if she'd discovered the stolen chocolates.

Would Georgia be at the meal that evening? Archie wasn't sure he wanted to see her amongst everyone else with all eyes on them. Or maybe it would be easier. He could gently find a way to talk to her again, apologise for his appalling lack of tact. He steadied the van down the track to Monarch's Lodge. The sleet had turned to full on thick snowflakes, some of which had lain on the ground leaving a ghostly sheen in the headlights.

As he drove closer, he squinted through the swirly flakes. Something glowed in the living room window downstairs. Was that Christmas tree lights twinkling? *But I don't have a tree.* Getting closer, Archie squinted. The shape became clear; it was definitely a tree. But who had put it there? Only one person would have the audacity. But why? An explosion erupted in his chest.

If she jumped out of a Christmas cracker, it really would be the best Christmas ever. He wanted to go inside, but at the same time he didn't.

He paused at the door, under the bright light shaped like a Victorian lantern. Blustery flakes lit up in its glow and beneath it on the door was a huge wreath, beautifully constructed using cuttings from plants which grew on the estate. 'Grandmother's wreath.' He shook his head. Only Georgia. She was the one person who knew, who could and who would.

Heart in his mouth, he pulled the door open and stepped inside.

CHAPTER 25

Georgia

Georgia picked her way down the path to Monarch's Lodge in the tracks of the van. She was frozen, having waited for Archie to come out of the house. She'd nipped into the van to hide.

Now she was about to spring the final part of the surprise. Her eternal optimism told her to keep believing. What could possibly go wrong, other than her slipping and breaking her neck?

The front door was ajar and light spilled out of the crack. Archie must be inside. Georgia hurried on. She stopped on the threshold and took a deep breath. It was now or never. She gently pushed the door and stepped inside. The rug deadened her footfalls as she made her way through the hall. Somewhere further inside, the dogs scuffled about, possibly chewing on a Christmas treat. The only light was the Christmas tree in the living room. Was Archie in there? She peered around the door. His silhouette stood tall, his shoulders broad in his dark wool coat; he stared at the Christmas tree, his back to her.

'Merry Christmas,' she whispered.

He turned like a shot, his coat swirling round. 'Georgia? There you are.' He crossed the room in a few short strides and pulled her towards him. Her head found the Arran sweater inside his greatcoat and she rested her cheek on it.

This was so much better than she'd expected. He rubbed her back with his leather gloves. 'I'm sorry I lied,' she said.

He released her and held her, looking into her eyes. 'I understand. And this is wonderful. It's so you. I knew you'd done it the minute I saw it.'

She held her hand to her mouth. 'I just wanted to say sorry and make things up to you.'

He tilted his head to the side. 'You already have, this is beyond anything I could have dreamed of. And I'm sorry too. I was pig-headed and I didn't listen.'

'All that stuff about Tony. It makes me cringe. It's so embarrassing I can hardly even think about it. He and I split up two years ago but we clung on to this idea that one day we'd get back together. When I heard he was coming back... Oh, I've been an idiot.'

'You just did what you thought was right.'

'I did what I thought I should more than what was right.'

'I've been guilty of that myself quite a bit this year.' He tightened his grip. 'But I'll never regret the day you knocked on my door.'

'I think I've cleared things up with your mum too.'

'Yes, she told me. I was rather surprised at her understanding.'

With a giggle, Georgia took his lapels and gently pushed him across the room. He tottered backwards until they bumped into the doorframe. Releasing him, she pointed up. 'But what's your understanding of this?'

Archie's eyes followed her finger until they landed on the mistletoe. 'I'm not quite sure.'

'Good.' She wrapped her arms around his neck and pulled him towards her. 'Because I want to show you.' The second his warm lips touched hers, she closed her eyes.

Somewhere she imagined bells jingling and soft snow falling, grazing against her cheeks. It seemed like hours had passed when they finally broke apart.

Archie ran his finger down her cheek and smiled. 'I wonder if…'

Georgia arched her eyebrow and pulled back. What on earth was he planning? He appeared to be psyching himself to say something.

'I wonder if you would do me the honour of helping me to assemble a bed frame?'

Georgia burst out laughing. 'Wow, how can I refuse? It's the most romantic proposal I've had all year. That's exactly how I want to spend Christmas Eve.'

He leaned in and kissed her again. 'Wonderful,' he said, breaking off the kiss, his lips still teasingly close. 'And once it's up, you can broaden my understanding on any other topics you care to choose.'

'Ooh, Archie, that sounds a little saucy.'

'I know how much you love my sauce. Now, come on, let's unload the van.'

It took some time lifting everything into the house with snow whirling around in great gusts. But it was fun. 'I like the bedding. Good choice,' she said, admiring the soft grey tones.

'I'm channelling my inner designer, and maybe after dinner I'll get cosy with my outer one.'

'I like the sound of that. I'd rather stay here and cuddle up than go back up there. We could put some presents under the tree and wait for Santa.'

Archie smiled and hope blossomed in Georgia's heart for a few seconds. 'That would make all my Christmas wishes come true, but I think we have to attend the dinner. I don't feel right leaving my mother.'

'With a pack of ruffians.'

'I said I'd spend Christmas with her.'

'Ok, let's go.' Georgia put out her hand.

'We can sit together.'

'And play footsie?'

'That kind of thing.'

Georgia didn't expect anyone in her family to notice she'd arrived with Archie. Why would they? They were far too wrapped up in their own concerns and trying to prevent the children from smashing something in their excitement. Mrs Crichton-Leith, however, gave them a broad smile. 'Everything all right now?'

'Better than,' said Archie.

'Good.'

They took seats in a row, Archie in the middle.

'Wonderful photographs, aren't they?' said Lavinia to the assembled guests, pointing to the huge sea eagle prints, decorating the main wall.

'Yes, quite so,' said Gordon. 'Stunning. Was it a local photographer?'

'It certainly was,' said Archie.

'It was Miss Rose,' said Lavinia. 'She's a fantastic photographer and a very talented artist.'

'I couldn't agree more,' said Archie.

Georgia felt the heat in her face and looked at her Christmas placemat as Gordon squinted at her. She could read his mind. He and all his other relatives couldn't believe she'd done anything like that. They all thought she was a waster who spent her life doing nothing but dragging down her family. She glanced up at Tamsyn who was rushing about with their mother. Their hair stood on end and they looked stressed.

'I should help,' said Georgia.

Tamsyn glared up from laying a platter on the table as though wanting to launch into an earful. Ellen clicked her tongue and shook her head.

'Absolutely not.' Mrs Crichton-Leith leaned across Archie and laid her hand on Georgia's arm. 'As we were invited to the meal, we shouldn't be obliged to help. That's extremely bad form. I would always suggest caterers for an event on this scale. It lowers the stress immensely.' She smiled at Tamsyn, who looked like she might short circuit at any second.

Finally, everyone had taken their places and the table was bursting with food. As Georgia lifted her napkin, she said, 'Isn't this a lot of work?'

Tamsyn took a seat beside her, throwing her a filthy look.

'I mean, you'll be doing turkey and all the trimmings tomorrow. Shouldn't we just have had a buffet tonight?'

'Well, darling, as you didn't bother to help, I don't see how it can make any difference to you. But if you must know, the reason I ordered so much food for this evening was that this was meant to be the celebration dinner for your engagement to Tony.'

Georgia nearly choked on her drink. Archie gave her a pat on the back and smiled. 'Do you realise it was Tony who left me two years ago, not the other way around? I was just stupid thinking he'd come back.'

Tamsyn gave her a withering stare. 'And he did. He's well-bred and knows how to act.'

'I'm not sure it was a particularly well-bred thing to do,' mumbled Archie into his wine.

Georgia bit her tongue and swivelled to face Tamsyn. 'So, let's get this straight. We're having this meal to celebrate something which was never guaranteed to happen, and now it's my fault that you've had to cook it?'

'Yah, I couldn't let the food go to waste.'

Georgia glanced at Archie and gave him a *see what I mean* look. He shuffled his hand along the table and touched his little finger against hers.

'Well, you've lost your chance now,' Tamsyn muttered, glugging a large mouthful of sparkling wine. 'This was the one opportunity to snare someone upstanding, and...' She leaned in and whispered, 'You know he's Gordon's cousin. It's put me in such an awkward place with the family.'

Across the table, Georgia's mother frowned and shook her head.

'God knows who you'll end up with now,' continued Tamsyn. 'Especially if you stay on this island. I've not seen any single men under the age of ninety.'

Archie adjusted his collar and pointed at himself in mockery. Tamsyn didn't notice, but Georgia burst out giggling. Her mother glared daggers.

'Well, I'll just take the best of what's available.' Georgia smiled. 'I don't want to be with one of the sleazy guys you'd like to set me up with. I want to be with someone I love.'

Archie lowered his hand under the table and pressed it on top of Georgia's thigh.

'Pfft.' Tamsyn snorted, grabbing a drink before embarking on a fresh onslaught. 'Love? I'm not sure you know the meaning of the word after what just happened with Tony.'

Archie's hand slid off Georgia's leg and an abrupt pinging sound stopped everyone talking. Georgia peered round to see him banging his spoon on his glass. She looked at him quizzically, but he smiled and stood up calmly.

'Everybody, I would like to wish you a very merry Christmas.' He raised his glass and everyone returned it. Georgia was aware of Tamsyn sitting up straight, preparing herself to drink in every word. Archie was the perfect yah, after all.

'And I would also like to thank you for being my first guests here. It's been a wonderful experience, especially as you've taken my mother and me under your wings and involved us in your fun.'

'Mother and I,' Tamsyn corrected, loud enough for everyone to hear.

Archie smiled benignly at her. 'I think you'll find in that sentence my grammar was correct.'

Red blotches blossomed on Tamsyn's cheeks and she tightened her fist around the stem of her wineglass. Georgia was on the brink of a laughing fit.

'The best part for me,' continued Archie, 'was when I discovered you were related to Georgia, my wonderful interior designer. In fact, if you would please stand up.' He took her hand and dragged her to her feet.

'Archie,' she muttered, smoothing her dress and meeting no one's eye.

'Let's have a big round of applause for this wonderful woman.'

He started it and everybody followed suit whether they liked to or not. Across the table, Georgia's parents whispered something between them.

'Without Georgia, I couldn't have made this place half as amazing as it is. In fact, without Georgia in my life, the past few months would have been nothing at all.'

She gaped at him, hoping she wasn't blushing, but the heat burned. She went to sit down but he took hold of her hand.

'A few minutes ago, Tamsyn told us she'd thrown this meal to celebrate Georgia's engagement.'

Tamsyn looked livid, but Georgia's heart raced at double speed.

'However, Tamsyn was disappointed the proposal hadn't taken place. So, I think we can rectify that now.' He turned and faced Georgia holding both her hands. She stared, speechless, guessing what he was going to do. Could she stop him? The room might self-destruct.

'Will you, wonderful, lovely Georgia, please do me the huge, the massive, the bigger-than-anything-in-the-world honour of marrying me?'

Her eyes widened, and her mouth dropped. No words came out. She simply stared, torn between laughing, crying and a desperate urge to melt into his arms and eclipse the watchers.

Archie waited, his lips curling upwards, his happily mismatched eyes twinkling. In the glint of the chandelier, it looked like he winked and Georgia felt like he'd passed her a secret note, telling her everything was going to be amazing. Utter silence filled the room, even the children were quiet.

'Ok, yes, I will.' She hoped the words had come out aloud. Before she had time to repeat it however, she was being kissed and the room had erupted. Whether into cries of joy or furious chitchat, she couldn't be sure and couldn't care less. She let the taste of Archie's lips filter into the deepest chamber of her heart.

'I haven't even told you, how much I love you,' he whispered into her ear, holding her hands so tight it almost hurt.

'Save it.' She put her finger to his lips. 'Why rush? Tell me later, or better still, show me.'

Archie's mother patted his back as he sat down. Tamsyn gaped at Georgia. 'Where did that come from? He's a millionaire, isn't he?'

Georgia pulled up her shoulder. 'I've no idea, I've not even had my hands on his wallet yet.'

Tamsyn didn't seem to have heard; she shook her head like a control had jammed somewhere. 'How did you do it?'

Georgia picked up her cracker and offered it to Tamsyn. 'Just the magic of Christmas, I suppose.'

CHAPTER 26

Archie

After so much food he could hardly move, Archie thanked his hosts and wished them a happy evening. His mother withdrew to his office wing to hide and watch some Christmas films of her own choosing.

'I bet she's a closet fan of *Love Actually*,' said Georgia.

'Probably.' Archie took her hand as they left by the main doors.

'You know Gordon's family will be gunning for me in there.'

'Who cares what they do. I've got you.' He squeezed her hand and started singing, 'Oh Come All Ye Faithful'.

Georgia joined in laughing and they continued all the way to Monarch's Lodge. 'We must sound like drunks,' she said as they reached the front door.

'I think we are a bit, but there's not a lot of people around here to disturb.' He ran his fingers over the wreath on the door. 'This is so beautiful. You really are the best.' He placed a lingering kiss on her cheek.

As they stepped inside and removed their boots and coats, Georgia looked at him. Archie pulled himself up straight and folded his arms. 'What?' Something about her expression was unsettling.

'You know I can't actually marry you.'

'Why not?'

'That was just a bit of fun, wasn't it?'

'It was fun, yes.' He stepped forward and took both her hands. 'But I was serious.'

'Archie…' She looked around, pinching her lips together.

'I won't force you into anything and of course, I'm aware how ridiculously sudden this is, but I know how I feel.'

'I know how I feel too. But I'm not made for this kind of life. I'm not my sister, I don't want to live in a castle with servants and be a dolly bird on your arm.'

Archie laughed. Her indignant face was too cute. 'Yes, I can see what you mean, and I don't want that either. When I said marry me, I was trying to please your family. What I meant was for you to be my partner. An equal partner, not living in a castle, though you're welcome to join me in this humble abode. But I'd like you to run the estate with me and do all the Georgia stuff you do so well, use your skills and talents while sharing in the profits. Plus, you can do your art and photography, there's plenty of space for a studio. You can open a shop, a gallery, whatever you like.'

Georgia looked serious for all of five seconds before turning to him with a wicked grin. 'You had me when you said I could live in this house.'

'This house is yours. I bequeath it to you, my princess. As soon as the solicitors open in the new year, I'll have it signed over.' He swept his arm around her and pulled her in for a kiss. 'You are very naughty, stealing my heart like this.'

'No, I swear I've been good.' She giggled and stroked his cheek. 'Though I can't promise to be any use when it comes to running an estate, I have no experience.'

'But you have initiative and that's more than enough.' He swooped in for another kiss. 'I'll put some music on, and we can dance.'

He set his phone onto the dock and the quirky opening notes of 'Jingle Bell Rock' burst out. Georgia took his hand and he spun her into his arms, bending her back so she was parallel with the floor. She squealed as he pulled her up and twirled her again.

'We need a piano in here,' he said. 'That's a priority for the new year. What about you? What do you think we need?'

'The piano's fine, I'll bring a tube of squirty cream.'

'You saucy minx. Maybe we should go upstairs and try out the new bed.'

'Oh gosh, let's,' she said, twirling under his arm. 'Can we hang up our stockings and listen for noises on the roof?'

Archie reeled her in close and kissed the top of her head. 'Yes. Let's do that. I never want to have a day of my life without you. You're the funniest, loveliest, craziest person I know.'

'Thanks... I think,' she said, rocking back and forward as 'Mistletoe and Wine' chimed out.

'You've made this my happiest Christmas ever.' He sealed his words with a kiss and they swayed towards the door, dancing all the way up the stairs.

CHAPTER 27

Georgia

After the second feast in less than twenty-four hours, Georgia sat in the drawing room of the main house, cosy on the sofa, curled up beside Archie, snuggling into his cashmere Christmas jumper. Wrapping paper chaos ruled, and she was glad she wasn't responsible for tidying up. She could relax this Christmas Day with gin, chocolate, and the man of her dreams.

'I got the best present,' he said, twirling a strand of her hair.

'As long as I'm not just for Christmas.' She rested her head on him as she leafed through her new book.

'Definitely not. You're the estate manager.'

'Ha, what does that make you?'

'I'm the landowner, darling,' he ruffled her hair.

'Oh, shut up. If you pull that card, I'll quit.'

'Ok, ok. I'm just a minion, you are in charge.'

Georgia arched an eyebrow. 'Can I have your wallet now?'

'I thought you already made a play for it last night.'

'I missed.'

He sniggered, raised his backside off the chair and pulled out his wallet. 'There you go.'

'Cool. Bribery will get you everywhere.'

'Good to know.'

Georgia's parents came in along with Tamsyn wearing two paper crowns. Some things never changed. Georgia flung the wallet back at Archie and sat bolt upright.

'Are you all right?'

'My mum and dad,' she muttered. They were heading over. 'I don't think they approve of us.'

Tamsyn clearly didn't. She slumped into the opposite sofa with a large glass of wine.

'But haven't they always wanted you to hitch up with someone rich? And here I am.'

'Oh, there'll be something wrong with you. There always is. They just don't want me to be happy.'

'I'm sure they do.'

'Nope. In fact, my mother will probably be angry you're richer than Gordon and this house is bigger than Tamsyn's. She'll never forgive me for that.'

'We'll see.'

Georgia deflated like a pin had been stuck in her bubble. Her parents took their seats next to her rather stiffly. She prepared herself for the barrage. Even the fact she was dressed like a Christmas fairy and it was Christmas Day was unlikely to prevent it. Maybe if she waved the little tinsel wand one of her nieces had left on the floor, she could magic them all away.

'Well, Georgia,' said her mother, looking at Archie. 'This was quite a shock to us.'

'Me too,' she said. 'I only met Archie a few months ago.' It was bad already, she may as well lay it on thick.

'Yes.' Her mother frowned. 'It does seem rather sudden.'

'It is,' Archie pitched in. 'But I knew I'd found someone special the first time we spoke.'

'What, when you told me to get off your land for trespassing?'

Archie's hand wavered above his knee. 'Around about then, yes. Maybe a little later.'

'You did what?' asked her father. 'Even though, there's a right to roam in Scotland.'

'Yes, I know,' said Georgia.

'And so do I,' Archie agreed.

'He was just being officious.'

'I was, and it was very mean of me.'

'Though it did make me notice you. You have a particularly fine pair of… dogs.'

'Well.' Her mother coughed, scrutinising her. Again Georgia waited for the attack. 'You both look happy. I hope it works out. And Mull is so beautiful. I'd love to come back in the summer and see it properly.'

Georgia's jaw hit the floor. Archie nudged her and smiled. 'You can come any time,' said Georgia. 'I invited you before, but you didn't seem interested.'

'Ah, more fool us. We're always afraid of new places, and this was just a step too far. I'm glad we gave it a chance.'

'When you come back,' said Archie, 'you can walk over the ridge with me and we can put up a little plaque in honour of the place where I first caught Georgia invading my territory.'

'Oh, we couldn't possibly,' said her father, 'we'd be trespassing too.'

'Not if I'm with you,' said Archie.

'Just my wee joke, son.' Her father winked.

Archie chortled. 'Good one.'

Georgia almost let a tear escape. Who would have thought it? All her Christmas dreams and more. As she looked up and glimpsed the Christmas tree, with waves crashing beyond, she melted back into Archie's hold and he resumed twirling her hair. This was where she belonged, a real house with a proper sea view, and Archie.

*

Darkness fell over Ardnish and sleety snow whisked around. The fun and games had finished when nobody had the energy for any more charades, quizzes or conundrums. Georgia and Archie collected their coats from the antechamber off the entrance hall, ready to brave the chill outside. Archie helped her on with her scarlet coat and smiled. With a grin, Georgia took her phone from her pocket and checked her messages. 'You see how wonderful messenger is,' she said, waggling her phone. 'I can keep in touch with my friends even on Christmas Day.'

'All right, I'll sign up.'

'Yay.' She pounced on him and stole a kiss, longer than strictly necessary, but why waste the opportunity? Returning to her phone, she laughed at the astonished faces and gifs. 'No one believes we're together. Haha, except Beth, she does, but says I'm a traitor and she'll never speak to me again. Joke. Phew! I think you've grown on her since you got her parcel.'

'Well, that's something.' His eyes lingered on Georgia's face.

'What?'

'Just you. Little Miss Christmas, making all my dreams come true.' He made as if to kiss her, then stopped and looked over her shoulder. 'Mother.'

Georgia turned to see Mrs Crichton-Leith. 'We haven't had a free moment to talk all day,' she said. 'Tomorrow I'd like to come and visit Monarch's Lodge.'

'Sure,' said Georgia. 'Come now if you like.'

'No, my dear. I'll leave the two of you in peace. I'm very happy you found each other. When I see you like this, you look so perfect together.'

Georgia glanced at Archie and grinned. His mismatched eyes twinkled. 'Thank you, Mother.'

'Oh, I need to get my scarf,' Georgia said, 'I think I left it on the coat stand in the kitchen the other day, let me run and get it.' Leaving Archie and his mother chatting, she darted down the corridor and pushed open the end door. Before she could check the stand for her scarf, she spotted Tamsyn at the Aga boiling the kettle.

'Are you leaving?' asked Tamsyn, turning around sharply. One of her paper hats fell off and drifted to the floor.

'Just to Monarch's Lodge.'

Tamsyn narrowed her eyes and Georgia saw the problem. Her sister couldn't stand the idea of her staying even one day at a place called Monarch's Lodge. Even if it was named after a deer and not Mary Queen of Scots. 'None of this is real, Georgia.' She lifted the kettle from the stove. 'Everyone is so caught up in Christmas glitter they can't see the gifts for the wrapping paper.'

'What do you mean?'

'All of this.' She gestured around the room, holding her arms wide. 'Is fake.'

'I don't follow.'

'It's a holiday house, not a home. The man who owns it is a big landowner, not your boyfriend. The job you did here is for Christmas, not for life. Once we've gone, this little world you've constructed from Christmas cards is going to fall around your ears and you'll be back where you started.'

Georgia blinked and shook her head. 'Wow, just wow. I know this has been sudden but—'

'Sudden? A man you hardly know proposes to you to appease me and you think it's sudden? It's not sudden, it's fake. And you ought to face up to that. He's bluffing and you're the one who'll suffer.'

'Why do you think he did it to appease you?'

'He said so. We all heard it. What an embarrassing charade. Gordon's family are quite disgusted.'

'You know what, I don't care. Maybe it started as a charade, but now it's real. I know how I feel about Archie.'

'Just like you knew how you felt about Tony?'

'No. I never knew what I felt about him. I liked him and I liked the idea that he brought me security and acceptance, but as a person, he and I weren't ever going to last.'

'And you think you'll last with Archie? A man whose family are mentioned in Debrett's?'

Georgia covered her face, trying not to laugh, or maybe cry. The door opened and she uncovered her eyes to see Archie's head poking around. 'Are you coming?'

'No, I'm arguing with my sister.'

'Oh,' said Archie.

'Please, darling,' Tamsyn said. 'How uncouth.'

'I am uncouth,' said Georgia. 'Not worthy of a man whose family are mentioned in doublets or whatever.'

'Debrett's,' said Tamsyn.

'Listen,' said Archie. 'Far be it from me to get involved in a sisterly feud, but as it's Christmas, why don't you call a truce? I promise to be good to your sister,' he told Tamsyn. 'I know some of my family probably have an abysmal record where their serving wenches are concerned.'

'Excuse me.' Georgia walloped his backside.

He grinned and continued. 'But I swear I will do the honourable thing. I'll also make sure to send her on elocution and deportment classes in the new year, but until then, we'll have to accept each other for who we are. It's these differences in Georgia which make her so special to me.'

Georgia was willing to bet this wouldn't settle Tamsyn a jot. If anything, it would enrage her even more. Tamsyn held her head high and looked between the two of them. 'Yah, of course, and good luck to you both.'

Georgia approached tentatively and put out her arms. They shared a brief hug. 'I'm not doing this to get one over on you,' said Georgia. 'I don't care if Archie has a big house, an estate, all the tea in China, or billions of pounds in his wallet. I love the man inside, the one who sings, dances, laughs, and has fun with me.'

'Yah, yah.' Tamsyn patted Georgia's back. 'I get that. Sure I do.'

As they broke apart, Archie leaned in a gave Tamsyn a peck on the cheek. 'Merry Christmas.'

She gave them both a smile and Georgia bent down and picked up the fallen paper crown. She stared at it for a second then placed it on Tamsyn's head on top of the other one. 'You better keep it,' said Georgia. 'It suits you better.'

Tamsyn raised her hand to it with a slight frown as Georgia waved goodbye.

'That was quite a trick,' Georgia said to Archie as they claimed the fresh air outside.

'What?'

'You got Tamsyn to be nice.'

'I doubt she's particularly happy, but I'll keep plugging away.'

'The crazy thing is, she loves men like you normally. She just doesn't like it that you prefer me.'

'She'll have to get used to it because I'm not going anywhere. Not without you anyway.'

Duchess and Dexter sniffed about in the sleet covered ground which glowed in the light from Monarch's Lodge. The shifting crash of the waves beyond the garden wall was the only reminder of where they were in the world.

'I have something for you,' said Archie.

'Oh? A Christmas present? Because you know I don't have anything for you… I mean I didn't exactly have the time.'

He put his finger to his lips and smiled. 'Shh. You already gave me the best present. Everything you've done for me over the past few weeks is all I could ask for, in fact, a whole lot more. But this isn't exactly a Christmas present.'

Georgia frowned as he dug about in his pocket. 'What is it?'

'Patience,' he said. 'I didn't want anyone else to see this but look.' Stepping towards the light glowing from the lantern over the front door, Archie produced a small red velvet box.

Georgia lowered her eyebrow and squinted at it. 'Does that have a ring in it? Are you going for a repeat of yesterday only with one knee in the slush this time?'

'Not exactly.' He flipped open the box. 'I want you to have this.'

'Wow.' Georgia slipped out a delicate chain with a filigree rose pendant. 'Is this your grandmother's?'

'Yes. I found the box in her old writing desk. I'm not sure why it was there but I'm glad. Laurence sold a lot of old jewellery to finance his gambling. Thankfully, this missed the purge because it's just so you and I know my grandmother would love you to have it.'

'It's beautiful.' Georgia held it under the light. 'Here.' She handed him the chain and pulled her hair and collar off her neck. 'Do me the honour, kind sir, and placeth the chain upon my neck.'

He chuckled and slipped it around, fastening the clasp at the back. She settled the rose in place and held up her head, pinning her collar low. 'Perfect,' said Archie.

Georgia took his face in her hands, leaned up and kissed him. 'Thank you.'

He put his arm around her shoulder. 'So Christmas in Monarch's Lodge is finally here. I didn't think I'd make it, definitely not this year,' Archie recited.

'Is that a poem?'

'I do fancy myself as a poet...' He looked about. 'Without further ado, we should go within, crack open some wine, some chocolate or gin...'

'That's bad.'

'Hand in hand by Ardnish Bay, with my one true love this Christmas Day.'

'Better.' Georgia rested her head on his shoulder.

He gently placed a kiss on her forehead. 'I love you,' he whispered, increasing the pressure of his grip.

'I love you too,' she replied, breathing in the cold night air and the true magic of Christmas.

Archie cleared his throat. 'All right, how about this?' he asked. 'When first on the bluff, I saw your trespassing self, sitting so cheeky like elf on the shelf. You became my enemy, so bold and so strong, changing my world with dancing and song.'

Georgia giggled, winding her arms around him as he continued.

'It seemed all was lost with your birthday surprise, but I needed that to open my eyes. And finally, I saw, right there was my fate; my partner, my princess, my forever soulmate.' He drew her in closer, pinning her tight to his chest.

Georgia let her eyelids fall and listened to his words slowly murmuring over the beat of the waves.

'And now you are both my lover and friend, to be with me always, right to the end.'

Together they held fast, laughing as the icy drops tickled their cheeks, ready to embrace the future with the glowing promise of love, laughter, and more than a stuffed stocking full of fun.

The End

SHARE THE LOVE!

If you enjoyed reading this book, then please share your
reviews online.
Leaving reviews is a perfect way to support authors
and helps books reach more readers.
So please review and share! Let me know what you
think.
Thank you

Margaret

X

You can review on Amazon here.

ABOUT THE AUTHOR

I live with my family in the beautiful county of Perthshire in Scotland. With impressive scenery everywhere you look, it's hard not to be inspired around here.

I'm mummy to a precious little boy who loves stories as much as me and always likes to know what I'm writing today.

I've been a closet writer for several years and have written stories, articles and poetry. In 2012, I won a short story writing competition at Pitlochry Festival Theatre with a faerie tale, Out of the Frame. It was an honour to have the piece read live in the auditorium.

As well as writing, I'm a keen photographer, and I also enjoy drawing. If you're looking for me, I tend to be either clacking the keys, scribbling in a notebook or reading - preferably with chocolate.

I can't wait to introduce my first series Scottish Island Escapes.

Join me on an adventure to the wild and remote Scottish islands from the comfort of your armchair and cosy up for some heart-warming reading.

To find out more visit:

www.margaretamatt.com

ACKNOWLEDGEMENTS

As always, I'd like to thank my husband, Ian, for putting up with my writing talk 24/7 and supporting me in my quest to become a published author. His encouragement has helped me pull through tough times and keep going. Also to my son, whose interest in my writing always makes me smile. To have him ask how my novels are getting along or about characters in the books is gold. I'm so proud to be your mum.

Throughout the writing process, I have gleaned help from many sources and met some fabulous people. I'd like to give a special mention to the following people. Stéphanie Ronckier, my beta reader extraordinaire, for giving me phenomenal feedback on my writing and helping me see everything from a fresh perspective. My lovely friend, Lyn Williamson, for her continued support. And fellow author, Evie Alexander, for her no-nonsense style of encouragement and all-round writing fabulousness!

Also a huge thanks to my editor, Aimee Walker, at Aimee Walker Editorial Services for her excellent work on my novels.

A shout out also goes to Anita Faulkner and the Chick-Lit & Prosecco Facebook group, which is a wonderful community of supportive people and a fun place to hang out.

MORE BOOKS BY
MARGARET AMATT

A WINTER HAVEN

She was the one that got away… Now she's back.

Career-driven Robyn Sherratt returns to her childhood home on the Scottish Isle of Mull, hoping to build bridges with her estranged family. She discovers her mother struggling to run the family hotel. When an old flame turns up, memories come back to bite, nibbling into Robyn's fragile heart.

Carl Hansen, known as The Fixer, abandoned city life for peace and tranquillity. Swapping his office for a log cabin, he mends people's broken treasures. He can fix anything, except himself. When forced to work on hotel renovations with Robyn, the girl he lost twelve years ago, his quiet life is sent spinning.

Carl would like nothing more than to piece together the shattered shards of Robyn's heart. But can she trust him? What can a broken man like him offer a successful woman like her?

A SPRING RETREAT

She's gritty, he's determined. Who will back down first?

When spirited islander Beth McGregor learns of plans to build a road through the family farm, she sets out to stop it. But she's thrown off course by the charming and handsome project manager. Sparks fly, sending Beth into a spiral of confusion. Guys are fine as friends. Nothing else.

Murray Henderson has finally found a place to retreat from the past with what seems like a straightforward job. But he hasn't reckoned on the stubbornness of the locals, especially the hot-headed and attractive Beth.

As they battle together over the proposed road, attraction blooms. Murray strives to discover the real Beth; what secrets lie behind the tough façade? Can a regular farm girl like her measure up to Murray's impeccable standards, and perhaps find something she didn't know she was looking for?

A SUMMER SANCTUARY

She's about to discover the one place he wants to keep secret

Five years ago, Island girl Kirsten McGregor broke the company rules. Now, she has the keys to the Hidden Mull tour bus and is ready to take on the task of running the business. But another tour has arrived. The competition is bad enough but when she recognises the rival tour operator, her plans are upended.

Former jet pilot Fraser Bell has made his share of mistakes. What better place to hide and regroup than the place he grew to love as a boy? With great enthusiasm, he launches into his new tour business, until old-flame Kirsten shows up and sends his world plummeting.

Kirsten may know all the island's secrets, but what she can't work out is Fraser. With tension simmering, Kirsten and Fraser's attraction increases. What if they both made a mistake before? Is one of them about to make an even bigger one now?

AN AUTUMN HIDEAWAY

She went looking for someone, but it wasn't him.

After a string of disappointments for chirpy city girl Autumn, discovering her notoriously unstable mother has run off again is the last straw. When Autumn learns her mother's last known whereabouts was a remote Scottish Island, she makes the rash decision to go searching for her.

Taciturn islander Richard has his reasons for choosing the remote Isle of Mull as home. He's on a deadline and doesn't need any complications or company. But everything changes after a chance encounter with Autumn.

Autumn chips away at Richard's reserve until his carefully constructed walls start to crumble. But Autumn's just a passing visitor and Richard has no plans to leave. Will they realise, before it's too late, that what they've been searching for isn't necessarily what's missing?

A CHRISTMAS BLUFF

She's about to trespass all over his Christmas.

Artist and photographer Georgia has spent two carefree years on the Isle of Mull and is looking forward to a quiet Christmas... Until she discovers her family is about to descend upon her, along with her past.

Aloof aristocrat Archie has let out his island mansion to a large party from the mainland. They're expecting a castle for Christmas, not an outdated old pile, and he's in trouble.

When Georgia turns up with an irresistible smile and an offer he can't refuse, he's wary, but he needs her help.

As Georgia weaves her festive charms around the house, they start to work on Archie too. And the spell extends both ways. But falling in love was never part of the deal. Can the magic outlast Christmas when he's been conned before and she has a secret that could ruin everything?

A FLIGHT OF FANCY

She's masquerading as her twin, pretending to be his girlfriend, while really just being herself.

After years of being cooped up by her movie star family, Taylor Rousse is desperate to escape. Having a Hollywood actress as a twin is about all Taylor can say for herself, but when she's let down by her sister for the umpteenth time, she decides now is the time for action.

Pilot Magnus Hansen is heading back to his family home on the Isle of Mull for his brother's wedding and he's not looking forward to showing up single. The eldest of three brothers shouldn't be the last married – no matter how often he tells himself he's not the marrying type.

On his way, Magnus crashes into a former fling. She's a Hollywood star looking for an escape and they strike a deal: he's her ticket to a week of peace; she's his new date. Except Taylor isn't who he thinks she is. When she and Magnus start to fall for each other, their double deception threatens to blow up in their faces and shatter everything that might have been.

FREE HUGS & OLD-FASHIONED KISSES.

A short story only available to newsletter subscribers

Do you ever get one of those days when you just fancy snuggling up? Then this captivating short story is for you. And what's more, it's free when you sign up to my newsletter. Time to get cosy and indulge in some Free Hugs & Old-Fashioned Kisses

Meet Livvi, a girl who just needs a hug. And Jakob, a guy who doesn't go about hugging random strangers. But what if he makes an exception, just this once?

MAP

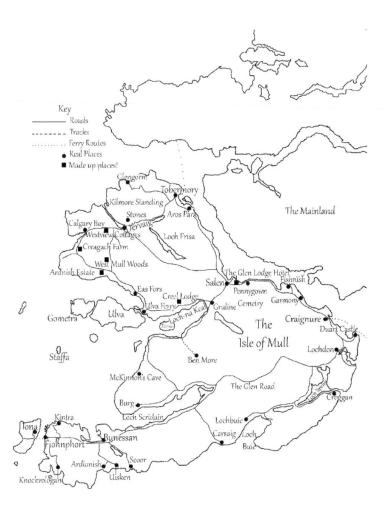

A CHRISTMAS BLUFF

Printed in Great Britain
by Amazon